PASS **IT** ON!

In the [REAL LIFE] series, four girls are brought together through the power of a mysterious book that helps them sort through the issues of their very real lives. In each of these stories, the girls find the mysterious RL book exactly when they need it. Each girl leaves the RL book for someone else to find, knowing it will help the next person who reads it.

While the RL book is magical, this book could be left in the same way for the next reader. Maybe this book needs to be read by someone you don't even know, or maybe you already know of someone who would really enjoy this book. Simply write a note with READ ME on it, stick it on the front of the book, and then get creative. Give the book to a friend, or leave this book at your church, school, local coffee shop, train station, on the bus, or wherever you know someone else will find it and read it.

No matter what your plan, we want to hear about it. Log on to the Zondervan Good Teen Reads Facebook page (*www.facebook.com/ goodteenreads*—look under the Discussion tab) and tell us where you left the book or how you found it. Or let us know how you plan to "pass it on." You can also let your friends know about Pass It On by talking about it on your Facebook page.

To join others in the Pass It On campaign, pick up extra copies of the [REAL LIFE] series at your local Christian bookstores and favorite online retailers.

Other books in the Real Life series:

Boyfriends, Burritos & an Ocean of Trouble (Book Two)

MOTORCYCLES, SUSHI & ONE STRANGE BOOK

[REAL LIFE]

book one

NANCY RUE

ZONDERVAN®

ZONDERVAN.com/
AUTHORTRACKER
follow your favorite authors

ZONDERVAN

Motorcycles, Sushi & One Strange Book
Copyright © 2010 by Nancy Rue

This title is also available as a Zondervan ebook.
Visit www.zondervan.com/ebooks.

Requests for information should be addressed to:

Zondervan, *Grand Rapids, Michigan 49530*

Library of Congress Cataloging-in-Publication Data

Rue, Nancy N.
    Motorcycles, sushi & one strange book / by Nancy Rue.
        p.   cm. — (A real life novel ; bk. 1)
        Summary: Fifteen-year-old Jessie Hatcher, forced to go to Florida with the father
    she thought was dead, finds that his faith, a book that seems to speak to her heart,
    and new friends help her get control of her ADHD and her life.
        ISBN 978-0-310-71484-2 (softcover : alk. paper)
        [1. Books and reading—Fiction. 2. Fathers and daughters—Fiction. 3. Christian
    life—Fiction. 4. Attention-deficit hyperactivity disorder—Fiction. 5. Family life—
    Florida—Fiction. 6. Florida—Fiction.] I. Title. II. Title: Motorcycles, sushi and one
    strange book.
        PZ7.R88515Mot 2010
        [Fic]—dc22   2009045132

Published in association with the literary agency of Alive Communications, Inc., 7680
Goddard Street, Suite 200, Colorado Springs, CO 80920. *www.alivecommunications.com*

Zonderkidz is a trademark of Zondervan.

Cover design: Rule 29
Cover photography: ©iStockphoto ©Graham Heywood 2007
Interior design and composition: Patrice Sheridan & Carlos Eluterio Estrada

Printed in the United States of America

---

10 11 12 13 14 15 /DCI/ 23 22 21 20 19 18 17 16 15 14 13 12 11 10 9 8 7 6 5 4 3 2 1

CHAPTER ONE

I guess my life was crazy even before the day it really lost its mind. I just didn't think it was.

I did think my friend Chelsea's life was a little weird. Her parents had been married to each other for twenty years and her family sat down at the table to eat supper together every night. They always had dishes like broccoli-and-cheese casserole or green beans à la mode. Or something.

I *definitely* considered my friend Marcus's life to be strange. His family went on a two-week vacation every single summer to places like Key West and the Grand Canyon. The day my world went insane, he was off with his parents and his little sister in California where they were staying in hotels and eating in restaurants that had tablecloths. Totally off the wall.

Okay, so I need to get to the point, which as you'll see I sometimes have trouble doing. I was like that even before that Saturday morning in late June—or was it early July? Doesn't matter. It was summer, so there was no reason to keep track of what month it was. At least not until August, when it would be time to think about going back to school. I tried not to.

It was going along like any other day in the life of Jessie Hatcher—that would be me. I was cleaning the house, sort of, and watching "I Love Lucy" reruns on TV Land—now *there* was a wacko, that Lucy woman—and talking to Chelsea on the phone. And she, as usual, was giving me grief.

"I wish you'd get a cell phone," she said.

"What's wrong with a landline?" I said, although I knew. We'd had this conversation before. I always pretended to forget.

"What's wrong with it is that you can't text on it."

"Why do I need to text? We're talking."

"No, you're whispering. I can hardly hear you. It's like you're in a library."

"Or a bank," I said. "Why do people always whisper in banks? Are they afraid somebody will find out how much money they have? Or don't have?"

"I don't *know!*"

I could imagine Chelsea raking her hand through that ginormous head of butter-blonde hair. She has enough for thirty-seven people. I barely have enough for me, which is probably good because it's bright red. The kind of red that makes people stare at you like you're Raggedy Ann come to life. So the less of it the better.

"Why are you whispering anyway?" Chelsea said.

I shifted the phone to my other shoulder so I could lift the corner of the dining room rug and slide a pile of crumbs under it with my foot. I'd already put the Swiffer away. Not that my mother would have noticed anyway. Those crumbs must have been there awhile, because the last time we ate in the dining room was probably four years ago on my eleventh birthday.

"I'm whispering because my mom's asleep," I said.

"At one in the afternoon? Oh, I forgot she works at night."

That wasn't exactly true. Okay, it wasn't true at all, but I must have led Chelsea to believe it at some point. I tried not to out-and-out lie. Usually.

"See, it would be so much easier to have a conversation if you could text," Chelsea said. "I'm totally getting you a cell phone for your birthday."

"Oh no—the whole thing's overflowing. I knew that was going to happen."

"What's overflowing? What are you doing, anyway?"

"I'm watching Lucy."

"Lucy who?"

I changed which ear was on the phone again and used my forearm to shove all the random stuff on top of the buffet into the drawer and craned my neck again to see the TV in the family room. Lucy and Ethel were knee-deep in suds pouring out of an industrial-sized washing machine. Speaking of which …

I darted for the laundry room.

"Lucy Ricardo," I said.

"*Who?* Never mind. I need to talk to you about Marcus."

Good. A safe topic. I hated it when Chelsea went off about text messaging. I couldn't have done it if I had an iPhone in my hand at that very moment. Not so anybody could understand it, anyway. Writing of any kind wasn't one of my talents. Actually, I hadn't really discovered any talents—

"Are you serious about him?" she said.

"Who?"

"Marcus."

"Define serious."

"You know what I mean."

Chelsea's voice dipped into that rich place where only the most delicious news can dwell. I knew her huge brown eyes were bubbling like chocolate fudge. My blue ones were so small compared to hers, I always imagined myself looking cross-eyed when I was around her. I looked in the round glass on the front of the washing machine. Okay, not exactly cross-eyed. But definitely too close together. My nose didn't help.

"Did you hear me?"

"What?" I said.

"I just think that for as long as you and Marcus have been together, it's time to either get serious or move on."

"Uh—hello—you know I don't do 'serious.'" I picked up a hunk of clothes out of the dirty clothes hamper and dumped them into the washer. "I want to be able to flirt with whoever I want. Aw, man, we're out of detergent. Can you use dish soap in a washing machine, I wonder?"

"Huh," Chelsea said.

"Is that 'huh, yes' or 'huh, you're an idiot' or 'huh, I don't know'?"

"Okay, could you focus for like ten seconds?"

That would be about it, yeah.

I heard Chelsea sigh like she was practicing to be a parent.

"Before Marcus left for California, he told me he was getting ready to ask you to go out seriously. Would your mom let you?"

I stopped with the thing of dish soap in my hand and considered that. Right now Mom might, since she was going through one of her In-Bed Phases. Actually, she might have let me take her credit cards and go to Acapulco if I'd asked her during an In-Bed Phase. Which I didn't, because I never knew when she'd emerge from her dark-as-a-movie-theater bedroom and go into one of her No-Bed Phases, where she polished the doorknobs and put the spices in alphabetical order. During her last No-Bed Phase, during which she didn't sleep for seventy-two hours, she "housecleaned" my room and found that letter from the school that said I needed to repeat ninth grade English, and the note from Adam Ackerson telling me he wanted to take me out as soon as he got his license in two years, and that other letter addressed to "Jessica Hatcher" that I got in the mail from somebody in Florida but never opened because it looked official and I was sure I wouldn't be able to figure out what it was talking about anyway.

Fortunately, that was all just a few hours before Mom returned to her bedroom. Most of the time I wondered which was better, the In-Bed Phases or the No-Bed Phases—but in situations like that, when she was too busy sleeping to call the school or Adam Ackerson's mother or whoever the stiff-looking letter was from, I had to go with the In-Bed Phase. I might have to clean the house, sort of, and do the laundry when I ran out of underwear, but it was better than having my space invaded and my CD collection arranged by album color.

"So would she?" Chelsea said.

"Would who what?"

"Would your mom let you date Marcus?"

"I don't know!" I said.

"Do you *want* to get serious with him?"

"Do I have to make a commitment this minute?" I squirted some dish soap into the washer.

"No," Chelsea said. I could picture her folding her arms like the guidance counselor who was constantly calling me into her office. "So what are you gonna tell him when he asks you? He's *so* going to when he gets back. Tonight."

I heard a door click down the hall, and I shut the door on the washer and tiptoed through the kitchen to peek. Mom was just crossing into the guest room, half-blonde, half-roots hair falling out of that attempt-at-a-bun thing she did when she was about to spend a week with the covers over her head. She squinted as she shuffled through the doorway. The sun was coming down on the west side of the house, which meant cracks of light were breaking in around the edges of the shades in the bedroom she'd just vacated. She was moving to darker territory.

Which put her closer to where I was. I padded to the back door and stepped out onto the porch, immediately scorching my bare feet on the blinding-white decking. It was hotter than the surface of the sun back there, so I slid down into the only corner where there was shade and let my feet stick out into the Alabama sunlight. My legs were as white as the floorboards, and they kind of reminded me of the skin on the chickens Mom had made two gallons of broth from during her last No-Bed Phase. I'd never figured out what she was going to do with all that juice, so I'd stuck it, pot and all, into the freezer.

"I wish I could get a tan," I said.

"Could we puh-leeze get back to Marcus?" Chelsea said.

"There's nothing to get back to. He's my best guy friend. Period."

"Then what about Adam Ackerson?"

"Why are you all over my love life today?"

"Because."

Silence. Which meant she was about to drop some bomb on me. As long as it wasn't, "You're too weird for me to hang out with anymore," I was okay with a bomb. It was better than discussing my mother and why I didn't text message and why I couldn't stick to one topic of conversation. Chelsea was my best girl friend, but I already knew what happened when somebody else figured out that my normal wasn't the same as their normal.

"Because why?" I said.

"Okay, I wasn't keeping this from you. I was just trying to figure out the best way to tell you."

9

"Tell me what?" I watched a spider swing on the tiniest thread from one porch rail to the other. I really did try to stay with Chelsea, but—had I taken my medication that morning?

"I'm just going to come out with it," Chelsea said. "Donovan and I are going out."

"Going out where?"

"Going *out*. He's my boyfriend. It's a serious relationship."

"Well—so?"

"Aren't you upset?"

"Why would I be? He's an okay guy. I think his teeth are kinda weird, but who am I to talk? Mine are like Bugs Bunny's." No, I had definitely not taken my meds. Later. Right now I toughed out the hot decking and stretched so I could prop my feet on the porch railing, just a few inches from the spiderweb. It would be cool if she would attach her web to my big toe. Not that I could sit still that long ...

"I like his teeth, but that's not the point," Chelsea said. "The point is, now that we're together, I'm going to be spending a lot of time with *him*."

"And not with me, chasing guys and getting them to chase us," I said. "I get it."

"You're mad."

"No, I'm not."

"Yes, you are, I can tell."

"How?"

"Because you're pretending you're not."

At the risk of waking my mother, I laughed out loud. The spider skittered up the pole and out of sight.

"What's so funny?" Chelsea said.

"Since when did I ever pretend not to be mad?"

Chelsea giggled. "Oh, yeah, huh?"

I didn't add that I pretended a lot of things, but that wasn't one of them. It was one of the curses of being a redhead. So people told me. Mostly the people I went off on.

"So you're really not mad that I won't get to spend as much time with you?" she said. "I know it's bad timing with Marcus being gone too."

The phone beeped its Call Waiting signal, and I could have kissed it. Maybe she'd get off the whole Marcus thing while I found out who it was.

"I'll call you back," I said, and punched the button. "Hello?"

"Is this Jessica?" a man's voice said.

"This is *Jessie*," I said. I got an automatic burst of bad energy up my back. Nobody ever called me Jessica except substitute teachers when they were taking roll. Or people who were about to tell me I was in trouble. Again.

"I'm sorry." The guy took in such a huge breath I wondered if he was locked in a walk-in refrigerator and was running out of air.

The big inhale turned into an even longer exhale. Okay, so maybe he was trying to sell me a yoga course.

"Well, Jessie," he said. "This is your father."

I froze, there in the cooking heat on the porch, and I forgot about spiders and Chelsea and Marcus and Lucy and Ethel. I tried to funnel what focus I had on that voice on the phone.

Because I didn't *have* a father.

Okay, so, weird. Very weird. My father died before I was even born. Were we talking psycho here? The man would have to be to want to be *my* father.

I stood up and shook my feet so the pant legs of my shorts would straighten out. "Sorry," I said. "I think you have the wrong number."

"You're not Jessica—Jessie Hatcher? Brooke Hatcher's daughter?"

"Yeah," I said—and only then remembered that you're not supposed to give out personal information to strangers over the phone. Or was that the Internet?

"Then I have the right number," he said.

It occurred to me that he sounded kind of nervous. Weren't psychos usually pretty jittery? In movies they always showed them sweating and pacing when they were holding people hostage in a bank vault.

"You didn't get a letter from me, Jessie?" he said.

"You sent me a letter?" Did that mean he had my address too? Now *I* was starting to sweat and pace.

"A couple of weeks ago. From St. Augustine."

"Where's St. Augustine?" I said.

"St. Augustine, Florida."

"Oh," I said. "That St. Augustine."

I could feel the perspiration running down between my shoulder blades, but I couldn't seem to get it together to go back into the air-conditioned house. I just stood there in the middle of the frying porch and saw the letter Mom had confiscated from my room wiggling in my memory the way the hot pavement ahead does when you're going down the road.

"Maybe we should start over," the man who claimed to be my father said. "If you didn't get the letter, I could see how this would catch you off guard."

"Ya think?" I said. "I got a letter but I didn't open it."

"That would make sense then."

Uh, no, none of this made sense.

"I'm Lou Kennesaw. Apparently your mom has never talked to you about me."

I added the psycho-pacing to the psycho-sweating. "No," I said. "I mean, yes, she told me about Lou Kennesaw, but you died before you could marry her. You're dead."

There was a silence so long I thought he'd hung up—which was fine with me because I was ready to unzip my skin and jump out of it. I even had my finger on the End button when he said— in a voice like that spider web I was toeing earlier as if I didn't have a problem in the world—"Jessie, I'm so sorry you were told that, but I am very much alive and I thought it was time I met you. If I'd known you thought I was dead, I never would have called you like this."

"Okay, so let's pretend you never did," I said.

I didn't mean to say it, but like most things I haven't meant to say in my life, it just came out. I called that a Blurt.

"I don't think we can do that," he said.

"Maybe you can't, but me, I'm great at pretending. Lou who? A wrong number, you say?"

"I know this is a lot to take in, so I'm going to let you soak it up a little—but I would like to see you."

He was actually sounding fatherly. Not that I'd had much experience with having a father. Okay, I'd had exactly none. Except my grandfather, who I hadn't seen much since he married that woman Mom didn't like, which was before I even started wearing a bra so he didn't count. But I'd heard Chelsea's dad say stuff like, "I would like for you to clean your room," in a way that sounded like she'd better do it or she was going to be placed under house arrest. This Lou person had that sound down. I always wondered why Chelsea went right up and cleaned her room instead of telling the man how stupid it was to tidy up a space you were only going to trash again an hour later. Until now.

But this dude was *not* my parent. I only had one parent, and even she—

Might come in handy at that moment.

"I'd have to ask my mom," I said.

"Well, of course. I didn't mean I was going to come by in the next ten minutes."

"Don't come by," I said. "Call. No, I'll call you. After I ask her. Which could be tomorrow, maybe Monday, depending on—"

I chomped down on my lip. When it came to certain subjects I did have *some* control over my mouth. But it never lasted long, and once again I had my finger on the button that could end this call so I could go back to arguing with Chelsea about Marcus and wondering how I was going to wash clothes without laundry detergent.

"I tell you what let's do," the Lou-person said. "You talk to your mom, and I'll call you later tonight. If you want me to talk to her, we can do that too."

"No," I said. "I'll do it. You can't do it."

"I'll call tonight," he said. And before I could beat him to it, he hung up. That ticked me off more than anything. Well, almost anything.

I went inside and pitched the phone onto a pile of laundry and charged down the hall to the guest room. I was about to break the one and only rule I had never broken before. I was going to wake up my mother.

CHAPTER TWO

If I had known that all it took to shake my mother out of one of her In-Bed Phases was to tell her my presumed-dead father called, I might have used that one a long time ago. If I could even have thought up such a weird story. I'd come up with some pretty big ones in my time, but even I couldn't have manufactured that one.

Mom sat up on the guest room bed, blinking at me with her eyes that lost all color when she was in a black hole. Even though she'd asked me to repeat myself four times, and I'd told her the very same thing four times, she was still shaking her head and staring like I was speaking Latin. Her face was going paler, which I hadn't even thought was possible. Mine, on the other hand, was, I knew, about the shade of a plum.

"So could it be for real?" I said—okay, yelled. "This guy might be my dead father?"

"What did he say?"

"Mom! I already *told* you what he said!"

She put both hands up and closed her eyes and licked her lips, while I thrashed around the room, picking up throw pillows and spiking them to the floor.

"Could you get me some water?" she said.

"*What?* Mom—"

"Jessie, just get me a bottle of water and let me get my head wrapped around this—"

"Did you read the letter?"

"What letter?"

"The one that you took from my room?"

She opened her eyes and gave me the look that apparently matched wrapping your head around something. It was a concept I never understood and I sure wasn't getting it now.

"That was from him?" she said.

"I don't *know!*"

"Jessie — just — sit down."

I did, and then got right back up and picked up the pillows I'd thrown so I could throw them again.

"You said he was dead," I said. "Was that a lie?"

Her face crumpled, which meant she was about to cry. Once that started, there would be no getting anything out of her.

"So was it?" I said.

"I did what I thought was right," she said. Every word dragged itself out like it didn't want to be there. "If he wasn't going to be part of your life, then it seemed like it was better for you not to know he even existed."

"He didn't want to be part of my life?" I said. "He didn't *know* me!"

"Please, Jessie, I just need some water, and I'll tell you every-thing." Her voice broke off, and here came the sobs.

I all but put my fingers in my ears. "I don't want to know *everything*," I said. I stood at the end of the bed, where I had once again run out of pillows. "I just want to know if I have to see him."

Mom fell back onto her own mound of pillows and covered her face with her hands. The crying was raspy, but it didn't make any tears. I always figured she'd cried so much she'd used up her life's supply.

"I guess I messed this up just like I've messed up everything else," she said. "I don't know what to do, Jessie. I guess you ought to meet him."

"I don't *want* to meet him! What am I supposed to say to him?"

"I'll talk to him," she said. "Just let me get a handle on this. I need a few minutes."

She was already headed into that curled-up thing, like

15

Chelsea's Chihuahua whenever anybody but Chelsea looked at him.

"Okay, I'm giving the phone to you when he calls," I said.

"When's he going to call?" she said.

"Tonight — tomorrow — I forget what he said."

I was so flipped out, I was actually about to forget my own name. What *was* my name, anyway? Was it still Hatcher — or was it now Ken-Doll or whatever it was he said his last name was? The hamster wheel in my head was turning faster than ever. And my mother was shivering under the covers and waving for me to close the door behind me.

Out in the hall I could hear water running in a way it shouldn't have been running, which probably meant the washing machine was overflowing or something. I didn't care. For once I could only think of one thing: I was going to meet my father.

Only not like Chelsea's dad was her father and Marcus's was his. This man had only given me his genes. He didn't make me clean my room or take me on vacations or tell me I couldn't bring the Chihuahua to the dinner table.

I froze with my hand on my bedroom doorknob. Did he think he was going to do that now? Come in and start telling me what to do?

Nah. I pushed into my room and flopped on the bed and did a shoulder stand so my toes touched the tassel that hung from the chain on my ceiling fan. Mom just said I had to meet him. He wasn't moving in. Besides, after ten minutes with me he'd probably deny he ever even knew my mother, much less — well, you know.

I dropped my feet to the mattress. Yeah, ten minutes was usually about all it took for adults to decide there was something "off" about me. They either fidgeted in their seats like I was making them nervous, or they nodded like they had made the same diagnosis made by teachers and counselors and that doctor my mother took me to when I was in seventh grade. I could read, "This is a classic case of ADHD" in their eyes. Which was about the only thing I could read — though most people didn't pick up on *that* even when I was in their class for a whole semester. I was pretty good at covering that part up.

I rolled over onto my stomach and crawled to the window seat at the head of my bed and looked out between the fancy black "security bars." My mother had called them that when she had them installed all over the house. I knew it was basically a way to make sure I didn't sneak out, which I'd never done after that one time in seventh grade. That had led to my visit to the doctor, who had said I had "poor impulse control associated with—" well, I forgot the rest. I watched a squirrel skitter up the magnolia tree in the side yard and totally identified with him. I always figured I'd have been a very successful squirrel. I wondered if my father liked small rodents.

Of course, it didn't matter whether he liked me or not. He wasn't going to be around that long. But I didn't want him to know I had a "disorder." If we just, like, sat in the living room and had a Coke, I could probably fool him like I did my friends and the adults who only saw me for a few minutes at a time. The UPS guy, for example, seemed to think I was pretty cool. Maybe this Lou person would just stay long enough to feel like he'd done some kind of duty by me and leave, and we could go back to normal.

Normal.

I squirmed off the seat and went to see how Lucy and Ethel were doing.

*

"Let me see what you decided to wear," my mother said.

I jumped halfway out of my skin. I hadn't even noticed that she'd moved from the guest room back into her own bed when I came in to forage for a pair of shoes from her closet. She'd gotten so thin she barely made a bump under the covers.

"Turn on the light," she said.

Actually, I could have opened the shades and it would have lit up the whole room, but she probably didn't know that Saturday night had turned into Sunday morning. Ever since Lou, father ghost from the past, had called the night before and she'd talked to him for thirty minutes with me stationed outside the guest room with my ear pressed to the door, she'd gone even further into her cave. When I'd asked her what he said, she mumbled something about him coming for me at noon to take me to lunch.

So while she was sleeping, I was tearing my closet apart trying to put together an outfit that didn't scream "I'm hyperactive!" but that didn't look too goody-goody like I was trying to impress him, or that wasn't too skimpy so he'd think he had to call social services. It took most of the night to make a decision, partly because I had a hard time making choices about anything and partly because I needed something to do since I couldn't sleep anyway. I could never fall asleep until like midnight on an average night as it was—and that was definitely not an average night.

"That's cute," Mom said about my lime green miniskirt and silver tank and arm full of bracelets. "Wear the silver sandals with the kitten heels. The Summer Brooke Line. SB–100."

"Okay," I said, and proceeded to open every box until I found the ones she was talking about. They were part of the line of shoes she'd designed before she had the In-Bed Phase before this one. They'd sold well enough to keep her accountant from coming over to say she had to get back to work.

I slipped the shoes on and modeled them for Mom as she squinted in the light from the lamp.

"You need a necklace," she said, and then shook her head. "No, you'll just fiddle with it and drive the man nuts. I don't think the bracelets are a good idea either, come to think of it."

I closed the closet and headed for the door.

"Jessie, wait," she said.

I decided to give her fifteen seconds. I wasn't done being mad at her over this whole thing—and if she was going to add her digs about my "condition" on top of it, I was so out of there.

"He's a nice man. You don't need to be afraid of him or anything."

"Nice?" I said. "As in leave-the-girlfriend-who's-having-your-baby kind of nice?"

"Jessie, that is so immature—"

Of course it was. I had the emotional skills of an eight-year-old. According to her.

"Look, I don't have the energy to argue with you about this," she said.

Good. That meant she wouldn't have the energy to yell at me when I slammed the door and stomped off down the hall, which I did, kitten heels and all. The grandfather clock in the foyer donged eleven times while I stood there counting.

I grabbed the phone and called Chelsea as I looked for my purse. By the time I told her where to meet me I still couldn't find it, so I just took off out the front door without it and started down the sidewalk toward Cahaba Road. Two steps out I realized I'd forgotten my sunglasses, but I wasn't going back to look for them. I probably wouldn't be able to find them anyway, so I just squinted into the glare.

I was mad enough to make it almost to Mountain Brook Village before I noticed that my feet were killing me. I took off my mother's designer shoes and held one in each hand while I marched the rest of the way to the Mountain Brook Creamery barefoot. The Fake Father could come to my house and have it out with the Messed-Up Mother while I was getting what I needed, which was ice cream and Chelsea.

She was already there when I arrived, standing at the counter with Donovan, who was looking down at her like, "Go ahead, try to make me smile." I hoped he wouldn't. He really did have funky teeth. Besides, what was he doing there? I'd made it clear on the phone that I had to talk to Chelsea in private.

Bent on getting rid of him, I started toward her. Somebody behind me said, "Fine. Don't say hi."

I whirled around into a T-shirt with a giant crab on it.

"Marcus!" I squealed, like a pig caught in a doggy door.

He picked me up, because he was six-foot-two and weighed, like, a lot. He swung me around while I held onto his neck, still clutching the silver sandals. After a mom holding two double-scoop cones for her kids glared at us, he dropped me into a chair at a table by the window.

"I am SO glad you're back," I said. "I thought I was gonna bore myself to death."

He smiled his big, sloppy smile and didn't say anything because usually I didn't give him a chance to anyway, which always seemed to be fine with him, because when most girls talked to him they expected him to actually contribute something to the conversation, and he wasn't that good at it. Not until you got to know him. Which I did. Which gave me an idea.

"I want to hear all about your trip," I said.

"It was good." His wide-as-a-plate face was pink under the dark stubble that dotted it like flecks of pepper, and his dark eyes that matched his hair were dancing all over my face. Unlike my mother, he did not seem to think I had the emotional maturity of an eight-year-old.

"I want to hear more than *that*," I said. "So can we go four-wheeling or something? You know—now?"

"No way, Jessie." Chelsea scraped another metal chair up to the table and stuck a scoop of mint chocolate chip on a sugar cone into my hand.

Donovan looked like he was about to slip into a coma as he leaned on the windowsill and dug into a sundae.

"You guys could come too," I said.

"Not before you tell me what's going on." Chelsea looked at Marcus. "She's avoiding something. You know she is."

Marcus shrugged. Chelsea glowered at him. She had her hair pulled up in a ponytail, which meant we were going to cut right to the chase. Otherwise, she would have it down where she could toss it at Donovan. Having ultrashort hair, I never mastered that technique.

"Come on, Jess, dish," she said.

"I had a fight with my mother, and I need to get out of the house," I said.

Chelsea shook the ponytail. "If you had a fight with your mother you wouldn't *be* out of the house. She'd have you on lockdown so fast."

That was true. Mom and I usually only fought when she was in a No-Bed Phase, and she always won.

"It's just weird right now," I said. "I need to go get wild—you know, get it out of my system."

"You never get wild out of your system. What's up with this—you've got something weird going on and you can't even tell your best friends?"

I darted my gaze to Donovan, who was looking at his sundae like it was disgusting even though he was practically inhaling it. What did she see in him anyway? The point was, *he* wasn't my friend.

Chelsea looked up at him too, and I could see a wrestling match start in her brain. Make Donovan go away, or not hear about my weirdness. I was betting she'd give up the weirdness for now.

"Okay," she said, "be that way—but I *will* get it out of you." She stood up and handed her cone to Donovan, who looked like she'd asked him to hold her Chihuahua. Then she leaned over and whispered in Marcus's ear while his face turned scarlet. It was like she was filling him up with red dye number 3.

"I'm calling you later," she said to me. She let her ponytail loose and did a toss toward the door. Donovan followed her without a glance at Marcus and me.

"I'm supposed to make you tell me," Marcus said.

I laughed, spewing mint chocolate chip across the front of his shirt and blocking out an entire crab claw.

"She thinks you can make me do something?" I said, tossing him a wad of napkins. "Has she actually *met* me?"

Marcus turned redder and looked at my ice-cream cone, which I handed him because I'd lost my appetite for mint chocolate chip. If I did tell anybody the embarrassing details of my secret life it would have been Marcus. He'd never breathe a word of it to anyone, and he'd never use it on me later during a fight because we never fought. I actually wanted to tell him about this father thing right that very minute—except that there was a problem.

I watched him lick at the scoop of green ice cream and felt my own face turn red. Way back in fourth grade when I was going through a Phase of my own—a Bald-Face Lying Phase—

I'd told Marcus and Chelsea and whoever else would listen this long tale about how my father died. I made up a story of him being a Navy SEAL and being blown up while he was rescuing an African princess and my mother having the only piece of his body that they found—and that it was preserved in a safety-deposit box at the bank. It was my finest hour as a Big Fat Liar.

Maybe nobody would remember it now. Oh, no, wait—back in May in history class the subject of Navy SEALs came up, and Chelsea raised her hand and said my father was one, and the whole class turned around and gaped at me. Except Marcus, who had smiled like I'd just given him one more reason to adore me.

"Do you trust me?" I said.

Marcus stopped licking and blinked at me. "Yeah. What's not to trust?"

You don't even know, I wanted to say to him. But instead I said, "I *have* to stay away from my house all day today, and I can't tell you why, but I need you to help me."

"Will I end up in jail if I do?" he said. "I can't go to jail—my dad'll kill me."

"No! It's not like I robbed a bank or something—I just need to get away for today."

"What if your mom sends the police looking for you?"

"You watch too many cop shows, Marcus." I sighed. "Okay, I'll leave my mom a note. What time is it?"

He glanced at his watch. "Eleven thirty."

The hamster wheel kicked into gear, but it didn't take me anywhere. Typically, the more stressed-out I got, the harder it was to think.

"Let's just go to my house," I said. "I'll figure it out on the way."

Which I didn't. Marcus did. He pulled the Jeep—that's what he drove, a red Jeep—onto the street that ran along the side of our house, which was on a corner. It gave me a straight shot to the back door.

"You're a genius," I said. "I'll be right back."

It wasn't until I slipped out of the Jeep that I realized I'd left the silver sandals at the Creamery. We could stop and get them after I grabbed a change of clothes from my room, which was the real reason I was here. It was pointless for me to even try to write a note to my mom—she probably wouldn't even get out of bed when Lee or Louey or whatever his name was rang the doorbell. I would be back before she even knew I went four-wheeling with Marcus instead of connecting with the father-who-wasn't-really-a-father.

None of that ever happened. When I rushed into the kitchen, a redheaded guy stood up from the table and said, "You must be Jessie."

I just stared at him like I was looking into a mirror.

CHAPTER THREE

He wasn't totally a mirror image of me, but if I had been a boy I would have looked like his identical twin.

He had the Raggedy Ann—well, Andy—red hair, cut short, and my same blue eyes that looked even closer together than they were because of the long-as-mine nose. He wasn't very tall—his skin was pale for somebody who lived in Florida—and in addition to looking like me, he looked absolutely nothing like a Navy SEAL. Any hope of telling my friends the government had mistaken that small body part in the safety-deposit box for his when it belonged to someone else faded almost before I could think it up.

About fifteen hundred questions crowded onto the hamster wheel, including, *Why are you early?* and *Where did you get that shirt?* and *Why didn't you marry my mother?* and *How did you get in here?*

I didn't actually have to ask that last one because I finally noticed that my mother was sitting at the kitchen table, bare feet propped up on the chair, knees under her chin, hair half in and half out of the bun thing. She'd managed to pull on a Brooke Line Shoes sweatshirt over her pajamas, but other than that she was exactly like she was in bed less than an hour before.

Well, not exactly.

"Jessie, this is Lou," she said.

Her voice was high and tight, as if she was forcing the last of it out of a toothpaste tube. She never got mad when she was in an In-Bed Phase, but she was obviously making an exception for Lou.

"It's nice to meet you, Jessie," he said.

His voice was so low I barely heard it. And when I looked at him, I could see him swallowing like he was trying to down a Ping-Pong ball. Something had gone on between the two of them before I walked in the door. Perfect.

"I'm sorry—I interrupted you guys," I said. "I'll just go—"

"Get some shoes on," my mother finished for me. "Lou is taking you to The Cheesecake Factory."

Yeah, if she didn't remember that I'd gone out wearing her designer shoes and came back without them, she was definitely still thinking about whatever it was they had been "discussing."

"You hungry?" Lou said to me as if we went out and grabbed a bite to eat together on a regular basis.

"I'll go get shoes," I said, and fled to my room where I gritted my teeth at those stupid security bars. If it weren't for them, I'd be out my window and—

I froze, head halfway into my closet. Marcus. He was probably still sitting out there waiting for me.

I dove for the window seat, just as my door opened and my mother slipped in and dangled inside the doorway like a skeleton.

"Just grab some flip-flops," she said. "He's ready to go."

"Who?" I said.

"Jessie, don't play that game with me."

Mom gave a weary sigh. I could never figure out how she could still seem so exhausted when she'd been sleeping 24/7 for days. Even now, after a week in bed, it looked like she had that black stuff football players put on under her eyes.

"Just go and get it over with," she said. "I owe him that much."

"*I* don't owe him anything!" I said.

She just shook her head. She wanted him out of there, and I had to be the one to take him. Period.

And Lou obviously wanted to get out of there as much as she wanted him to go. He was standing at the front door jangling his car keys when my mother escorted me to the living room, me wearing neon orange flip-flops she wouldn't have let me be caught dead in on a normal day. This day didn't qualify. I'd already left behind my shoes, my best guy friend, and my usual ability to weasel out of a situation. Even thinking, "What would Lucy and Ethel do?" didn't help.

*

"What's good here?" Lou said to me from behind the menu.

I couldn't remember. I read the paragraph-long descriptions of every dish, but I couldn't remember any of the words the minute I moved on to the next one. The more stressed I was, the less success I had with reading—which was why I was lousy at taking tests, writing book reports, and today, ordering from a menu with my I-thought-you-were-dead father sitting across the table from me.

"I'll have the special," I told the server, although I couldn't remember what he'd told us it was.

"I'll have the same," Lou said. He smiled at me when the waiter was gone. "So you like eggs Benedict too."

I had no idea what that was, but I just nodded and groped for a way to get through this. How did I get through anything difficult—trips to the discipline office, after-school detention, teacher-mandated tutoring sessions with geeky seniors? Of course ...

I wrinkled my nose at Lou and laughed. "I don't even know what eggs Benedict is," I said. "I just got it because it sounded funky."

He sat back, one hand flat on the table, and gazed at me. "So where do we start, Jessie?" he said.

"I'll start," I said, and picked up a spoon to give myself something to fiddle with while I talked. "I'm fifteen. I won't be sixteen for ten months, which means I'll be like the last one of my friends to get a driver's license—my friend Marcus already has his, *and* a car—" I paused a second to consider whether Marcus was still sitting at the curb waiting for me, then plunged back in. "I just finished my freshman year; my favorite subject is art—and lunch. No, I don't have a boyfriend—adults always want to know that, like it's any of their business. No offense, but I mean, do I ask grown-ups, perfect strangers, if they're seeing anybody? What's up with that?"

26

"I have no idea," Lou said.

He wasn't laughing yet, but his eyes were sparkling and he didn't have the ADHD diagnosis on his lips. This could be working.

"I've lived in Mountain Brook since I was six," I babbled on, "and my mom's designer shoes made it big, so we could move out of my grandfather's garage apartment in Birmingham, which I don't remember that much anyway, and besides he doesn't live there anymore because after my grandmother died he married some younger chick, and they sold the house and moved to Fort Myers or some other old people town, although I don't know why she would want to live there except maybe she's not that young—just younger than him, but, then, who isn't?"

"I knew your grandfather," Lou said.

"Oh," I said to the bowl of the spoon. "Did he run you off with a shotgun? Is that why you didn't marry my mother?"

It was a Blurt, but maybe somewhere in the wrinkles of my brain I'd kind of planned it. Maybe being "socially immature" had its benefits. I watched to see what Lou would do with it. He rearranged the silverware at his place and then sat back, both hands flat on the table this time, and nodded at me.

"I guess we should get it out there, huh?" he said.

"Whatever," I said. "It's probably none of my business. My mother obviously doesn't think so—"

"Of course it's your business."

Nobody had looked at me like that since my English teacher said, "Of course you're getting an F. You didn't turn in a term paper!"

"Look—I would have married your mother if I'd known she was pregnant."

"You didn't notice her getting fat?"

"She broke up with me before she was even showing."

"So what about later?" I said, as long as we were on the subject and he didn't look ready to pitch a fork at me.

"'Later' was long after I was married to someone else," he said. "I offered to help, but she said you two were all set, thank you very much."

Just as I caught an I-have-tasted-something-disgusting curl on his lip, he rubbed his palm in the air like he was erasing everything he'd just said.

"I should have insisted on being part of your life then, Jessie, and I'm sorry," he said. "But I'm older and wiser now, and I'm here—for whatever you need me for."

Can you get them to pass me to tenth grade English without going to summer school? I wanted to say. And then I didn't want to say it, because I didn't want him to know I was the worst student in the history of high school because I had a "disorder." People found that out—certain people—and they—well, whatever. The point was, he wasn't going to be around that long. He did, after all, have a wife.

"Does she know about me?" I said.

"Who?"

"Your wife."

"I'm divorced."

I exchanged the spoon for a saltshaker and examined the bottom, of course, spilling salt on the tablecloth. "Was it because she found out about me?"

Lou shook his head. "We had other issues. Back to you now."

Fortunately the food came then, and I stopped and stared at the eggs Benedict, which had some kind of gross-looking sauce drizzled over them. When I looked up, Lou was watching me.

"I'll go ahead and bless it," he said.

He closed his eyes and propped his chin on folded hands and had "Father, thank you—" out before I realized that he meant he was going to pray. Not that I had never seen somebody pray before. Up until sixth grade when the Richardsons who'd lived across the street moved away, I'd gone to church almost every Sunday. I went with whoever on our cul-de-sac was going, so for a while I rocked with the Pentecostal Holiness people and then I watched people get baptized in the pool at the Baptist Church and after that I got into chancel drama with those people who didn't call themselves anything except Christian.

Even when the Richardsons left I still prayed to God the way they taught us in Methodist Vacation Bible School. Or

28

was it Presbyterian? They said just talk to him so I did, and even though my mind went all over the place—big surprise—and I didn't know what I was doing, it felt like Somebody was there and it kept me from feeling like I was going crazy.

Until hormones kicked in, and then nothing kept me from going off the wall. And besides, I figured out that God wasn't answering when I said, "Please help me pass this test" and "Please let me throw up so I don't have to go to school tomorrow" and "Please make my mom stop having Phases." So I gave up praying. I missed it at first, but I hadn't thought about God in a while.

But here was Father Lou, talking about blessing the hands that prepared our disgusting-looking eggs Benedict. I glanced around to see if anybody was staring at us and got my hands folded and my eyes closed before he said the amen. Why I cared whether he thought I was praying or not, I wasn't sure. I just did it.

*

I had no idea what time it was when Lou pulled his pickup truck into our driveway, but I was sure it had to be, like, the next day. I was wiped out from talking so much, which I had to do to keep him from asking me questions I didn't want to answer or couldn't answer or wouldn't answer if he'd pulled a gun on me. I wondered if it had occurred to my mother that this guy could have developed into some kind of psycho over the years—although he seriously didn't look or act like one. Not that I had known any psychos.

Anyway, I was so ready to jump out of that truck, say, "Good-bye, it's been nice," and forget this whole thing ever happened. I even had my hand on the door handle—but he turned off the motor and drummed his fingers on the steering wheel and said to the windshield, "Is everything okay here for you with your mother?"

"She won't let me get a learner's permit, and I have to do the laundry," I said, "but other than that, it's all right."

"That's not exactly what I mean."

He looked straight at me, the way Chelsea's father looked

29

at her, and I got the definite feeling that he had done this kind of thing before. Or maybe men just got the dad thing when they reached a certain age.

Although I knew what he meant, I shrugged and opened his glove compartment and examined the contents. He reached over and closed it without a word and left his hand on the dashboard. I snapped the seat belt against my chest and said a loud "Ow," but he completely ignored it.

"It's pretty clear your mom is depressed," he said. "I just wondered how that affects you."

"She's freaked out because you showed up," I said, which was part of the truth.

"And are you okay with her 'freaking out'?"

"Oh, yeah, I have a lot of fun with that."

"Who's there for you when she can't cope?"

"Look, I'm fine," I said. "I've been fine for fifteen years, so I really don't need you to come in and fix my life."

That was more than a Blurt. I was bordering on a meltdown. I jerked the door handle and tried to get out of the truck without unfastening the seat belt, and when I fumbled at the stupid thing, Lou put his hand on my arm and I shoved it away.

"Okay," he said. "I'm sorry — I shouldn't have pushed you. We don't have to have this conversation now."

"We're not having it ever," I said. "I'm going in."

He let me get out, but he met me at the front door where I was hating myself because I hadn't brought my key and I was pretty sure I'd lost the one that used to be under a rock in the flowerbed.

"Are you locked out?" he said.

"I can get in. You can go," I said.

He didn't say anything. He just reached up and rang the doorbell.

I folded my arms and jiggled my knees back and forth. He probably thought I had to go to the bathroom. I reminded myself that I didn't care what he thought, but that got lost on the hamster wheel, which would have thrown even the toughest rodent off by now.

"I'm planning to stay in town for a few days," he said. "We could go to the lake—"

"I'm pretty busy," I said, and rang the doorbell again myself. And pounded on the door with my fist. And then yelled, "Mom! Let me in!"

"You think she's in the shower or something?" Lou said.

I didn't tell him my mother didn't take showers during In-Bed Phases.

"I'll go to her bedroom window," I said, putting up my hand to keep him from following me.

He did anyway.

Of course, once I was there I couldn't do a whole lot. It was like Fort Knox with those bars on the window, and I wasn't tall enough to see in anyway. I just yelled "Mom!" over and over, and although I didn't mean for it to, my voice got higher and more freaked-out sounding every time. This was weird, even for her.

Finally Lou stepped past me and peered in. I could tell by the way his fingers tightened around the bars that he didn't just see my mother with the covers over her head.

"Is she there?" I screamed at him. "What's wrong? Is she— what's going *on*?"

I was clawing at the back of his Hawaiian shirt, trying to pull him out of the way. He turned around and pressed me against him with an arm that was surprisingly strong. Even as I struggled to get away, he fished a cell phone out of his pocket and punched in three numbers. I didn't have to see them to know they were 9-1-1.

CHAPTER FOUR

T wenty-four hours before, I didn't even know I had a father. Now I was in the UAB Hospital hallway with him, waiting for somebody to tell me if my mother was going to survive swallowing half a container of pills. My hamster wheel spun with what had happened in between: him busting through the back door—okay, so maybe he *had* been a Navy SEAL—and giving her CPR, paramedics putting a mask on her face and hauling her off in an ambulance, and me screaming, "What's wrong? What's *wrong*?" until finally, in the truck, this man who said he was my father told me she'd tried to commit suicide, only he didn't think she really wanted to die or she would have taken the whole bottle.

"Is there somebody we need to call, Jessie?" he said now.

I stopped pacing a path on the floor in front of him and said "Chelsea—no, wait, not Chelsea."

"Who's Chelsea?" he said.

"My best friend. Maybe Marcus. No, I can't tell him—he's probably mad at me for—no, I can't tell him."

"And Marcus is ...?"

"My other best friend."

I went back to pacing.

"I was talking about an adult," Lou said. "Is your mother seeing anybody? Does *she* have a best friend?"

"She used to," I said. "They had a fight. There's Garry—he's her accountant—"

"No other friends? Relatives?"

I looked at him over my shoulder. "My grandfather."

He almost made a face, I could tell.

"He's in Cancun or someplace," I said. "He sent me a post-card. Mom would ground me for the rest of my life if I called him."

"You two are really alone," Lou said.

I didn't answer him because he sounded like he was talking to himself. Besides, for once I couldn't argue.

"Don't worry," he said. "I'll stay until we figure something out."

What was to figure out? I would go home and do what I always did when my mother was In-Bed. Her not being there for a night or two wouldn't make that much difference, right?

I got a weird chill up my back.

"You cold?" he said. "I can get you a blanket."

The door we were guarding swung open, and we both pounced on the guy in green scrubs who came through.

"You're Ms. Hatcher's family?" he said.

"I'm-Jessie-I'm-her-daughter," I said as if it were all one word.

"I'm Jessie's father," Lou said.

The guy in the green looked at both of us and nodded. "I can see that. Okay—well, the news is partly good. She's physically stable—no brain damage that we can determine at this time—"

"Brain damage?" I said. "Like, a vegetable?"

"There is none, thanks to whoever gave her CPR."

I looked at Lou, but he didn't say anything.

"Her vital signs are good," the guy said, "so we're going to move her onto the—"

"Why can't she just come home?" I said. "I can take care of her."

The guy—who I'd figured out by now was a doctor because he wasn't actually answering our questions—looked at me and then at Lou.

Lou rubbed the back of his head. "Jessie's very protective of her mom."

"She'll be in good hands here. I'm sorry—" He reached out his hand to shake Lou's. "I'm Dr. Blah-Blah. I've been taking

33

care of Ms. Hatcher, and I'm turning her over to Dr. Blah-Blah, who is a psychiatrist …"

I'm sure their names weren't Blah-Blah and Blah-Blah, but that was about all I was catching. This guy was talking about them putting my mother in the loony ward, so I didn't care who they were.

"She isn't crazy," I said. "She doesn't need to be locked up."

"We aren't going to 'lock her up,'" Dr. Blah-Blah said. "We're just going to make sure she doesn't hurt herself again, and we're going to try to figure out why she wanted to in the first place."

I turned my glare on Lou, but he was nodding at the doctor like he totally agreed.

"You don't get it!" I said. "She just got upset. She never did this before. She'll get out of bed in a couple of days and start cleaning our house with a toothbrush and staying up all night designing purses—"

I stopped, because the doctor was gazing at me like I'd just discovered the cure for cancer. He said, "That helps a lot—Jessie, is it?"

No. I'm not Jessie. I'm some idiot who blurts stuff out and gets her mother in more trouble and—

And—I didn't know what. Because Lou was right. Without her, I really was alone.

"You okay?" Dr. Blah-Blah said.

"How about a blanket?" Lou said—probably because I was shaking so hard I could barely stand up. I didn't have any choice but to let him put his arm around my shoulder and half-carry me to a chair in the hall. I couldn't say what happened after that, except that Lou kept saying, "God's got this handled, Jessie. He's got it handled."

Why, I wondered, should I trust that God would all of a sudden show up now and make everything okay?

That anybody would.

*

I didn't wake up until noon the next day. When I did, I smelled bacon cooking, and I sat up straight in the bed and looked around to make sure they hadn't checked *me* into a hospital. I had never smelled that in our house, not even during a No-Bed Phase. It would have made too much of a mess.

I dragged myself into the kitchen. Lou was at the stove using a black bath towel as an apron and flipping a pancake into the air. It landed perfectly on the spatula, like something you'd see on a cooking show.

"You want blueberries in yours?" Lou said without looking at me.

"We don't have any blueberries," I said.

"We do now. There's juice for you on the table."

I glanced over at the glass filled with orange juice I also didn't think we had. It was on a green place mat—where had that come from?—next to a cloth napkin with the letter *H* stitched on it. Nobody had set the table since Heidi left—or was it Tammy? One of those nannies my mother had fired when she was No-Bed—until she'd stopped hiring them at all four years ago.

I drifted to the table, and Lou put a plate with a stack of pancakes in front of me. They were melting their own butter. My mouth watered.

"When's my mom coming home?" I said.

Lou handed me a warm pitcher full of syrup and watched me pour it before he said, "Not for at least two weeks."

I left the syrup dripping over my plate. Lou took the pitcher from me and wiped off the spout.

"There's good news, though," he said. "She told the doctor this morning that she wants help."

"I said I'd help her!" I said. "I do it all the time. Except when I made the washer overflow—which wasn't my fault. We were out of detergent and I tried to use the dish stuff—"

"Not that kind of help, Jess," Lou said.

He sat down across from me. It didn't look right, a man in our kitchen.

"What kind of help then?" I said.

"Psychiatric help. Doctors who can get her on medication and therapists who can work through her issues with her."

"She won't do that," I said. "She doesn't believe in it."

Lou's auburn eyebrows went up. "She's been told before that she needs treatment?"

I chomped down on my tongue so I wouldn't say, "No. She's been told *I* need treatment—and I am NOT telling you what happened with that."

Lou sat back and put his hands flat on the table because he was getting ready to say something heavy. It bothered me that I was already getting the way he talked with his body.

"You know," he said, "sometimes you have to hit rock bottom before you'll admit you need help."

"Yeah, well, thanks for that," I said, stabbing the stack of pancakes with my fork.

"For what?"

"For making her hit rock bottom. She wouldn't have taken those pills if you hadn't shown up."

He didn't even blink. "How many days had she been sleeping all the time before I came?"

"Not that many."

"And before that, was she 'cleaning the house with a tooth-brush'?"

"No." She was going through my room with a garbage bag.

"I may have been the last straw," Lou said as he leaned on the table to look straight at me with those eyes like mine. "But if it hadn't been me, eventually it would have been something else. I'm actually glad it *was* me—that I was here for you."

I gave the pancakes a slap with the fork and sent syrup splashing over the side of the plate.

"I know you're used to taking care of yourself," he said, "and you obviously don't do that bad a job of it."

"Is that supposed to be a compliment?" I said.

"But two weeks is a long time, and by law you can't stay alone without adult supervision. I think you should come home with me, Jess, just until your mom gets back on her feet."

I left the fork standing up in the stack and scraped my chair back. "I'll find my own adult supervision," I said, and left him there with his bacon and his butter and his bad ideas.

I called Chelsea first, because she had more adult supervision than anybody I knew.

"My mom has to be away," I told her. "Do you think I could stay with you for two weeks?"

She loved the idea. Her mom hated it. She said the last two times I spent the night with Chelsea, we got in trouble. How was I supposed to know that website we ended up in was going to be way beyond PG–13? And that the phone calls to try to talk to the Jonas Brothers were going to run up a two-hundred-dollar bill? My mom paid it, but that obviously wasn't enough for Chelsea's mom.

I actually tried my grandfather next, but he evidently didn't get cell phone service in Cancun or Aruba or wherever he was, because my calls went straight to his voice mail, and then I didn't know what to say so I hung up.

That left Marcus. I couldn't ask him if I could stay with him. I mean, even though he was my second-best friend he *was* a guy. And after I left him sitting outside my house for hours in the heat, I was afraid to call him and have him tell me to get lost. I couldn't actually imagine him saying that, but I didn't want to hear it if he did.

My only hope was that when I told my mother, she would hire somebody to stay with me. There was no way she was letting me go off to St. Somewhere with a guy I hardly knew—a guy who, for some reason I still didn't get, had suddenly decided to become the poster boy for fatherhood.

So I asked Lou if I could see Mom. That evidently required the passing of a law or something, because it took a whole day and about a hundred phone calls conducted in Lou-whispers to get me to the hospital. About three steps into the wing that had a name so long I didn't even try to figure it out, I was so creeped out I was sorry I'd ever thought this was a good idea.

We—Lou and I—had to go through three sets of locked doors that clanged shut behind us like they do in prison movies. All of them had tiny windows in them and buzzer things that had to be pushed before anybody would let us go any farther. Dr. Blah-Blah had lied when he said my mother wasn't on lockdown.

Finally the guy leading us—who looked like he should be in the ring on WWE instead of in a hospital—told us we could go into this one room, and that he would be right outside in case we needed him.

"For what?" I said.

Lou started to go in with me, but I planted my hand on the doorjamb.

"I want to talk to her by myself," I said.

WWE shook his too-big head. "You have to have an adult with you."

"Why?"

"Because you're underage."

I opened my mouth to tell him *he* was the one who was nuts, but Lou nudged me into the room. I made a mental note to tell him later that I didn't like people touching me, and then I forgot, because I saw my mother.

She was sitting in front of a window in a blue chair. It was the only piece of furniture in there except for the bed. The walls were blue too, and the bedspread was flowered, and I was pretty sure she hated that décor.

And then I knew she hadn't really noticed it. Although her hair had been washed and brushed into a neat ponytail and the light-green sweats she was wearing didn't look like she'd slept in them, her eyes were still smudgy underneath and her bony shoulders seemed to be reaching for each other in front of her. If she was any better than she was before they stuck her in here, I sure couldn't see it.

Especially when she looked at me and burst into tears-without-tears. She put her rickety arms out to me.

My mother and I were never snuggly with each other, so it took me a second to figure out that she wanted to hold me. I leaned over and sort of patted her back while she hung on. It was like hugging the coatrack in our foyer.

"I've messed up my life, Jessie," she said into my neck. "I have to fix it."

38

"You will," I said. "You always do."

She pushed me to arm's length to look at me. Her almost-no-color eyes seemed to have a hard time focusing.

"I really have to fix it this time," she said. "It's going to take a while."

I shrugged, which was hard to do with her hanging onto my shoulders with hands like claws. "That's okay."

"Longer than you can stay by yourself."

I glared back at Lou, who was leaning against the wall and staring at the floor like he was trying to be invisible. But he was listening to every word—I knew it.

I knelt in front of Mom and tried to get my face up close to hers. "That's what I wanted to talk to you about," I whispered. "You could get somebody to stay at the house with me until you get fixed. I was thinking Millie. I know you fired her a long time ago, but she was the best of all of them and you didn't fire her because she did anything wrong—you just thought I was old enough not to have a nanny anymore, which was true, but since they say I can't stay by myself for two weeks"—I tossed another glare back at Lou—"she would be perfect . . ."

My mother was shaking her head. "No, Jessie. In the first place, you can hardly be trusted to stay two hours by yourself, let alone two weeks."

I clamped my teeth together to keep from screaming. Even when she was at—what did Lou call it?—rock bottom, she could still reach up and scratch my heart out.

"And I don't know how long I'm going to be in here," she was saying, "or what kind of work I'm going to have to do when I get out—just—no, that isn't going to work for me."

"I'll cooperate—I swear I will. I'm not going to drive a nanny nuts like I did back then."

No, I did not just use the word *nuts* on the psych ward. I put my hand over my mouth, but Mom didn't appear to have noticed. Her eyes were losing focus again.

"I don't have what it takes to argue with you," she said. "I've already agreed to send you home with Lou."

What happened to me then can only be described as a *nuclear* meltdown. WWE came in from the hall. Lou pulled me off my mother. Mom herself turned back to the window while somebody hauled me out of there. By the time Lou deposited me into the front seat of the truck, I was hoarse from screaming at him.

Through it all, he never said a word—not until we were back in my driveway. Even then, all he said was, "I'm so sorry, Jessie."

"You're not that sorry," I said, "or you wouldn't make me go with you."

"That's not what I'm sorry about," he said.

*

Over the next two days, as Lou did all the stuff he had to do to become my temporary guardian, I didn't ask him what he *was* sorry about. It wasn't going to change anything, and I was too busy doing what desperation made me do. I wasn't good at planning. I just knew that if had to go to St. Somewhere with this almost total stranger, then I had to do whatever it took to get back here to my own life as soon as possible. Back to where I had at least a little bit of control over what happened to me. I had to have that, or I was going to end up in the room with my mother. I might even have gone for that if I hadn't wanted to flush her down the toilet for setting this up behind my back. Like she said, she'd messed up her life. Now she was messing up mine.

I could only come up with two things to do. First, I called Marcus.

"I know you probably hate me now, and I don't blame you," I said the very second he answered the phone. "And I swear I'll make it up to you when I get back—"

"Where are you going?" he said.

I stopped and blinked because Marcus never interrupted me when I was on a roll.

"Uh, my mom's … away," I said, "and she's making me go off with this … relative I hardly even know—"

"How long are you gonna be gone?"

His voice was sounding panicky, at least for Marcus.

"Not long if I can help it," I said. "Or if *you* can. I know the last time I asked you for help I ditched you, but that wasn't my fault, trust me—"

"What do you need?"

I finally figured out that he must be interrupting me not because *he* was panicking but because *I* was. Even I could tell my voice was climbing up the wall.

"I only have to go with my—this relative because there's no place for me to stay here and I can't stay with Chelsea because her mom's a control freak, so if you could maybe find me a place to be for, I don't know, a week, that would be great."

There was a long-time silence.

"Marcus?" I said.

"Okay," he said.

All of a sudden I wanted to cry—not meltdown scream, just curl up in a ball and bawl. Maybe I would have if it didn't sound like what I'd seen my mother do.

"I owe you," I said. "And I will pay you back for this, I swear. Maybe we can even talk about seriously—well, whatever you want."

"You don't have to," Marcus said.

"I want to. So think of something."

I left him thinking and hung up and went on to the only other thing I could think of to do. Marcus was going to find me a place to come back to. All I had to do was make Lou's life so miserable he would be happy to let me go. The thing was, I knew it wouldn't be that hard. Most adults were ready to get rid of me within the hour of meeting me. Maybe even half an hour.

Granted, Lou hadn't gotten that "Oh, I know what's the matter with you" look in his eye. He probably hadn't been around that many kids. He probably thought we all acted like we had hamster wheels in our heads. Or he just hadn't seen me at my worst. The scene at the hospital didn't count. Anybody would have lost it under those circumstances. No, I needed for him to see me do my "normal" thing when the world *wasn't* going ballistic around me. The only challenge was going to be keeping him from knowing why. I had to keep the label ADHD out of it. It had done nothing but mess me up ever since it got stuck on me.

I peeled myself off the bed and went into my bathroom and opened the medicine cabinet. I'd convinced myself I was the only kid I knew whose toothpaste and zit cream had to share a shelf with a controlled substance. This wasn't going to be so bad. I hated taking it anyway, hated having to pop pills just so I could concentrate on what my friends were saying to me (much less my teachers) and stay in my desk for forty-five minutes at a time and not fall asleep in sixth period because I was so wiped out from pretending I was okay all day. Not only was I going to drive Lou crazy without even trying, but I was going to get a break from feeling like a freak at the same time.

The pills were only part of the freakiness—and not the worst part. Without them I'd be just wacko enough to make Lou want to send me home—but not enough to set me up for ridicule and humiliation and all those other multisyllable words I always got right on vocabulary tests because I knew them so well. If I could keep him away from the label, I could keep him away from doing what my mother had done to me. Her and everybody else who knew.

I popped open the container and lifted the lid on the toilet seat.

"Good-bye, little green pills," I said as I poured them in.

I pulled down the handle and watched them swirl away, and wished it was that easy to get rid of the rest of my problems. Maybe this was the beginning.

I had no idea.

CHAPTER FIVE

"You can sit down," Lou said. "The flight's been delayed again."
No, I could not sit down. Climb the post I was leaning on. Run down the up escalator. Those things I could do. Sitting down was out of the question.

I guess I didn't know how much those little green pills were helping me until I stopped taking them.

Besides, I already knew from the fifty-two minute flight from Birmingham to Atlanta that I wasn't going to be able to handle having a "father" for two weeks. I felt like I was being questioned on *The Closer*.

"So tell me about Chelsea and Marcus. What do you do after school? Do you play sports? Do you have any hobbies?"

Was he serious? Teenage girls do not have "hobbies"—at least none of the teenage girls I knew. As for "What would you do if you could do anything you wanted?"—I didn't even have to think about that one. I would get out of this airport and hitchhike back to Mountain Brook and pray that Marcus had found me a hideout.

And that was another thing. The praying. I was always catching Lou with his hands folded and his eyes closed—before the plane took off, when the plane landed, and basically whenever he thought I wasn't watching him.

Yeah, I definitely had to get out of here, in case praying did work for him and he was asking God to make me want to stay with him in Senior Land. I'd learned that much from Chelsea before I left: that any place in Florida that wasn't Disney World was full of old people.

I looked down to find Lou watching me. Which wasn't all that surprising since I was twirling one of my flip-flops on my finger.

"The good news is I got us on an exit row," he said.

"Why is that good news?" I said, returning my shoe to my foot.

"We'll have more leg room." His lips twitched. "I think you're going to need it."

"Why's it called an exit row?" I said.

"That's where the door is that we'd all go through in case of an emergency."

"Oh," I said. "So we'd get out first."

"No. We'd open it and help get everybody else out."

"I don't know how to do that!" I said. "I've never really flown before!"

The bald guy next to Lou glanced up from his laptop.

"See?" I said, pointing to him. "He's not gonna feel safe with me trying to get the door open. Are you?"

Baldy shook his shiny head. "Leave me out of this," he said.

"I'm serious," I said to Lou.

"They'll give us instructions—"

"Then I'm definitely disqualified," I said. "I don't follow instructions that well."

That was true, and for once it was a good thing. I didn't even regret the Blurt.

"I'm *serious*," I said again. "You've gotta get us a different seat."

Lou gave me a look so long I almost thought he wasn't going to buy it. But he finally got up and said, "I'll see what I can do. Stay here with the stuff."

I had no intention of doing that. As soon as he got up to the counter, I was going to take off—just beat it out of there and find a way to get back home. I even hoisted my backpack over my shoulder and was about to lose myself in a herd of high school kids going past our gate when Baldy said, "Is this yours?"

I looked back with a no already formed with my tongue. He was holding out a leather book that looked like it had been run over by a luggage cart.

"It was on your seat," he said. "I didn't want you to forget it."

He was a lying sack of cow manure. There was no book on my seat when I got up from it. Did I look like somebody who would be carrying around something from the Dark Ages?

Evidently so, because he was still holding it out to me, and he was starting to look impatient. That was the adult reaction I was used to.

I took it from him, only because I was losing my chance to blend in with the field trip or whatever it was. What I was going to do with it I had no idea. Maybe drop it back on the seat when Baldy went back to his magazine. Which he didn't do. He just kept watching me and glancing up at the counter and looking at Lou's bag parked on the floor and then back to me. What—he overhears one conversation between my "father" and me and he thinks he has to babysit me now?

I stuffed the leather book in the outside pocket of my back-pack and looked to make sure Lou was still at the counter arguing for a seat change. He wasn't. He was already on his way back to me.

Great. Now I had lifted somebody else's book. Any minute, airport security was going to come and shake me down—

I felt a smile taking shape on my lips. Perfect. The Father of the Year wasn't going to want a criminal in his house, even if she was his daughter. A night or two in juvie and my mom would have me back home so fast.

"Thanks," I said to Baldy, and sat down to wait for our plane.

*

"How long 'til we land in Jacksonville?" I said.

Lou's eyes crinkled at the corners. "Not as long as it was five minutes ago when you asked me. Don't you wear a watch?"

I didn't. The art of telling time had always escaped me, unless it was in digital, and even then I was always late anyway so I never saw the point in a wristwatch. I'd lost the one Mom bought me in one of her No-Bed Phases when she was on a campaign to straighten me out.

"You okay?" Lou said.

45

I swallowed back the lump that formed in my throat every time I thought about my mother and pulled down the tray table and put it back up again.

"Seriously," I said. "How long?"

"Fifteen minutes," Lou said.

"Oh. Then I have time to read."

I pulled my backpack out from under the seat in front of me and took the leather book from the pocket. Now that I had time to look at it, I decided it hadn't been run over by a luggage cart. It had taken at least an eighteen-wheeler to do that kind of damage. The cover was cracked like somebody—a lot of some-bodies—had curled it back to read, and more than one person had carved stuff into the leather. The only thing that looked like it was supposed to be etched into it were two letters in the middle, RL. Whose initials were those? If it was some famous dead person, forget about it. Last semester was the first time I'd ever learned anything in a history class, and that was only because of Mrs. Morse. She brought in costumes and had us acting stuff out and making 3-D maps and building models. Chelsea and Donovan and Adam and everyone else said it was lame at first, but I secretly dug it, and I was glad when they finally got into it so I could too. Mrs. Morse herself was all right too. At least she never said I was "operating far below my potential," like my English teacher Ms. Honeycutt. We had to keep a note-book in her class, and half the time I couldn't find mine. I got like a fifty on it. I'm not that organized and she was so boring. She talked the entire period, and we were supposed to be taking notes and I would always end up drawing spiderwebs. I felt like I was caught in one, and she was the black widow.

"What are you reading?" Lou said.

I had to look at the book for a second to remember what I was doing with it. Maybe I should have kept one or two pills.

"I don't know," I said.

"You brought a book but you don't know what it is?" Lou said.

"I didn't bring it." I took a breath. Here goes. "I stole it."

His eyebrows shot up. Finally. I'd started to think he was a robot.

"You stole it," he said. "From where?"

"From the airport. It was lying on the seat and I just took it. I do stuff like that."

Actually, I'd never done anything like that before, but from the look on his face, it was worth a little white—okay, a big fat lie. Any minute now he was going to call for the flight attendant and tell her to have social services waiting when we arrived in Jacksonville.

"Let me see it," Lou said, mouth in a straight line. Gotcha.

I handed it to him and tried not to look too smug while he opened it and looked at the first page. The straight line turned up at the ends, and he made a husky sound in his throat. Was he laughing? He was holding a stolen article, and he was laughing?

"Did you read this?" he said.

"No, I didn't read it," I said. "I haven't had a chance. I just stole it."

He pulled a pair of glasses out of his shirt pocket and put them on. They made him look smart.

"'If you've found me,'" he read, "'you need me. I was left for you for a reason. Read and discover what that is.'"

He tilted his chin down to look at me over the top of the glasses. "I've got a pretty good idea what you had in mind, Jessie, and I don't think this was it."

I snatched the book from him and stuffed it back in my backpack. The skin on my face was about to burn off.

"Aren't you going to read it?" he said. I could hear the chuckle still lurking in his throat.

"Later," I said.

I folded my arms and jiggled my foot and turned the knob on the tray table so it would drop and bounce.

"Why don't we just see what God does with the next two weeks?" he said.

I jerked my face to the window. I didn't know what kind of thing God did if God did anything. But I wasn't giving up on doing what I had to do.

CHAPTER SIX

The first words out of me when the light went on were, "No! Turn it off!"

"It's a little hard to turn off the sun," Lou said.

I pried open my eyes and glared into the light that glared back at me from the window where Lou had just yanked open the lime-green-and-hot-pink-striped curtains.

"Why?" I said.

"Why what?"

"Why are you waking me up?" I rolled over and peered at the clock, which, thankfully, was digital. "At eight o'clock! That's the middle of the night!"

"It's an hour later than you're going to get up tomorrow," Lou said in a voice so cheerful I wanted to pluck his nose hairs out. "I let you sleep in."

I didn't inform him that this was not sleeping in. Not when I'd been up until three wandering around a house so tiny you practically needed a microscope to see it.

I'd spent half the heebie-jeebies night discovering everything there was to know about it, including the fact that there was no air-conditioning. I was sweating so badly I had to change out of my pajama top, which really wasn't pj's but the shirt I'd worn on the plane because I couldn't find anything in my suitcase. I'd put on a T-shirt with the sleeves cut out that was hanging on the back of a chair in the bedroom and explored in that. I found out there was also no TV—only a monitor for watching movies— no video games, and no food that didn't look like somebody had grown it.

And that there *was* an alarm system, which made steal-ing away into the night impossible. Lou didn't have bars on his windows, but I still felt like I was in a cage. A very small cage with two bedrooms, one bathroom, a kitchen, and a room that was evidently used for everything else, including pray-ing. There was this thing to kneel on in there. I'd seen one when I went to Lutheran Vacation Bible School. Or was it the Church of Christ one? Anyway, I had everything figured out except why a man living alone had painted his spare bedroom pink and hung foo-foo curtains on the window to match the comforters.

"We're leaving in half an hour," Lou said from the doorway. "You need to wear long pants and long sleeves and bring cooler clothes in your backpack. I've got breakfast ready."

"I'm not hungry," I said. "Where are we going?"

"To work," he said, and closed the door behind him.

He was taking me to the place where he worked. It was official, then. He was going to treat me like the eight-year-old my mother said I was, and I was going to die of boredom. I started to pull the covers over my head, but I stopped—partly because that reminded me too much of Mom, and partly because it couldn't be any more boring there than it was here.

I threw back the comforter and sat up on one of the two twin beds. Okay. I could make his life chaos at work. Get his boss to threaten to fire him if he didn't get me out of there. That should take a day, max. Because during the night, when I was tossing and turning and getting myself tangled up in the flowered sheets and the big T-shirt, it came to me that I really hadn't shown Lou what I was capable of when I didn't have something to do. He hadn't seen anything yet.

*

"I told you long sleeves," Lou said when I walked, backpack over my shoulder, from the kitchen into the garage—which, I'd discovered the night before when we arrived in the dark, was as big as the whole rest of the house.

"I forgot," I said. I'd gotten the jeans right, although I *didn't* get the point. It was already so hot out my hair was going to frizz like a poodle. Who wore long pants in Florida in July?

"Never mind," Lou said.

He reached up and took something denim from a hook and tossed it to me.

"A jacket?" I said as I caught it. "I'll fry!"

"I don't think so." He had that chuckle-thing going in his throat again. "Put this on too."

I stopped, one arm in a sleeve, and looked at what he was holding: a white helmet with a pink rose painted on the side.

"Why do I need that?" I said. "You don't drive that bad."

"It's the law. Come on—we're burnin' daylight."

He looked like he was about to give me a surprise party or something. I wasn't in a party mood. I stuck the helmet on my head and followed him under the garage door, which was halfway down. When I stood up straight, he was grinning and holding out one arm.

"Meet Levi," he said.

He was pointing to the biggest, reddest, shiniest motorcycle I'd ever seen. Not that I'd ever actually seen one up close—

"You ever been on a Harley?" he said.

All I could do was shake my head.

"Good—and don't ever *get* on one unless it's with an experienced rider. An *adult* experienced rider." He erased that with his hand in the air. "No, don't ever get on one unless it's with *me*. How does that helmet fit?"

"I'm riding on that?" I said.

"That was the plan." He picked up a black helmet from the seat of the bike and studied my face. "Are you afraid? Because if you are, we can wait."

I found myself shaking my head. No, I wasn't afraid. In fact, the thought of climbing onto that monster thing was thrilling right up my backbone. Before I could stop myself I said, "Are you serious? This rocks!"

"I thought you'd see it that way."

Even though he looked pretty satisfied with his sweet self, I didn't try to hide the fact that I was jazzed as he adjusted the strap on my helmet and showed me where the pegs were that I was going to put my feet on and told me I had to sit still and just look where we were going so I would lean naturally.

He got on and revved up the motor. It purred like a lion who rocked the world—and I squealed.

"Did that scare you?" he said. His voice was all concerned.

"No!" I said. "It's just sick!"

He nodded like he actually knew what *sick* meant and said, "All right. Get on."

I swung my leg over the seat and sat down, feet on the pegs.

"Where do I hold on?" I said.

"You can lean back," he said. "You've got a sissy bar. Or you can hold onto me if you want. Just remember, you have to pay attention. Okay?"

It was a promise I couldn't usually make, but I said, "Okay."

The engine snarled, and we were suddenly going down the driveway and turning onto the street. The bike leaned and I grabbed the back of Lou's jacket.

"Just lean with me!" he said through the visor that covered his face. "You're not going to fall off."

So I leaned, and then when he straightened back up, I did too. The air floated around me, and the bike growled beneath me, and Father-Man drove us straight ahead with nothing around us but sunlight. It was loud and crazy and I felt the whole world on me. I could even smell—

"Are we near the beach or something?" I yelled through my own visor.

"When I tell you, look to the right," Lou yelled back. "Now!"

I turned my head and I saw it. Blue water that stretched all the way to the sky and splashed it with its waves.

And then it was gone, swallowed up by a giant building— a hotel or condos or something.

"Was that the ocean?" I said.

"That was it. You've seen it before, haven't you?"

"No. Not for real. Only in movies."

His helmet nodded, and it seemed like his shoulders got bigger.

"We're going to get into some traffic so I have to pay attention," he said. "We'll talk when we get there."

I wanted to look back to see if I could get another glimpse of the ocean, but I was afraid of not watching the road. It was a little freaky when cars passed us, and I found myself curling my fingers around the sides of Lou's jacket. But then we came to a bridge, and I forgot I was even on a motorcycle.

We had to be flying. I mean, we were in midair except for a strip of concrete. "Ha—I laugh at your bridge," I wanted to shout. "I have wings!"

Lou pointed toward the other side of the water—at a building that looked like something out of a Mel Gibson movie where he wears armor and jabs a big spear at people on horses.

"Is that a fort?" I said.

"Castillo de San Marcos. I'll tell you all about it."

"I want to go there!" I almost blurted. But for once I caught myself. I couldn't be showing all this interest. I wasn't letting him think I was staying. Harley or no Harley.

Still—that fort. It looked so real, guarding the bank with its thick stone walls and lookout towers like it was expecting a band of pirates to attack any minute. They probably did build it for a movie. Either that or I was in a time warp.

We turned in the direction of the place, and I smothered a, "Yes! I can get a better look!" But when we drove right along the road that passed beside it, I couldn't help it. I blurted out, "Dude, it's real!"

"It's almost four hundred years old!" Lou shouted over his shoulder.

Too bad I wasn't going to get to go inside. There was no way I could get to it on my own, and I was still determined not to let him know how completely cool this all was to me. Still—

I chanced a glance back over my shoulder before we rounded a curve. We immediately slowed down, and then stopped.

"You go ahead and get off," Lou said, "and I'll park him."

"We're there?"

We'd pulled into what looked like it used to be a big gas station, only it had been turned into something else and now

52

looked better than a filling station ever did. There was a mob of scooters on one side of us and a whole row of motorcycles on the other, staring us down like a gang.

"Jess," Lou said. "Go ahead and hop off."

I was still staring at the scooters as I stood up on the pegs and tried to swing my leg back over the sissy bar. For some reason it was harder to get off than on. My foot got caught on something, and the next thing I knew, I was lying on my back on the ground.

"That's one way to do it," somebody said.

I opened my eyes to a boy-creature with a grinning mouth. All I could really tell about him was that he had a space between his two front teeth big enough to drive Lou's Harley through.

Above me, Levi's engine died.

"Is she okay?" Lou said.

"I don't know," the guy said. "Are you okay?"

"Hello—yes," I said. "I'm only still down here because you're in my way."

Boy looked at Lou. "Yeah, she's okay."

He put down a hand, but I batted it away and scrambled to my feet. My head barely came to the dude's armpit, which meant he could look *down* at me with one of those smirky grins that goes all the way to the eyes—glitter-green in his case—and say, "Are you a ditz or what?" I already couldn't stand him, even if he *was* tall (way taller than Lou) and muscle-y in a skinny kind of way and probably old enough to drive.

"That's why you wear a helmet," he said.

"Let me have it, Jess," Lou said. "You go ahead and look around. I'll catch up to you."

I yanked the helmet off and thrust it at Lou, but he too grinned. "Maybe you ought to keep it."

Very cute. Hilarious. I pushed the thing into his chest until he took it, and then I stomped off. I could hear Boy-Creature hissing through his tooth-gap behind me.

*

There was definitely more to see where Lou worked than where he lived. Not that I cared. But checking it out was better than standing there letting some skinny boy with sun-bleachy hair laugh at me like I was an idiot. The fact that I felt like one made absolutely no difference. It was one thing for me to point at my*self* and say, "I am such a loser!" and make everybody else laugh with me. That's how I handled being a complete klutz-airhead-motormouth. That's how I had friends and a reputation for being a blast at parties. That's how I got some teachers to cut me slack.

But when somebody *else* took it upon *his* jerk-self to tell the world I was a klutz-airhead-loser, that was something totally different. I stayed away from people like that—just so I wouldn't rip their lips off. The only time I ever got in real, serious trouble was when one of them refused to leave me alone—and then I figured he had it coming to him.

Which was why I put as much space between me and Boy-Creature as I could in thirty seconds. I left him *and* Lou—who wasn't innocent in this as far as I was concerned—to their grinning and marched down the driveway we came in on until I found myself in the wide-open doorway of a garage-looking thing where some guy was taking a piece off a motorcycle that was even bigger than Lou's. Black with fenders that curved up at the edges. It reminded me of Darth Vader.

So—Lou was a motorcycle repair guy.

When the man looked up I said, "Sorry" and took off for the next thing I could find, which was a long office kind of place that was all windows across the front. It was sort of inviting, actually, as I looked through the glass—palm trees in pots and red couches and a counter where a short line of people was standing but not looking grouchy the way people usually did when they were waiting in a line. A white sign with red letters on the wall read *Scooter Rentals.*

Oh. So Lou was a rental agent. That must have been why he'd gone out of his way to be decent to the man at the car rental place when we returned that pickup truck at the Birmingham airport. My mother wasn't usually that nice to clerks and salesmen and other people who waited on you. Of course, when she was in a No-Bed Phase, she wasn't that nice to anybody.

I didn't go in there. I was still too prickly to talk to anyone—and I had to be pretty prickly not to want to run my mouth. I went to the end of the building and found a garden—one of those kind with trees cut in shapes and little statues like you see in a kung fu movie. There was even a tiny stream with a bridge over it about big enough for Chelsea's Chihuahua. It was the last thing you'd expect to see at a we-fix-motorcycles-and-rent-them place.

So Lou was a gardener? Uh, no. Even I couldn't imagine that.

What I also couldn't imagine was me hanging out here for two weeks doing nothing but watching other people take off on scooters like the man and woman who had just come out of the office and were climbing onto a pair of matching yellow minibikes. When they started them up, they sounded like sewing machines compared to Lou's roaring Harley, and it only took the guy about ten seconds to explain how to ride it before the lady was peeling out of there, laughing back at him with her hair flying out behind her.

Another couple came out and then two guys and then a pair of women who were the coolest yet. They got pink ones, not my favorite color, but who cared if it meant scooting away, free as—

Free as I needed to be.

As soon as the two chicks on pink scooters were out of there, I made my way over, straddled a red one, and turned the key. It didn't occur to me to wonder why it was sitting there in the ignition. I was too busy figuring out what was the gas and what was the brake. When turning the handle like Lou did on Levi hurtled me forward, I did it again and broke from the pack.

I squealed with delight when I sailed off the curb. I landed on both wheels just in front of a red blur that blew its horn at me. Leaning like Lou, I rounded the corner and belted down the same street we'd arrived on. A cemetery shot by me on the right. A couple and their kids jumped back onto the sidewalk to let me pass, which was a good thing, because I still hadn't figured out where the brake was. All I knew was that the huge pair of stone pillars ahead of me weren't going to be as helpful. The pavement turned into a wide sand path. I turned the handle on the other side, but that wasn't the brake. The scooter surged forward even faster, and the back wheel flipped sideways like the tail of a fish. A man walking toward me with a little boy grabbed the kid and jumped up on the low wall that bordered the path, just in time for the scooter to lay down with me on it and slide—forever—in slow motion, until we hit a pillar. I didn't need the brake then.

"Are you all right?" somebody—probably the terrified dad—called to me.

"I'm fine," I called back, although I had no idea if I was. I added a laugh so he wouldn't come over and try to help me.

Seriously, though, I couldn't wriggle out from under the scooter. Footsteps were pounding toward me from several different directions, but I couldn't see who they belonged to. All I could see was the front of the red scooter, crunched into the wall, six inches from where I thought my head might be.

When I heard the growl of a motorcycle, I closed my eyes and prayed that I would die immediately. Not until it stopped and *those* footsteps headed toward me did I realize that I had just accomplished what I'd set out to do. Lou was going to have a meltdown of his own, and I was as good as on my way home.

Yes.

I even had a smile on my face when the footsteps stopped next to me.

"Oops," I said—and opened my eyes—and saw a face with a space between its teeth, smirking down at me.

Hadn't I already *had* this nightmare?

He squatted beside me. "Are you hurt?"

"No," I said.

"I can't say the same for the scooter. Dude, that's totaled. You're gonna be too when your dad finds out."

"He's not my dad," I said.

I gritted my teeth as he got on the other side of me and pulled the scooter so I could get my legs untangled and stand up.

"He told me he's your dad."

"He's my biological father," I said, examining the large hole I'd ripped in the sleeve of the jacket that wasn't even mine. One more reason for Lou to put me on the next plane.

"Yeah, well, he's gonna be your biological prison warden when he—"

"You know what—nobody asked you, okay?"

I reached down to stand the scooter up.

"What do you think you're doing?" he said.

"I'm going to take this back and—"

"How are you planning to get it there?"

I didn't have to look at him to know he was grinning that hideous gap-tooth smile.

"I don't know," I said. "Just leave me alone and I'll figure it out."

"Like you figured out how to stop it?"

"Did somebody die and leave you in charge of me?"

"No. But I'm your only chance of getting away with this."

I did look at him then. He was standing there with his hands on his hips, like he had the answer to every question before you even asked it. I hated that in a person.

"I don't *want* to 'get away with it,'" I said, making those quotation mark things with my fingers.

"So, what, you did it on purpose?"

I hoped he didn't hear me catch my breath.

"It's none of your business!" I said. I leaned over and tried to pick up the scooter, but it was heavier than it looked. Especially with a pain shooting down my arm.

"Yeah, well, it's my business to take care of the scooters," he said, "so you go make your confession or whatever it is you're gonna do, and I'll get this back to the shop."

"I can—"

"Touch it and you're toast," he said.

"Are you threatening me?" I said.

"I don't have to," he said, and grinned the biggest, stupidest version yet.

*

Just as I suspected, the boy-creature didn't know absolutely *everything*. Lou did not "total" me when I found him in an office at the cycle place and showed him the jacket and told him about the scooter. Even though I made the story as dramatic as I could—including the father and small boy I ran off the road and the red car I pulled in front of—Lou didn't even get bulgy veins in his neck or raise his voice or in any way come close to having a meltdown. As a matter of fact, when it was his turn to talk, his voice just kept getting lower and quieter until I had to practically crawl up on the desk we had between us to hear it.

"First of all, are you injured?" he said.

I swore I wasn't. My arm did hurt some, but a trip to the emergency room would only slow down my exit.

"The bike's totaled, though," I said. "That's what that guy said."

"What guy?"

"The one with—" I put my finger up to my two front teeth.

"Rocky," Lou said.

"His name is Rocky? Are you serious?"

"So, you just thought you'd take a little joy ride, is that it?"

"I do stuff like that," I said. "This one time, my mom's assistant that she used to have came over to work on some purses, and she brought her teenage niece who wanted to be a designer like Mom—only she didn't seem that interested in it. Anyway, her aunt said she could take her car and go to the mall, and the girl—I forget her name—said I could go with, and we stayed there 'til it closed. And then she said since the parking lot was empty she would teach me to drive, even though I was, like, twelve. I got the brake and the gas mixed up and ran into a pole." I shook my head. "It wasn't good."

I didn't add that that was when my mother finally decided, after two different doctors had told her, that I needed medication.

Lou waited until I was done, and even a little longer than that, before he nodded and said, "All right, so, it looks like you need to have everything laid out for you ahead of time so you know what you're dealing with—what the rules are."

No, that wasn't what I needed at all.

"Knowing that," he said, "then I'd better prepare you for what's going to happen tomorrow."

Ah. At last.

He sat back in the chair and laid his hands flat on the desk. Oh, yeah, this was going to be deep. He was going to say, "Jess, I think I've made a mistake and—"

"You have a sister," he said. "Half sister, if you want to get technical. Her mother and I are divorced—I told you that—but I have her every weekend. She's going to join us tomorrow night."

I was still back on "you have a sister." The hamster wheel was going at warp speed.

"She's ten," he said. "Her name's Louisa, but we call her Weezie." Lou leaned forward and parked his folded hands under his chin. "Finding out you have a father and a sister, and your mom's situation—this is a lot for you to process in a short period of time, which I think accounts for stealing books and taking off with scooters and—"

"Yeah," I said. "That's it. And I don't want your boss to fire you—especially since you have a kid. So … what?"

He was smiling. Bordering on that chuckle thing. What was *wrong* with this man?

"I can't get fired," he said. "I own the business. I *am* the boss."

"You're not the boss of *me*!" I said.

All he did was tilt his head. "Then who is, Jess?" he said.

I didn't answer.

I didn't know.

CHapTer SeuEn

By the next morning, the hamster wheel in my head was spinning so fast I couldn't even think about *thinking* about another plan. If crashing into what Lou told me were the two-hundred-year-old city gates didn't even get him to twitch an eyebrow, much less turn me over to social services, I didn't know what would.

And now I was going to have a little sister to deal with. Even when I told myself she was only a half sister—even just a biological sister—it didn't slow down the drag race that was going on in my brain. She was another relative I hadn't known about. I wondered if Mom knew about her. I thought about Marcus's little sister, who was also ten, and who was annoying as a bumblebee and said things like, "Ooh, Marcus has a girlfriend," every time she saw me. Which was as little as possible if I had anything to do with it.

The thing I kept coming back to as I went around and around on the hamster wheel most of the night was that instead of getting rid of me, Lou was trying to plant me deeper into his life. I knew that for a fact when we got to the shop Friday morning—in his truck because we had to pick up "Weezie" on the way home. Weezie. What kind of name was that anyway? It sounded like she had asthma.

I was heaving a huge what-am-I-going-to-do-all-day sigh when Lou turned off the ignition and said to me, "I have a job for you."

"I don't know how to do anything," I said.

"Oh, I doubt that," he said. "But you definitely don't know how to do this. Most people don't."

"Then how am I supposed to do it?"

"They'll teach you."

"Who's 'they'?" My stomach was already in a knot. *Teaching* meant I was supposed to learn something. I didn't do that well. And even though this could be yet another move toward home, I still hated the humiliation I was already feeling at the very thought of getting instructions I didn't understand and making an idiot out of myself trying to follow them.

"You okay?" Lou said.

"No," I said. "I don't want a job."

"Nobody does, really. But we all have to make a living, right?"

"A living?"

"You don't think I'm going to put you to work and not pay you, do you?"

"As in money?" I said.

"Seven fifty an hour," he said. "You're barely legal working age but—"

I missed the rest. Money. Of my own. That meant I could buy a plane ticket. Bus ticket. Cab fare.

"Okay," I said. "But I'm not good with mechanical stuff. I don't think. I never tried it."

"You don't have to be mechanical for this," Lou said. "Follow me."

I did—over to the funky little garden thing and down a path to a building behind the garage and connected to it by another one of those bridges—although this one was big enough for actual people to walk over.

On each side of a red door was a bush clipped into the shape of—were they motorcycles? A sign *over* the door said something like *Ride American*, but we went in too fast for me to get the rest of it.

Once I was inside, I forgot all about trees shaped like Harleys and signs that made no sense. We were standing in a restaurant with tables that had miniatures of the shape-trees on them and chopsticks rolled up in napkins and that music that sounds like there's something wrong with it playing in the background.

"Bonsai!" Lou called out—followed by a bunch of other words that made him sound like Jackie Chan.

Somebody answered with words just like them from behind a curtain made out of wooden beads, and then a small man with black spiky hair and crinkly eyes came out. He not only sounded like Jackie Chan, he looked kind of like him.

"Bonsai," Lou said, "this is my daughter Jessie. Jess, meet Bonsai."

"Hi," I said, lamely.

He said something to me in whatever language it was they were speaking and then looked at Lou and said, in perfect English, "She can't be your daughter. She's too pretty."

"She is, isn't she?" Lou said. "Where's Rose?"

It was like we were in a play. The beads rattled and a woman came through—dressed in a red kimono like my grandfather brought me when he and New Wife went to Japan or someplace, and which was way too small because he hadn't seen me for a year and he still thought I was, like, five. This lady wore it as if it was her regular clothes, you could tell that. And the hair folded up on top of her head and held there with chopstick-looking things—that looked like it was for real too. And then she folded her really tiny hands at her waist and came toward me and bowed. Bowed. Like I was the president or something.

I didn't know what to do so I bowed back.

"Rose, my daughter Jessie," Lou said. "Jess, Rose."

She murmured something so low I couldn't tell whether it was English or what. I kind of murmured back at her.

"She's all yours, Bonsai," Lou said.

"I'm all his for what?" I said.

"You're going to learn the sushi business. Bonsai's the best sushi chef I know."

"I'm the only one you know," Bonsai said. "Get out of here before you insult me any more."

Lou laughed—why, I didn't know—and told me to have a good morning and he'd see me at the end of the day. My heart was pounding right out of my chest before he even got through the door.

I looked at Bonsai. "I don't know anything," I said.

"Good," he said. "Then we won't have to break any bad habits. Rose, take her back in the kitchen."

Rose bowed again, and I bowed back and wondered if we were going to go through that every time we looked at each other. By then I'd fallen completely off the hamster wheel.

*

It was a disaster. Seriously. And for once I didn't cause it. Well, I caused it, but not on purpose.

In the first place, I didn't understand a thing Rose said as she pointed to all these things on the shiny metal counters in the kitchen and named them. I guess that was what she was doing. I saw a bamboo place mat and chopsticks as long as my arm and some kind of evil-looking toothbrush, but I couldn't have said what any of it was called by the time we were done with that lesson. Besides the fact that she barely moved her lips when she talked, I kept getting hung up on the sight of the knives. They looked like smaller versions of the swords Tom Cruise used in that samurai movie. And when I watched Bonsai cut a fish's head off like he was slicing butter, I thought I was going to faint—except that I didn't want to fall on the unidentified fishy stuff on the floor below him.

Apparently that was all the introduction I was going to get, because Rose bowed at the end of it and tied a white apron around me and demonstrated rubbing some kind of root thing across a bowl that had teeth on it until the root thing came out in thin, wide curls. She made it look easy. I ended up losing control of it twice, and when I finally did get it going, I scraped my knuckles on the teeth and got blood in the shavings and they had to throw it all away. Bonsai wasn't amused.

Then Rose switched me to the evil toothbrush and showed me how to draw it up the body of a fish, from its tail to its head. That didn't make me want to faint. It made me want to throw up. I was pretty sure the fish was dead, but that eye kept looking at me the whole time I was scraping its scales off. I was freaked-out enough to quit when Rose stopped me anyway because Bonsai barked something to her in what I finally figured out was Japanese. She bowed to me and took the scaler away from me, and then Bonsai barked at *me*, "You were bruising the fish."

"It's already dead," I said. "Isn't it?"

She put me on another scraping duty—this time it was something green that I had to rub with something that looked like the skin of some other fish.

"Shark," Rose said, pointing to the skin.

"I definitely hope *that's* dead," I said.

She bobbed her head and handed me the green thing. "Wasabi," she said, and bowed.

I of course bowed too, and said, "Wasabi."

Yeah, well, wasabi did not turn out to be my friend. I grated until my eyes started watering, and when I rubbed them I about went blind and ran screaming to the bathroom in pain. This time they didn't put me on another job. Bonsai shot me evil looks and called Lou.

"You've never had wasabi?" Lou said as he dabbed at my eyes with a wet towel.

"I don't even know what it is!" I said.

He chuckled. "You do now."

"I can't do this sushi thing," I said.

"What do you mean you can't? You've only been at it for two hours."

"Is that all?" I said. I was glad my eyes were already running because I thought I might be crying too, and I didn't want him seeing that, because I had come to the conclusion that he was trying to break me down.

"The biggest part of learning a new thing is finding out what not to do," Lou said. "Maybe you could just watch Bonsai for the rest of the day. Get the big picture. How does that sound?"

It sounded horrible. Bonsai obviously wasn't thrilled with me being there—but there wasn't any point in arguing. Lou was denser than—than me.

*

Rose evidently didn't understand the word *watch*.

As soon as Lou was gone, she handed me a pair of industrial-size tweezers and smiled and bowed and made me pick the bones out of fish.

Then people started coming in for lunch—most of them guys in sleeveless T-shirts like the one I slept in and bandanas tied around their heads. Seeing them eat little bite-size rolls of rice and raw fish was like watching a football team take a ballet class.

Rose practically washed my hands for me and had me put glasses of water on tables and wrap more chopsticks in more napkins. But Bonsai wouldn't let me get near the sushi. He acted like every dish was a work of art or something. They kind of were. Some of them looked like dragons, complete with paper heads and tails. Some of it was more like cones with all this colorful stuff sticking out. Although, once I found out the cones were made of seaweed, I didn't care what they looked like. That was just gross.

I got out of eating any of it, even though Rose offered and Bonsai gave me the evil eye when I said I wasn't hungry. I drank about three Cokes to fill myself up, which meant that by the time I was waiting at the end of the day in Lou's office for him to get ready to head for "Weezie's" house, my whole *body* was on a hamster wheel. I sat on the desk and swung my legs and wished I had some chocolate.

"Hey, Crash."

I glared at the door. Rocky—was that his name?—was getting ready to do a pull-up on the door frame. Show-off. I hated that in a guy. Okay, usually I liked it, but I hated it in him.

"So they put you out at Rosie and Bonsai's so you couldn't hurt anybody, huh?"

"Shut up," I said.

"They aren't letting you touch the knives, are they?"

I rolled my eyes and jumped off the desk and knocked over a cup full of pens.

"Dude, you need a padded room," he said.

He strolled over and tried to put some of them back in the cup, but I smacked his hand away. He curled his fingers around my wrist and laughed into my eyes with his.

65

"You are one crazy chick," he said.

"Let go," I said.

"You promise not to hit me again?"

"Let go."

"Rock. Back off."

Rocky pulled both hands up like he was surrendering to the army and grinned at Lou, who was smiling and shaking his head and moving from the doorway to his desk.

"We were just messin' around," Rocky said. "Sorry."

"*You* were messing around," I said. "*I* was not. Just so we're clear."

"What are your plans for the weekend?" Lou said.

I whipped around to look at him. He was *not* going to ask this creature to join us, was he?

"A bunch of us are going to the movies tonight," Rocky said. "You've got me working tomorrow. Saturday night's the pizza thing—which you're not gonna be at because you're totally ditching us. Then church Sunday."

He was such a liar. He was going to party and make some girl think he was cool, putting his hands on his hips and showing the hole in his smile like he did. What was up with the "church Sunday"? Was he trying to impress Lou because he was his boss?

"Sounds good," Lou said.

"You got Lou-WEE-za this weekend?"

"Yep. We're going to pick her up now."

Rocky placed his devil-smile on me. "Have fun with that," he said.

*

I had no intention of "having fun with that." In fact, the minute I saw the little shrimp of a girl-child fly down the front steps of her mini-mansion and into Lou's arms, I found another plan. She gave him a loud kiss on each cheek and hung her arms around his neck while she chattered into his face. This was so Daddy's Girl, it would have been sickening if it hadn't been absolutely perfect. If *she* didn't like me, I was as good as gone by Monday.

Lou carried her over to the truck where I was still standing and put her down in front of me. She was so small her head barely came to my shoulder, and I was no runway model my own self. She tossed her not-quite-as-red-as-mine bob of hair back from her face and smiled at me. Sort of. Let's just say it wasn't only the braces on her teeth that made me think of plastic.

"Weezie, this is Jess," Lou said. "Jess, Weezie."

"I *know*, Daddy," Weezie said, rolling her huge blue eyes. They were the same color as his—ours—but twice as big. It was like she got the same genes and then had them upgraded. Even the freckles on her nose looked like they had been perfectly placed there.

"I mean, who else are you gonna be, right?" she said to me.

"I could be an imposter," I said.

"No, you couldn't," she said.

"Get your stuff, Weez," Lou said.

She skipped back to the house, hair swinging, and Lou shook his head. "They're so literal at ten."

They're such brats at ten, I wanted to say.

CHAPTER EIGHT

I didn't have to do much to turn Weezie against me. She was halfway there before we ever got to Lou's house.

She sat right up next to him in the truck and chattered longer than I could listen to her about this sleepover and that birthday party and when was he going to take *her* to work with him and were *they* still going to do all *their* Saturday-night traditions. Between every sentence she glanced over at me like she was making sure I was getting what an intruder I was.

Like I could miss it.

At the dinner table — Yay! Daddy had fixed her favorite coconut shrimp just the way she liked it — she pointed out to me that she was named after him. "He's Louis — I'm Louisa. Who are you named after?"

"I don't know," I said. "I'm just Jessie."

"Is that short for Jessica?" she said.

"Yeah."

"I like that better. I'm calling you Jessica."

"Why don't you ask her if she wants to be called Jessica?" Lou said. "You don't like anybody calling you Louisa."

Weezie shrugged and went back to eating the coconut off of her shrimp.

Did he know this kid? I'd only been around her for an hour, and I already had it down that she didn't care what I wanted or didn't want. It was all about her.

There was no doubt about that when it was time to go to bed and she put it together that I had been sleeping in *her* room and was going to sleep there that night too. At least now I knew why it was pink and had foo-foo curtains. She had probably picked them out herself.

"You trashed it!" she said.

I looked around. I'd dumped my suitcase on the floor looking for something to wear that morning, and I'd collected several dishes on my midnight raids on the kitchen—but it didn't look that different from my room at home.

She went after it like my mother in a No-Bed Phase, while I looked for the big T-shirt to sleep in and discovered Lou must have put it in the wash. I wasn't used to somebody else doing the laundry. I stuck on sleep shorts and a cami and flopped down on one of the twin beds and watched Weezie go after the room.

After she piled all my stuff back into the suitcase and plumped up the pillows on the other bed and did everything but get out the vacuum cleaner, she stood there and stared at me.

"What?" I said.

"Are you, like, hyperactive or something?"

I almost swallowed the fingernail I was chewing on.

"No," I said.

"Then why are you all wiggling your foot and biting your nails and stuff?"

"Why are you cleaning up the room like the Tasmanian Devil?"

She arched an eyebrow, just the way Lou did. "You are weird, Jessica," she said.

"Right back at ya, kid," I said.

Weezie pulled the covers back on her bed, and something thudded to the floor. She leaned over and picked up the leather book. That RL thing.

"What's this, your journal?" she said.

"No," I said.

She gave me a long, blue-eyed look. "I know. If it was, you'd be fighting me for it. My babysitter went nutso one time when I picked hers up. Besides, you aren't the journal-writing type."

"How would you know that?" I said, in spite of the fact that I had silently vowed not to get into a conversation with this child.

"Because you're hyperactive."

"Would you get off that?" I said.

"There's this boy in my class and he's hyper and he can barely read."

"Yeah, well, I can read, okay?"

"Here." Weezie tossed the leather book onto my bed. "Read this."

I wanted to throw it back at her. The only reason I didn't was because she wasn't going to let this go until I proved to her that I wasn't something that I actually was.

I flipped open the book. Fine. It wasn't that I couldn't read words—I just couldn't remember them ten seconds after I read them because, let's face it, concentration wasn't my thing. It was usually pretty obvious when I had to read something out loud. This little chick would be on that like white on rice.

I turned to the first page, which didn't have a lot on it. I opened my mouth and my lips froze. It came right up to me like somebody else was already reading it to me.

"I knew you couldn't," Weezie said.

I waved her off. "'This is going to sound very strange to you,'" I read, "'but I want you to take this book from the one who gave it to you and eat it.'"

"*What?*"

"'It's going to taste sweet, but stand by, because it will also upset your stomach.'"

Weezie made a disgusted sound in her throat. "It does not say that."

Yeah, it did. But it wasn't what it said that had me blinking at the page. It was the fact that I had just read it without stumbling over any words. And that five seconds later I still knew exactly what it said.

"Let me see that." Weezie climbed over onto my bed and hung over my shoulder. "Okay, it does say that. But it doesn't make any sense."

"You just told me to read it," I said.

"So are you going to do it?" she said.

"Do what?"

"Eat the book."

"No, I'm not going to eat the book. That's not what it means."

She folded her arms and narrowed her eyes. "What does it mean then?"

I looked back at the page. A chill shivered up my spine—because I did know what it meant.

"I'm supposed to, like, read it the way you eat food. So it gets inside me."

Weezie tossed her bob. "I don't get it."

Neither did I, totally. But the weird thing was, I wanted to.

*

Weezie's only good quality was that she slept like she was dead. I turned on the light and polished my toenails and ate Rice Krispies, and she never even rolled over. I could have picked her up and carried her outside and she wouldn't have woken up. I was tempted.

I think the only thing that kept me from doing that was the RL book. I took it out into the kitchen and dropped it on the counter and then just looked at it.

There was definitely something weird going on with the thing if I could understand it. That was something I'd envied in Chelsea and Marcus and every other person I'd ever sat in a classroom with who opened books and read them as easily as I opened potato chip bags and ate. If I could have done that, it would have made my whole life different. The only reason I didn't snatch this book back up again was because I was afraid that it had only been my imagination—that I would open it and find out that as usual it was just words that wouldn't mean anything in the next breath.

It wasn't a good enough reason. I grabbed it and opened it to a random page and stood by the light from the oven hood and read.

He traveled to several different towns, but Capernaum was basically his central location.

Already a word I didn't know—Caper-where? I almost closed the book right then, except that the next sentence explained it:

Don't get hung up on the name. For now, just know he went to real places that you could still go to today. He wasn't just a figment of somebody's imagination.

I got another chill. Okay—was this book reading my mind? Either that or I was losing it.

He was teaching, and the people were blown away. They were used to teachers who used bigger words than Capernaum and took every sentence apart and made everything so confusing the students' eyes glazed over.

I heard *that*.

But this man—he taught so they could actually understand it—as if he understood it—as if he knew it so well it was him.

"You're going to have to run that by me again," I said out loud.

He didn't say, "This might mean this or it might mean that." He said, "It is this. Live it. Do it. Be it."

I still didn't totally get it—

Read on and you'll understand what that means.

I hiked myself up on the kitchen counter. This was getting freaky. I considered putting the whole book down the garbage disposal. But I read more. Because I could.

In the meeting place where he was teaching and people were hanging on every word, there was a guy who was mentally disturbed. As in psycho. He stood up and screamed, "Hey! What's up with you, Yeshua? You Nazarene!"

Nazarene? Was that some kind of put-down?

"Nazarene" meant Yeshua was from Nazareth. Like if you're from Alabama, you're an Alabaman. Nazareth was a Podunk town, so this was like calling him a redneck. Anyway, this guy kept yelling like he was possessed, "I know what you're doing! You're the Holy One, and you're here to take us down!" He was saying all this stuff right in the middle of church. You'd think the ushers would've escorted him out of there, but Yeshua said, "Be quiet. Come out of him."

Who was he talking to?

See, the guy was possessed by a demon. Maybe we'd call it the schizophrenic demon or the psychopath demon, but whatever it was, it did what it was told. It threw the guy down on the floor in front of everyone and it left. Now here was this "crazy person"—probably

homeless, out screaming nonsense on the street an hour before—sud-
denly sane, just because this Yeshua told his psycho-demon to get out.

The people who saw what happened were completely flabbergasted.
Somebody who spoke and something actually happened? He could
just order an evil spirit to come out and it did? It was like he was the
words he was speaking. Nobody could stop talking about it.

Ya think?

I closed the book and sighed and slid off the counter. Too bad this was just a story. If it were real, I'd be calling this Yeshua person up and sending him to UAB Hospital.

*

The only other good thing about Weezie was that she got up early, and I was left in the coma I'd finally gone into around three in the morning. Lou didn't come in and pull the curtains open, and I slept until the sun was way up. Then I took a long shower, just to avoid having breakfast with Daddy and his little girl. Maybe they'd go off and do something and let me do my thing. I still hadn't gotten down to the ocean, and I was starting to believe I'd only dreamed that it was out there. Besides that, there was the RL book. I wasn't sure now that it hadn't been a dream too, and I wanted to find out.

But Lou and Weezie were in the Everything Room when I tried to slip through to the kitchen without them seeing me. They were on the couch with their backs to me, Weezie kind of sideways, probably with her legs draped over his lap, and both of them chatting away like they'd been saving up things to tell each other.

A pang went through me—sort of like what I felt the one time I didn't get invited to THE sleepover back in sixth grade. The way I felt when Chelsea and Marcus talked about Christmas at their houses, while I pretended mine with my mom was just as good. The way I felt when they threatened to put me in the special ed. class ...

I shook myself away from that. Weird that I should feel it now. I didn't want to be part of Lou and Weezie's daddy-daughter thing. I wanted to get away from it.

I made it to the kitchen and then stood there wondering how I was going to open the refrigerator without them hearing me. It was in that moment of stillness that Weezie said, "You know what I think?"

"Do I have a choice?" Lou said.

"No. You don't. I don't know, like, for sure, because I've only known her for—"

"Two hours?" Lou said. I could hear that chuckle thing in his voice.

"I just spent a whole night with her, Dad. She's all hyper and unless she's taking drugs—"

"Weezie."

"I'm just saying."

She stopped as if she were pouting. Good. I didn't appreciate being discussed before I even had my eyes completely open.

"Don't say anything if you don't know it's true," Lou said.

"Then I'll ask it like a question. Do you think Jessica has ADHD?"

CHAPTER NINE

"You little liar! Shut up!"

By the time those words had been screamed out, I was standing in front of Lou and Weezie, breathing like a freight train. Weezie hugged a couch pillow—as if *that* was going to protect her—but she was nodding like the little know-it-all she was.

"I knew it, Daddy," she said.

"You don't know anything about me!" I screamed at her. "So just—"

"Whoa, whoa, whoa." Lou folded Weezie's legs back into her own lap and stood up.

I backed away from him so he wouldn't touch me. I knew I'd smack him if he did. He put up both hands and shook his head.

"Relax—we're cool," he said.

"We are not cool! She's a lying little brat—"

"I am not! You're crazy!"

"*I'm* crazy?" I shouted at her, until I could feel the veins in my forehead popping out. "You're the one who's—possessed!"

"All right, enough," Lou said.

He turned to Weezie, who was by now standing on the couch, holding the pillow like a shield. I didn't know if he saw it, but the I-just-won-this-round shimmer in her eyes was clear to me.

"Sit down," he said to her.

"Make her back off me!"

"I said sit down."

His voice got lower with every word, but it dropped Weezie to her seat. It did not, however, shut her up.

"I'm not staying if she's gonna be here, Daddy," she said.

75

"Not a problem!" I said. "You can have your 'Daddy' all to yourself. I'm gone."

Where I was going, I had no clue. I just turned around and fumbled with the latch on the glass door until I could slide it wide enough to get out, and then I ran—across the deck and down a set of steps and up a narrow road past an apartment building—all in bare feet. When I hit sand, there was a wooden walkway with railings so I took that too, running and stumbling and choking on the sobs I was *not* going to let through my throat if it killed me. The way it hurt—it just might.

Why hadn't I tossed that kid into a dumpster in the night when I had the chance? All I wanted her to do was hate me. I didn't expect her to out me. She could have said anything else in the world to make Lou send me home. She could have told him I was a serial killer for all I cared, but not that I had a "disorder," not that I was a mental case—like my mom.

My side was about to split when I got to a turn in the wooden walkway and I had to stop, doubled over, to catch my breath. I wanted to keep running away from the memory that was pounding in my head, but it wasn't working anyway. It was right there in front of me, just like it was the day it happened.

That doctor in the emergency room after my car accident wasn't the first one to tell my mother I had Attention Deficit Hyperactive Disorder. He was just the only one who threatened to call child protective services if she didn't do something about it—since I was obviously a danger to myself and others. She had to sign a statement saying she would give me medication and get me special help.

I didn't think she'd really go through with it. Nobody told my mother what to do, especially when she was in a No-Bed Phase, which she was at that point. But there must have been something on that paper that freaked her out, because Monday morning she was at the middle school, and three days later we were all in some kind of meeting that had initials—who knows. The guidance counselor and the district psychiatrist and two teachers talked to my mother about me like I wasn't there. I drifted off into my own mind-thing until somebody said the words "special ed."

I almost turned the table over coming out of the chair. I was already yelling before I got to my feet—and that shrink was already scribbling stuff on his little form. Even at the time I wasn't sure what I was screaming at them all, but it was something about not being stupid and not belonging in a special classroom.

It didn't matter that they kept saying special education didn't mean I was stupid, that it just meant I "needed some assistance in dealing with my special challenges." I don't care what anybody says, no kid wants to be "special," especially not a twelve-year-old girl who already feels like she's walking through a pillow because of the drugs they're giving her.

My mother told me later that, as usual, I had acted like a two-year-old. At least I'd progressed to eight years old in her eyes by the time I was fifteen—but at the time she said she didn't think I needed any special help, thank you very much, and that she would deal with me on her own. But when one of the teachers said they couldn't guarantee that I would ever graduate from high school if she didn't address my issues, Mom actually folded. She told me to wait out in the hall—which was where I was, right in front of that door that said Special Education Department, when Chelsea and Grace showed up and stared at me and stared at the sign as if it said, "Anyone standing here is untouchable."

"What were you doing in *there?*" Grace said to me.

"I wasn't in there," I said. Lying was always my first option back then.

"Then why are you standing here?"

I opened my mouth, but nothing would come out, not even a big fat lie. I was frozen by the disgust that was already curling up her lip, and worse than that, the suspicion that narrowed Chelsea's eyes. My best friend's eyes. The best friend I wouldn't have if I turned out to be "special."

"I'm going to be an aide for one of the teachers," I blurted out.

For the longest moment of my life they continued to stare at me while I silently begged the door not to open, pleaded in my mind for my mother not to come out and destroy my seventh-grade life completely. And then the moment ended and Chelsea said, "That's cool."

Grace moved away a couple of weeks later. Then I only had Chelsea to fool every time I had to go check in with the special ed. teacher whose name I refused to learn. At least I didn't have to go to special classes. At least it only lasted for the rest of that school year, and then my mother got mad at the way they were doing things and I didn't get special help anymore. But no one can say something that threatens your social existence at twelve goes away at thirteen or fourteen or fifteen. It was there, always—the lip curling, the name-calling that could start at any moment if somebody found out.

And now somebody had.

I pulled my forehead up from the railing, ready to run away again, and that's when I saw it. The ocean. Stretching out just beyond the hills of scrub brush and sand I'd been cutting through on the walkway. Sparkling its eyes at me. Begging me to come and see.

I did. Only I didn't run this time, because I didn't want to look away from that ocean as I made my way to it. I never knew there were so many shades of blue, like the sky was melting into the water and leaving its trail of color behind until it washed up on the sand with only a memory of blueness in it. All that blue was rolling toward me and then curling back on itself. I had to get to it before it rushed away for good.

I didn't stop until the water was slipping over my toes, cold and foamy. Then I just stood there and let it talk to me.

Come on—jump in—I'll take you away—I'll bring you back—I'll take you away . . .

I was in up to my knees, the waves teasing at the hems of my shorts, before I heard the growl of an engine. When I turned around, Levi was coming toward me, right down the hard-packed sand. Only the unbelievable fact that Lou was driving *on* the beach kept me from diving into the surf and swimming for China. That and the absence of Weezie on the seat behind him. I had the random thought that the white helmet with the pink rose on it must be hers. I reminded myself never to wear it again. Not that Lou would be taking me anywhere on his motorcycle, now that he had the suggestion in his head that I was "challenged."

Lou stopped the bike about six feet from the water's edge and turned off the engine and removed his helmet. He hung it on the handlebar like he was going to stay for a while and climbed off. I groaned inside when he pried off his boots and rolled up his jeans to his knees.

With no place to go, I watched him wade into the water and stop just close enough so I could hear him say, "You came to the right place."

I grunted.

"This is where I always come when it gets to be too much. I should have brought you down here sooner, but it's been a little—"

He stopped, but I knew he'd been about to say "crazy." The fact that he *wasn't* saying it made me feel more like a freak than ever. It was like me saying *nuts* on the psych ward.

"I guess you're mad because I yelled at your kid," I said.

"It was interesting to see Weezie meet her match," Lou said.

I stared at him. What did it take to make this man go off?

"Listen," he said, "I think it was too soon to put you two together. I shouldn't have done that, and I apologize."

"You apologize?" I said.

"Yeah. You've had too much at one time, and I didn't prepare *her* like I should have either. I messed up, and I'm sorry."

In spite of myself, I said, "I don't get it."

He shot up an eyebrow. "What's to get? I made a mistake and I'm asking you to forgive me."

"No way."

"Yes, way. I don't understand, Jess."

I leaned over and splashed some water out to sea. "I just never had an adult tell me they were sorry, that's all." Usually it was them telling me I needed to apologize to somebody else. Now *that* happened a lot.

"So you're expecting me to tell you to apologize to Weezie."

"Yes, and you can save your breath. No offense, but she shouldn't have said that about me—that I was crazy and weird."

79

"No, she shouldn't have. Nor should you have said she was a lying little brat. I'd say you came out about even."

"Good," I said. "So you're not going to try to make me tell her I'm sorry."

"Are you sorry?"

"No."

He shrugged. "Don't say it until you mean it. The same goes for her. I hope that'll happen at some point, but it isn't going to be today."

"Yeah, well, about today." I swung my foot back and forth through the water and watched some foam collect on my leg. "I don't think I can be around her without getting in her face, unless she just doesn't talk to me. Or about me. Like that's gonna happen."

"That won't be an issue. Her mom came and got her."

I felt my eyes spring open.

"I told Weezie the same thing I told you—this was too much too soon, and we'll try it again next weekend."

I grunted again. "I bet she pitched a fit."

"She tried. We worked it out."

"Okay, so, like, are you even human?"

He broke into a sun-squinty smile. "What makes you ask that?"

"Nothing."

"You know how to bodysurf?"

"Huh?"

"Bodysurf. Ride the waves in."

All I could do was shake my head at him.

"Come on. I'll show you."

I so did not want to do that—or anything else he suggested—but he acted like I'd just said, "Yippee, Daddy!" He looked over his shoulder, toward the horizon, and put a hand up like a stop sign. "We have to wait for just the right one," he said. "Not too big, not too small—"

"One what?" I said.

"Wave," he said. "Not this one."

The water swelled, and Lou grabbed my arm so that we

both floated up and came down in the same place. Our clothes were soaked by then.

"Okay—this is a good one," he said. "When I tell you, swim for shore like a mad dog. You can swim, right?"

"Yeah—"

"Okay—now! Swim! Go!"

It was either do what he said or drown. I pointed myself at the shore and dug in with my arms and kicked like that mad dog he was talking about.

"Pull—pull—pull!" I could hear him yelling right behind me. "Okay, now—let go and ride it in!"

I stopped swimming and prayed I wasn't going to my death. The wave caught up to me and lifted me up—until I was on top of it, shooting toward the beach. When it started to drop, Lou yelled, "Keep going! You're doing it!"

I let myself fly until I was completely out of the water, on my stomach in the sand. I dropped my head and giggled from way down somewhere in the hollow of myself. When I lifted my face, there was a small potbellied bird, just a few feet away, looking at me.

"Cut me some slack," I said. "I never did this before."

I heard Lou whooping behind me, and then he slid onto the sand and laughed at the bird as it freaked out and skittered away.

"I talk to them too," he said. "They're plovers. A little neurotic, but, then, we all have our issues."

Uh-oh. I started to get up.

"Sit down," he said.

Unlike Weezie before me, I went with it on the first command—partly because I was too out of breath to run. Lou spread his hands out on the sand, which I could have predicted he was going to do.

"So what pushed your buttons was Weezie saying she thought you had ADHD—or you were on drugs." His lips twitched. "Like she knows that much about either one. But that set you off—we agree on that?"

"That I got upset?" I said. "Yeah."

"Is it something you're ashamed of?"

"Then you believe her. She's, what, ten?"

"Jess." Lou tilted his head. "I didn't need Weezie to tell me. I already knew."

I felt my eyes narrow. "My mom told you."

"Nobody told me. It's just there. Nobody had to tell me you have blue eyes, either."

"So you're saying I act like a crazy person!"

"No, you act like a person who'd climb right out of her skin if she could." He kind of smiled. "I know the feeling."

"You have it?" I said. "I got it from you? Gee, thanks for that, 'Dad.'"

Lou patted the sand I was rising from, and I sat back down. But I wouldn't look at him. I dug a hole with my fingers.

"No, I don't have ADHD," he said. "I have other demons, trust me, worse than yours."

I jerked my head up from the hole. "Did you say demons?"

"It's just a figure of speech. It means I have things to deal with too, so I know how hard it is. And I think I can help you."

I smothered the hole with my hand. I so did not want to hear him tell me that if I just concentrated and tried harder, I could be like any normal human being. I'd heard it all before. The hair on the back of my neck went up and stayed there. I reserved the right to bolt if he kept this up, out of breath or not.

"I have to ask you some questions," he said. "I'm not interrogating you—I just need information so we know where we need to go from here."

I could tell him where I needed to go. Him too, for that matter.

"Have you been officially diagnosed by a doctor?"

"Yes." I gave an explosive sigh. "Several times."

"Are you on medication?"

"Yes. No."

The eyebrow went up. "Which is it?"

"I'm supposed to be taking it. I flushed it all down the toilet before we left Birmingham."

As usual, he just nodded. "And you did that because ..."

"I wanted to drive you crazy."

He laughed. He actually laughed. "That's not a drive, Jess, that's a putt."

"Huh?"

"I'm already pretty crazy. It would take more than you crashing a scooter into a wall to send me over the edge. Unless you'd been hurt. That might do it." He immediately stuck up his hand. "And don't start thinking you're going to break a leg or something so I'll put you on a plane back to Alabama, because it isn't happening."

I was really starting to hate him.

"Look, Jess, I didn't just fall off a turnip truck. I don't know you the way I'd like to, but don't you think I can see that you don't want to be here with some strange guy who shows up after fifteen years and tells you he's your father? I don't blame you. And you're worried about your mother. Plus you didn't want me to find out your secret. Now you have a smart-mouth little sister who's jealous of you—"

There was so much in that that I wanted to scream at, but since I only had one mouth, I went for, "She is SO not jealous of me."

"I do know Weezie. She's having a hissy because you're here with me all the time. That's why she turned into a sea witch with you."

I felt my eyes squinting in that way that made my mother say I was pulling attitude. "So, do you, like, know everything?" I said.

"Not even close. All I know is that I want to help you." He squinted out over the water. I saw him swallow that Ping-Pong ball he seemed to have in his throat at moments like this. "I've been praying about it, and I think I know what to do. But for today—" His eyes came back to me. "What do you say we spend some time together?"

I would rather have been shot. I shrugged my shoulders all the way up to my earlobes and squinted until I could hardly see. But it was like he was wearing some kind of emotional armor.

"How about a ride?" he said. He nodded toward the motorcycle.

Great. Now he was learning my weaknesses and playing on them. And I thought I hated him before. I started to shake my head. And then he said—

"We could do the beach before it starts getting crowded."

Aw, man. How totally delicious would that be—if it wasn't with him. Although, who else was it going to be with at this point? I pretended to be gazing at the horizon.

"Don't I have to have a jacket and pants and all that?" I said.

"Got it. And your helmet."

I let my lip curl. "Okay, so, no offense, but I'm not wearing Weezie's helmet. She'd have a meltdown if she found out."

It was the first time I saw Lou look confused. "Why would you wear Weezie's helmet?"

"I wore it the other day."

"No you didn't. That was yours." He got the Ping-Pong ball going again. "I bought that before I went to Birmingham. I just hoped you'd come here and wear it someday."

He got up and went toward Levi. I told myself I didn't have any choice but to follow, and I kicked at the sand as I went, just for the sake of 'tude. One ride didn't mean I was taking his "help." It just meant that if I didn't do something—anything— I was going to go as crazy as my mother.

CHAPTER TEN

I had hardly ever used the word *perfect* to describe anything about myself or my life. But that day that I spent riding on Levi the Harley with Lou, it came into my head a dozen times. Maybe more.

Going down the beach — the *beach*, not just the road *beside* the beach — and smelling the salty-fishy-seaweedy mixture that didn't exist anywhere else I had ever been: that qualified as perfect.

Sitting in the F. A. Café at a table shaped like a fish, peeling steamed shrimp and eating them and being assured by Lou that I was doing it right because there was no way to do it wrong: that was also perfect.

And parking Levi on a low bridge that had the Atlantic Ocean on one side and what Lou told me was the Intracoastal Waterway on the other so we could watch the sun set and hear the gulls cry to see it go: that might have been the most perfect thing of all.

I could hardly admit to myself that he was okay to be with. I still got my hackles up every time I caught him looking at me like he was about to tell me how he was going to help me, change me, turn me into a smart little daughter like Weezie. But hours went by and he didn't say another word about it. And so the word *perfect* could stay in my head.

I crashed on the couch while Lou was cleaning the barbecue after our grilled salmon supper, and I didn't wake up until Sunday morning when he pulled up the shade on the sliding glass door. That was not perfect.

"I let you sleep as long as I could," he said as he set a glass of orange juice next to me on the coffee table.

"We're going to work *today*?" I said. "Isn't it Sunday?"

"Yes, it's Sunday, and no, we're not going to work. We're going to church."

I peered into the juice. There were seeds and pulpy things floating in it like he'd squeezed it out of the orange himself. I was pretty sure I'd never had it that way.

"I didn't bring any church clothes," I said, neck hairs fully extended again.

"What are church clothes?" he said.

"I had to wear dresses and matching socks when I used to go," I said. It had been so long since then, I'd probably worn hair bows too.

Lou grinned. "I'm having a hard time imagining that. And I don't think you'd want to wear a dress on a Harley anyway."

"We're taking Levi?"

"In thirty minutes."

I was in capris and a top in twenty. There was no doubt that I had a boring sermon in my future, an hour of trying to sit still and not nod off and fall out of the pew. But if going meant I got to ride on the back of Levi, I was there. The rest ... well, I never planned that far ahead.

When we crossed the bridge we went straight, instead of turning like we did to go to the shop, and headed into a part of St. Augustine I hadn't been in before. The town acted as sleepy as I was, with only some gray-headed people strolling through the big park with their coffee cups, which made me want caffeine. Maybe while Lou went to the service I could spend the hour in that coffee shop on the skinny brick street we turned onto ...

Fat chance. He pulled Levi into a parking space right next to a gray building with a red door and a steeple, and there was a cross on top of every part of the roof that came to a peak. The stained-glass windows were a dead giveaway: this was the place. As we went up the front walk, with Lou herding me like a sheep that was about to make a break for it, bells chimed so loud they made me jump. The whole thing couldn't have been more old-timey. I looked longingly over my shoulder at the coffee shop and sniffed.

"Smells great, doesn't it?" Lou said. "We'll go over there after."

"Do they make lattes?" I said.

He stopped on the first step and twitched his lips. "Yeah, but I think the last thing you need is espresso."

"But I love—"

"Make it decaf and you've got a deal."

It was the only thing that got me through the front door. The only thing.

I'd actually loved church when I was a kid. We got to sing songs with motions and stick flannel people and camels and donkeys on boards to tell stories and make stuff out of Popsicle sticks. It was way better than school. I even still believed in God, although I pretty much figured he'd lost my address or wasn't speaking to me, because I couldn't concentrate on sermons about seeds growing and Jesus coming back to tell me I wasn't going to heaven if I didn't shape up. But if the Richardsons—the last family that took me to church—hadn't moved away, I might have quit going anyway, because I'd gotten too old for children's church and had to go to the adult service and pretend like I had some clue to what the preacher was talking about. I didn't have much hope that this, today, was going to be anything but a snooze session.

To make matters worse, it was quiet when Lou and I walked in, except for a guitar playing. Which meant any sound I made squirming around in my seat was going to bounce off the stained-glass windows and have people going, "Shh," and giving Lou dirty looks.

That, however, wasn't the worst of it. I'd barely slid into the pew when somebody else came in from the other end and sat next to me. Rocky.

The word *perfect* vanished from my vocabulary.

He leaned across me and shook hands with Lou and then smirked into my face. I could see straight through the gap between his front teeth. Wasn't there some kind of commandment about thou shalt not go to church just to torment somebody?

"You got rid of Lou-WEE-za already?" he whispered to me. "You're good."

I started to tell him to shut up, but the music got louder and an organ and a violin joined in and everybody stood up. I basically forgot about Rocky because there was so much going on—singing, and then kneeling down, and then sitting to listen to people read something about fig trees, and then standing up to sing again, and finally sitting for a sermon that was preached by a guy in a white robe and sandals. If he was supposed to look like a saint, he wasn't pulling it off. The guy was taller than Marcus and had gristly gray hair and shoulders like the dudes who came in to eat sushi. The only thing that sunk into my mind before it wandered off was him saying something about the story of the fig tree really being about the manure. I didn't know you could talk about fertilizer in church.

I was just starting to peel off my nail polish when the sermon was done and we were singing again. If I remembered right, this should be just about over, which made it the shortest service I'd ever been to.

But then we were up again, and Lou and Rocky were both looking up at the front where Big Shoulders was standing behind a table with a pottery goblet and a round loaf of bread, like he was about to fix lunch. I was still holding out for coffee when he put his hand on the loaf and said, "On the night before he died, our Lord Jesus Christ took bread."

He picked up the loaf and lifted it. "And when he had given thanks he broke it," which Shoulders also did. "And gave it to his disciples saying, 'Take, eat—'"

Whoa. So he was acting out what he was saying up there. That was kind of cool.

He went on to raise the cup, and said, "Drink this, all of you, in remembrance of me."

I'd obviously missed something—in remembrance of who?—but it looked like other people were going to get in on the act too, because the two rows in front of us emptied out, and people went up to the front and stood in a semicircle while Shoulders gave out pieces of bread.

"Have you ever seen communion before?" Lou whispered to me.

"I don't know what that is," I whispered back. I glanced at Rocky, sure he was going to have something to say about *that*, but he was looking down into his lap.

"Just come with me and watch," Lou whispered. "You'll receive a blessing."

"Okay," I said.

I had no idea why. But I kind of wanted to be part of the acting out. It reminded me of those plays we did in Sunday school when we pretended to be animals on the ark or cows at the manger. Those were the only times my mother ever came to church—to see me in a play. And then we booked out of there before, as she put it, they could get their hooks into her. At the time, I didn't remember any hooks. Only later did I figure out she meant they were going for her checkbook.

So I followed Lou up to the front and watched every move he made as he cupped his hands and held them up so Shoulders could put a bite-size piece of bread into them and then dipped it into the cup somebody else brought around. Big Shoulders stopped and put his hand on my head and whispered something, but I was busy looking across the circle at the other people dipping their bread. I felt like I knew them. It was deliciously strange.

That lasted until after we sang the last song. It was obviously okay to talk in a normal voice then, and Rocky said to me, "You got through the whole service without breaking anything, Crash. Minor miracle."

"Shut—"

"Join us at the Galleon, Rock?" Lou said. "I'm buying."

Rocky's eyes glittered across my face. "I would, but I've got plans."

Okay, so maybe God was rewarding me for coming to church.

"Too bad," I said, plastering on my best killer smile.

"But I can be late. You want me to round up everybody else?"

"Sure," Lou said. "We'll meet you over there."

I didn't ask who "everybody else" was. I was afraid he was

going to say it was a posse of Rocky clones. Besides, I was still getting over the fact that the kid actually had the nerve to show up at church and even act like he was praying, when he was obviously a poseur. I'd caught him with his head bowed and his eyes closed several times during the service. Didn't you get struck by lightning for stuff like that?

I followed Lou across the street to the coffee shop—the Spanish Galleon, the sign said—where he ordered me a decaf vanilla latte with extra foam. I was sitting on a high stool under a pair of crossed swords on the wall, hoping they would fall down and stab Rocky in the heart when he walked in, when he did come through the door, followed by two other teenage guys and three girls. He actually had friends?

Then I watched with my chin hanging almost into my foam as they all shoved their way past Rocky and crowded around Lou, the girls hugging him, the guys punching at him the way boys do when they like somebody and don't want to go so far as to say, "I love you, man."

"I miss you, Lou!" one girl said.

"When are you coming back?" a guy said.

I could barely see Lou because most of them were taller than he was, but I heard him say, "Cut me some slack, guys. You're killin' me."

"Thanks for hogging your old man." Rocky hopped up onto the stool next to me. I considered knocking him off of it.

"I'm not hogging him," I said. "And he's not my old man."

Rocky picked up my coffee cup and sniffed at it. "So he's not your old man and he's not your dad. What do you call him—Bio-Dad?"

I snatched the cup back and splashed foam on both our hands. Rocky laughed out loud. I might have poured the whole thing over his head if a blonde girl hadn't poked *her* head out of the mob around Lou and said, "We gotta go, Rocky. We're already late."

"Hey, before you guys go," Lou said. "I want you to meet Jessie."

They all turned to me at the same time, as if they'd rehearsed it, and said, "Hi, Jessie!" in one big loud voice and then laughed like we were all on *Saturday Night Live*. I didn't get it.

"Get out of here, you bunch of Bozos," Lou said. "And stay out of trouble."

"I'll watch 'em," Rocky said.

That clinched it. They'd all be calling Lou to bail them out before this day was over.

"Bye, Jessie," a couple of the girls said as they all headed for the door.

"Nice talking to you," one guy said. He punched Lou's arm. "Like you even gave us a chance."

I craned my neck to see if he was remotely cute, but Rocky was already wrestling him out onto the sidewalk. Who had stepped down and left him in charge?

I had a feeling it was Lou. Okay, one day at the beach with the guy was fine, but, hello, I needed some time with somebody under forty—preferably under eighteen. And evidently that wasn't going to happen, because it sounded like Lou had given up whatever it was he usually did with all of them on a Sunday afternoon—go figure—to spend it with me. That one guy *was* kind of cute, and the girls didn't act like I had leprosy, the way girls could when somebody new showed up.

But it sure looked like I was going to be locked up with Lou again. I loved the Harley and all that, but cut me some slack. Back at the house he packed sandwiches while I changed into my swimsuit and shorts, and then we carried a cooler and blankets and boogie boards down the wooden walkway through the dunes and set up a mini-camp in the sand. We had the lunch spread out on a blanket with a Harley Davidson logo on it, and I was squinting down the beach, hoping maybe some bronzed surfers would show up, when Lou said, "So, Jess."

He unscrewed the top from a bottle of water and handed it to me.

"You remember yesterday I said I could help you."

I felt my eyes practically squinting shut. So it was all a ploy to get me to "trust him" so he could come in and do a personality transplant. I took a long swig of the water and wished it were a Coke. I was having caffeine withdrawal, among other things.

I set to work on peeling the label off the water bottle. He took it from me and put it down and looked right at me.

91

"I want you to hear me, Jess," he said, "because if you don't, this isn't going to work."

"What isn't going to work?" I put my hand up. "No, don't tell me because I can already tell *you* that if helping me means you lecturing me about how I need to pay attention and try harder and do better, it *isn't* gonna work. Been there, done that — didn't want the T-shirt."

I stopped to take a breath. Lou rubbed his chin. "If you could do that, you would have already," he said. "And we wouldn't be having this conversation."

"Right — but I can't do it, because I'm lazy and crazy and hopeless and stupid. Does that pretty much cover it?" Because if it did, I was going to go find some surfers myself.

"You can't do it," Lou said, "because I don't think anybody has given you the right tools. I could be wrong — I'm not an expert — but there are some things we're at least going to try."

"Do I have a choice?" I said between my teeth.

"Yes, actually, you do."

"Right."

"You always have a choice between doing the thing that's going to help you or doing the same thing you've been doing that makes you miserable. But since you don't know what the thing is that's going to help you, you haven't been able to make that choice. Until now."

It still didn't sound like a choice to me. I nodded because I figured he'd do his thing and then find out it didn't work, and by then the two weeks would be over. Still, I turned so that he had to talk to one of my shoulders.

Lou picked up a plastic knife and got on all fours in the sand. *Now* what was he doing?

YOUR ROOM, he wrote in the sand with the knife.

"We're going to get you organized in there," he said. "And then every morning before we leave for work, you're going to put everything where it belongs."

So that was where Weezie got it. He *was* trying to turn me into her.

"My mom tries that," I said. "She goes in there and puts everything in baskets and color codes my CDs and then I just

92

mess it up again. Not on purpose. It just happens." I folded my arms. "I don't see the point anyway. It's *my* stuff."

"It is your stuff, which is why I'm going to *help* you organize it, not do it for you. And the point is, can you ever find anything when you need it?"

"Sometimes," I said stubbornly.

"And when you can't find it, do you get anxious? Start freaking out?"

"Doesn't everybody?"

"And then you can't think so you lose something else or forget something important and everybody's in your face." He raised his eyebrows like he was waiting for an answer.

"Okay, yeah," I said. "So?"

"When your environment is cluttered, so is your head," he said. "Trust me."

I didn't. "I'll never be a neat freak like Weezie," I said.

"Nope. You won't. Nor do I want you to be. But you can get some control over the chaos."

As he bent over to write something else in the sand, I came as close to screaming as I had the morning before when I went off on the little Weezer. The first time I met him I was afraid he was going to get all fatherly and tell me what to do—and now he was doing exactly that. Only then, I could go home to my mother who only tried to run my life when she actually got out of bed. This guy was so in my business.

I looked down at what he'd written.

"NAME LABELS?" I said. "What—?"

"I'll help you put your name on everything—your jacket, your helmet, your phone—"

I stopped in the middle of actually starting to stand up and leave this control freak in the sand. "What phone?" I said.

"The one I'm giving you so we can communicate when I lose track of you." His lips did that twitchy thing.

"You're giving me a cell phone?"

"It's just basic; no bells and whistles."

I smelled a bribe, but I bit anyway. "Can I call my friends in Birmingham?" I said.

93

"Yeah. But your name's going on it so if you misplace it, it will have a better chance of finding its way back to you."

A cell phone. Chelsea would freak. I was even about to.

"Jess," Lou said, "stay with me."

I glued my eyes to his sand list. Maybe this had possibilities.

ROUTINE, he wrote.

Or not.

"Everybody needs rhythm in their life," Lou said, sitting back on his heels. "I know your body wants to stay up until two in the morning and sleep until noon, but the world doesn't operate on that schedule. I'd like to see you in bed by—"

He started writing times in the sand—for going to bed and getting up and going to work and coming home and having supper. With every number that got etched into the beach, another hair stood up on the back of my neck. I was at full porcupine status when he said, "Jess."

"*What?*"

He put his hand on my shoulder to stop me from rocking back and forth.

"Okay," he said, "let's go at this another way." He drew a large square around the numbers he'd carved in the sand. "Inside here are the things that are pretty much set up for you because that's the way it is. That's the way it is for just about everybody. But—" he pointed outside the square. "There is plenty of time beyond the box when nobody's telling you what you have to do."

"What—like ten minutes out of the whole day?" I said.

He shook his head. "For example, when we get home you have three hours after supper before lights-out. Plenty of down time there. It's a good balance—work, play, rest."

"You don't seriously think I'm going to sleep at ten o'clock."

"Not at first. It'll take your body awhile to get used to that. We'll get you into a slowdown routine in the evening, which should help."

In your dreams. I looked down to see my hands digging in the sand so hard I was already up to my wrists.

Lou tossed the plastic knife onto the blanket and smiled at me. "Okay, well, that's a start. You want to try out the boogie board?"

A *start*? This whole I-have-your-entire-life-scheduled-for-you talk was just a *start*? What else could he possibly have planned to "help" me?

Cell phone or no cell phone, I couldn't do it. Not now that I knew that the spend-the-day-with-Jessie thing yesterday had all been a setup for this — this — takeover.

I stood up and brushed the sand off the seat of my shorts and hoped some of it got into his sandwich.

"I'm gonna take a walk," I said.

I turned to march off.

"Jess," he said.

"*What?*"

"Take this with you." He pulled a blue cell phone out of the pocket of his T-shirt and tossed it to me. "It has my number programmed in. And your mom's."

I looked at it and at him and wanted to scream for about the tenth time in the last hour.

"It's okay," he said. "This is a lot of change. No pressure — we'll walk through it together. One day at a time."

I took off down the beach, running until my side hurt, until I was far enough away that no one could hear me. Then I planted myself at the base of a dune and punched buttons on the phone until I found an entry called *Mom*.

She didn't answer at first. The ringing went on and on until I was ready to throw the phone into the Atlantic. The thing looked prehistoric anyway ...

When she did pick up, I thought it was someone else. Someone with a voice that was more breath than words.

"Mom?" I said.

Long pause.

"It's Jessie," I said.

"I know — Jessie — what are you doing?"

"Calling you." I bit my lip. I couldn't cry, not now.

I heard her switch the phone to her other ear. "What's up?" she said.

"I just want to know — how you are."

She sighed long and hard. I'd never known her to do that

before. "I'm not good, Jessie. Look, I don't think it's a good idea for us to be talking right now."

"Well, when?" I said.

"I don't know. When I'm better than this. I'm sorry, Jessie. Are you okay? You sound okay."

I sound okay? Or you *want* me to sound okay? I'm not okay!

"We'll talk when I'm better," she said. "When I get my mind around this."

"Mom—"

"Bye, Jessie."

The phone went dead.

I kind of wished I would too.

It wasn't bad enough at home when I always felt like a flake? At least there my friends accepted it and liked me when I played it up. At least my teachers just told me to try harder and then gave up on me. At least my mother only cared about any of it when she was in a No-Bed Phase that was sure to end soon.

But here—here I had one kid calling me Crash and another one calling me Crazy, and I couldn't get away from either one of them because they were both attached to Bio-Dad at the hip. And he—

I kicked at the sand and kicked at it and kicked at it again. He was trying to turn me into somebody I couldn't be—and he was going to do it until he found out I was a loser-airhead-moron—and …

And who cared? So he had a Harley and a house on the beach and he didn't mind saying he was sorry …

I stopped kicking, and I looked back down the shoreline where Lou was standing ankle-deep in the water, shading his hands against the sun like he was trying to find me.

Okay. Fine. I would try to do all the things on his list and he would see that he was wrong—that it wasn't going to work because it never did. Then he *would* be sorry.

And I could go back to being the crazy chick I knew how to be.

I smoothed out the sand I'd kicked and strolled back down the beach toward Bio-Dad.

CHAPTER ELEVEN

Ten o'clock at night felt to me the way noon probably felt to everyone else. I was ready for a lunch-size snack, including something that didn't have the word *natural* printed on its wrapper—although there was almost nothing in Lou's fridge that even had a wrapper. And while everyone else was winding down, I was just gearing up to do—something. Anything. Except lie in bed staring at the ceiling and wishing for the thousandth time that I wasn't cursed with ADHD. People could talk all they wanted about what a common "challenge" it was. They only said that because they didn't have it.

I threw back the covers and sat up and looked around the room in the moonlight that made its pale way through the pink-and-green curtains. Lou said he'd already had it figured out before the Weezer opened her big mouth. Now it was like he'd googled it on the Internet and read all about what to do for the "victim" and was following it like an owner's manual.

He didn't own me—I was clear on that. But he sure acted like he did. We'd just spent an hour going through each section of the room and putting away my stuff. And then he'd given me hot Sleepytime tea—when I was ready to sell the cell phone for a supersize Coke—and turned on what he called "soft rock"—which sounded like geezer rock to me—and left me alone to do what I was doing right now, which was going slowly insane. I yanked off the big T-shirt, which now smelled like fabric softener, and threw it in the corner. He'd obviously bought it for me, like he had the helmet, to make me think he cared that he had another kid. I wasn't wearing it.

I pulled on a tank top and paced around the room. I considered short-sheeting Weezie's neat little bed but decided she wasn't worth the energy, even if she did have a mouth the size of an Olympic-size pool.

I went to the table Lou had put on my side of the bed and opened the drawer and pulled out the cell phone "we" had decided I should keep there at night so I could find it in the morning. I looked at the screen, but Marcus hadn't called, even though I had left him four messages. Chelsea hadn't returned my phone call either. She was probably out with Donovan. Doing normal stuff. Not undergoing a treatment plan like me.

I flopped back down on the bed. Too bad you couldn't just have an operation to take out your messed-up brain part, like they did when somebody had sick tonsils or something. Just reach in there and pull it out so the person—me—could be normal and not have to—

I sat back up. This was reminding me of that story in that RL book. The guy telling the demon to come out and it just did. *That* was what I was talkin' about.

Where did "we" put the book anyway? Ah—"we" didn't put it anywhere. "I" had stuck it between the mattress and the box spring so the little Weezer wouldn't see it next time she came. For some reason, I wanted it to be private.

I slid it out and sat cross-legged on the bed and opened it. My stomach felt suddenly queasy. What if I couldn't understand it anymore? What if it had just been my imagination and I really was nuts?

But when I opened it, the words came up to me again as if they were reading themselves to me.

So you came back. You're hungry for more, aren't you? You want to know if there's any more of that demon freeing.

The usual chill went up my back, but I was starting to like it.

Check this out. That night at sundown, everybody who had anybody sick brought them to him—fever, paralysis, skin disease, you name it.

Brought them to who? The same guy?

98

Yeshua. He put his hands on every single one of them and healed them.

I had a quick flash of Big Shoulders' hand on my head. But what about the demons?

There was a mass exit of those. All these people everyone said were out of their minds were sane again, which did not make the demons happy at all. After all, they didn't have anyplace to go now. They left screaming because they knew who he was. He shut them up. He didn't want them telling everyone.

Why not?

Keep reading the story and you'll get it. Really get it.

I turned the page, but the words looked foggy. A yawn came up out of me and I couldn't keep my eyelids from slamming shut. That happened a lot when I tried to read. With a sense of disappointment, I slid RL back into its place and conked out.

*

Rose did her usual bow to me when I got to the sushi restaurant the next morning. I bowed back, and that seemed to be all the conversation she expected, which was good because I wasn't in the mood to chat—for once. After going through the check-list with Lou before we even got on Levi—phone, flip-flops, shorts, snack—and having to go back inside for the flip-flops, and having to admit to myself that now I knew exactly where they were—anyway, after all that, if anybody had said to me, "Do this," or "Do that," I probably would have had a serious meltdown and taken them with me.

I started to put on my apron, but Rose shook her head and picked up a cooler and nodded toward the back door. She bowed and smiled—the other thing she seemed to do constantly—and led me out and down the street. I couldn't stand the suspense.

"Where are we going?" I said.

"Buy fish," she said and, of course, smiled.

We wove our way among the early morning senior citizens out walking with their little yappy dogs and their to-go cups of coffee. It was all I could do not to grab one from a lady when she stopped to let her Yorkie sniff my foot. Speaking of sniffing, I didn't have to ask Rose where we were going to buy fish because I smelled it long before we got there. I would rather have gone into the cool shop where they were selling shell jewelry or the bakery that had cupcakes with an inch of frosting displayed in the window, but she skittered into the cold, dark place that was lined on both sides with tanks full of creatures—moving creatures.

"Rosie!" said an almost-bald guy at the far end who stood behind a counter wearing an apron covered in ... I didn't want to know what. He had more knives on the wall than Bonsai and the Spanish Galleon put together.

I could have predicted that Rose would bow to him, which she did.

"Who've you got with you?" he said.

"Yes!" Rose said.

"Hello, Yes!"

"It's Jess," I said.

"Close enough. I sent your order down, Rosie. Was there a problem?"

"No." Rose smiled and shook her head and smiled some more. If I'd been the guy in the nasty apron, I would have been pulling out what little hair I had left.

"Need more squid," she said.

"Squid?" I said. "Are you serious?"

She just smiled—again—and pointed to the tank we were standing in front of. Ew—they were squid, all right, except they were smaller than the gigantic ones in the middle-of-the-night movies I'd seen, and less evil looking, but still very strange.

Apron Guy lifted a metal lid with holes in it from the top of the tank. "Go ahead and check it out, Rosie. Let me know what you want."

Rose nodded, but she looked at me.

"What?" I said.

"You pick," she said.

I looked at the squid, and several of them appeared to be staring back at me with eyes that bugged out from clear blue skin.

"Okay," I said, "I'll take that one that's looking at me."

Rose shook her head.

"Why? What's wrong with him?"

"Touch tentacles," she said.

"Are you serious?"

"You have to make sure the suckers are still active," Apron Guy said. "That's how you know they're fresh." He winked at Rose. "I tell her they're all fresh, but she's suspicious, that Rosie."

"So what do I do, stick my hand in there?" I said.

"Yep."

"Do they bite?"

"Nah."

They both looked at me like it was perfectly normal to put your fingers in a tank full of squid. It actually sounded kind of cool. I stood on tiptoes and poked my hand into the water. When I grabbed for one, they all scattered.

"They shy," Rose said. "Go slow."

"Shy squid. Okay." I let my hand float toward one pink guy hiding in a corner. His tentacle slid out and curled around my finger and hung on with his little sucker cups tickling my skin. It was so weird and delightful I giggled out loud. "This guy's definitely fresh. That feels so cool. You want me to pick out another one?"

Rose nodded, and Apron Guy said, "You've got the touch, Yes."

I selected four and rejected one whose suckers seemed a little sluggish to me. Rose also let me pick out some live shrimp—the active ones, she said. I chose a bunch that looked like they could have had ADHD. She taught me how to nudge open the shellfish to see if they'd close by themselves and how to check the eyes on the tuna—which I had never seen anyplace outside a Starkist can—to make sure their pupils weren't "like clouds." Took me several tries to understand that "crowds" were "clouds."

We both did a lot of bowing and smiling while we were translating, but I got out of there knowing that you had to stroke fish to make sure they weren't stiff and sticky and didn't have droopy tails and did have tender heads. Who knew all that went into the little roll things Bonsai made like they were craft projects? I was pretty sure the people at Captain D's didn't go through all that when they made fish sandwiches.

"Now we clean," Rose told me as we scurried—she pretty much always scurried like a chipmunk—back to the shop, me swinging the full cooler and checking out the windows of the shops full of pirate stuff and beach furniture and art that looked like someone real had actually painted it.

"Yeah," I said, "I definitely need to wash my hands."

"No. Clean fish."

"I don't know how to do that," I said.

"You will," she said, and bowed to me for no apparent reason.

It sounded icky—but, then, it couldn't be any worse than sticking my hand into a tank full of suckery sea creatures. So I put on my apron and cleaned the cutting board and was practicing saying "san-mai oroshi" with Rose—which she said was the name for the way we were going to cut the fish—when Lou poked his head into the kitchen.

"How's it going?" he said.

"Don't disturb me," I said. "I'm trying not to bruise the fish." I held one up by its tail to show him.

"Can you spare her at lunchtime?" Lou said to Rose.

"Where are we going?" I said.

"To the doctor," he said. "Meet me at twelve thirty."

"The doctor! Why?"

But I already knew why, and I let the fish flop to the cutting board.

"Careful," Lou said. "You're going to bruise it."

*

It was a miracle I didn't bruise something besides a tuna that morning. Napkins and chopsticks. Hunks of wasabi and ginger. The glasses I yanked out of the dishwasher. Everything took it heavy as I beat up on Lou in my head for pulling the doctor thing on me. Even Rose stopped smiling. Bonsai told her, "Don't let her near my dragon rolls. Everyone will get indigestion."

I definitely had indigestion by the time we got to the doctor's office. I was biting my nails and swinging my feet and doing whatever else it took not to karate chop Lou while we sat in the examining room.

"You're going to make me take medication, aren't you?" I said.

"I'm not going to 'make' you do anything," he said. "I want us to hear what the doc has to say about it, and we'll decide from there."

"'We'?" I said. "Don't you mean 'you'?"

"No, I don't. You'll have a say."

I swung my legs harder off the side of the examining table. "And then you'll decide what I'm going to do."

Lou tilted his head at me. "Is that the way it works with you and your mom?"

"Yeah. It did." I stopped swinging. "I don't know how it works now."

"So, until now, you haven't been allowed to make any decisions for yourself."

"Except when she's in an In-Bed Phase. Then I make all the decisions—until she gets up and changes everything, so what difference does it make?"

I chomped down on my lip. I hadn't meant to Blurt all that out. But, then, when did I ever mean to Blurt? I folded my arms into my middle and went back to swinging. Lou was now making more decisions for me than my mother ever did.

The doctor came in then. He was sort of young looking, and I could tell he and Lou already knew each other because they called one another Lou and Jason and looked like they could play tennis together or something. Great. It was already two against one.

"You must be Jess," he said to me.

"I must be," I said. I gave him my bubbling-over-like-a-soda smile. In spite of how annoyed I was, it just kind of kicked in when I was in doctor's offices and other places where it might get me out of something. It had worked before.

He asked me a bunch of questions that I answered with

103

the truth because what else was I going to do with Lou sitting there checking off my answers in his head? Doctor—I couldn't remember what he said his name was—listened and nodded and then looked at the folder he'd walked in with.

"How was the medication working for you?" he said. "Before you stopped taking it?"

I glared at Lou. He hadn't missed telling him anything, had he? Traitor.

"I could get through a class without having to go to the pencil sharpener twelve times," I said. "I could finish a test without forgetting what subject I was in. It was okay, I guess."

"And without it?"

I waited for him to glance at Lou for an answer, but he just kept looking at me as if I had actually been speaking intelligently. It gave me a funny feeling in my throat.

"Without it I'm a ditz-queen-airhead-moron," I said.

He looked like he might have a funny feeling in his throat himself. He closed the folder and cranked up a stool so he could sit on it and look at me at eye level. "I think we can do better than that," he said. "I'd like to try you on a new medication. It lasts longer, doesn't have as many side effects. It should give you more concentration so you can keep working on your coping skills."

"Oh," I said. I shot Lou a killer smile. "Is that what we're doing?"

"The meds aren't going to do it all," Doctor Tennis Player said. "Have you guys talked about counseling?"

I stopped smiling. Lou shook his head. Lucky for him. I couldn't have controlled myself if he had said, "That's next."

The doctor squeezed my shoulder and stood up. "This is entirely up to you two—and in terms of the meds, that's your call, Jessie. Unless your dad plans to shove them down your throat."

He hit Lou on the arm with the folder and left. I barely waited for the door to close.

"I'm not doing counseling," I said. "If you make me go, I'll just sit there and not say anything."

Lou's lips twitched. "I have a life-size picture of that."

"Don't laugh at me—it's not funny! I'm not going to some shrink and have him tell me I'm crazy. I'm not doing it!"

"No, you're not. I wasn't even going to suggest it."

"Oh," I said, and felt stupid. And I was about to cry, which made me feel even stupider.

Lou leaned forward. "But I would like to see you try the medication, Jess," he said. "Life isn't an endurance test, you know? Why make it any harder than it already is? If there's something that can help take the edge off all this frustration, why not use it?" He looked down at his hands for a second. "If there were something I could take for my own stuff, I'd do it in a heartbeat."

What stuff? I wanted to know—as he sat back and held onto his jaw and watched me. I shook that off. Whatever "stuff" he had, he was wrong about mine. But I'd told myself I'd let him find that out for himself—and be sorry.

"I'll take the pills on one condition," I said.

He answered me with his eyebrows.

"You have to promise not to tell the—tell Weezie about it—or about us doing all this other stuff that we're doing for my—you know."

"ADHD."

"Yeah. That's the only way I'll do it."

"I'll go you one better," he said. "I'll make sure she doesn't even bring it up again. Deal?"

He had his hand out like he wanted me to shake it. What adult had ever done that? I put my hand inside his and he squeezed it, and I said, as best I could with a lump in my throat, "Deal."

*

Okay, so he wasn't wrong about the pills. Although I didn't tell *him*, I knew, like, the second day that they were working. A little.

Like, I learned how to fillet a whole fish by myself—without "bruising" it. I kind of liked saying "WHACK!" when I chopped off a head and cut away the fins. Bonsai gave me a lot of out-of-the-side-of-his-eyes looks, but Rose always giggled. Although, she giggled at everything I did, including when I shrieked, "No, not the skin—not the skin!" as I skimmed it off a salmon, and when I danced the squid around a few times before I started to clean it.

That was still as close as Bonsai would let me get to the sushi—except to taste it. Before the lunch crowd came in Wednesday, he made me sit at the counter and work the chopsticks until I could pick up a single piece of rice with them, and then he put a roll in front of me and waited.

"What is it?" I said.

"Maki-zushi," he said. "Tekkamaki."

I wrinkled my nose. "What's in it?"

Bonsai rested his forearms on the countertop and shook his head at me.

"I just want to know what I'm eating," I said.

"You picked it out and cut off its head and pulled off its skin and you still don't know it?"

I picked up a roll with the chopsticks and brought it close to my nose. "Tuna?"

"Tekkamaki. Tuna roll. Thin and light and perfect for lunch." He craned his neck at me. "Eat it."

I started to put it in my mouth, and then I said, "What are the little red beads on there?"

"Fish egg," Rose said beside me.

Bonsai glared at her.

"Are you serious?" I said.

"Eat," Bonsai said. "Dip it in the soy sauce first."

I did, and then I closed my eyes and inserted it in my mouth. Maybe if I just swallowed it whole, I wouldn't taste it and I wouldn't throw up.

But I immediately knew it was the most delicious thing I'd ever had on my tongue. "I think I died and went to heaven," I said with my mouth full.

"You irritating child," Bonsai said. But I saw the corners of his mouth twitch. He must have learned that from Lou.

I also knew the pills were working—a little—when by Thursday morning I made it onto Levi without having to go back inside and get something I'd forgotten. And when I got back to the house after my usual sunset visit to the beach before Lou had to come looking for me. And when I only checked my phone four times a day instead of a thousand, to see if Marcus or Chelsea had called me back.

Or maybe that last one was just because I was giving up hope. Chelsea I could understand—she was wrapped up like a mummy in Donovan. No wonder she'd warned me when she started going out with him. That seemed like such a long time ago now.

But Marcus—that brought me down. He always called me. He was always there. The only thing I could figure out was that he hadn't found any place for me to stay, and he was afraid to tell me because he knew I'd go off like a bottle rocket.

That I could still do, as I found out Thursday afternoon.

I was wiping off the last table after lunch when Lou came out to score some leftover salmon rolls from Bonsai.

"Take them, you mooch," Bonsai said, giving him a plate of them decorated with bamboo leaves cut into the shape of turtles. I kind of wanted to learn how to do that, but I knew it wasn't happening with Bonsai, who still gave me as many evil looks as he did blank ones.

"Don't go there with me, Bonsai," Lou said. "I know you throw them away anyway—which seems like a waste to me, but what do I know about sushi except how to eat it?"

"Not much evidently," I said.

Lou looked at Bonsai and then at me, a curl of pickled ginger hanging between his chopsticks.

"If you keep them too long the yaki-nori gets soggy," I said. "That's the seaweed it's wrapped in. Thirty minutes max, even rolled in a paper towel and plastic wrap."

"Is that so?" Lou popped a piece of salmon roll in his mouth and chewed and grinned at the same time. "You'll make a sushi chef out of her yet, Bonsai."

Bonsai grunted. Rose giggled. I bowed, just for the hang of it.

Lou glanced at his watch. "It's about free time for you, isn't it, Jess?"

"Excuse me?"

"You only have to work until three. It's that now. Don't you want to explore St. Augustine a little bit?"

"Are you serious?"

"It's part of your schedule."

"You didn't tell me that!"

"It was written right there in the sand." He dipped his roll in the soy sauce. "Of course, you were so busy ranting about how I was taking over your life that you might have missed it."

"I never said that!"

"You didn't have to."

I did that thing he always did and erased the conversation with my hand. "Okay—so I have 'til, like, five?"

"Not 'like five'—exactly five. Use your cell phone as a watch."

"So, do I get to use a scooter?"

He looked at me as he chewed.

"Just asking," I said.

"Just answering."

I tore off the apron and headed for the kitchen and stopped. "I don't even know where to go," I said.

"That's okay," he said. "You'll have a guide."

"What, you mean, like a map? I'm really bad at reading maps—I could get lost in a closet with a map."

"No, not like a map," Lou said. "Like a personal guide."

"Who?"

"Rocky," he said.

CHAPTER TWELVE

T hat was when I went off. Not to Lou's face. That would have made him think he was right about me—that I needed all these rules and schedules and babysitters. No, I saved the blow-up for Rocky.

After all, Rocky had probably set the whole thing up so he could try to drive me off the deep end, which was apparently his new career. That was why I'd made it a point to avoid him all week, why I always stayed out in the restaurant even when there wasn't anything left for me to do there. The thought of spending two minutes with him, much less two *hours*, sent me straight to the restroom where I flushed the toilet four times in a row and turned the water on and off and destroyed several paper towels until I stopped wanting to do all of the above to that gap-toothed weasel. Hottie weasel—but still a weasel. And definitely not my type. At all.

Rocky was sitting on one of the scooters when I emerged from the building, and for a second I thought maybe my tour of St. Augustine was going to be on the back of one of those. That would mean being really close to him. Not gonna happen.

But he stood up and sort of strolled toward me like he thought I couldn't wait for him to get there and he was making me suffer. Whatever.

"So you want to see St. A," he said.

"Yes," I said. "But not with you."

"Not even on the back of my bike?"

"I am SO not riding on a bicycle with you."

"No, my motorcycle."

"Oh," I said. "You have a Harley too?"

"An old Sportster." He shrugged. "But a Harley's a Harley. I've seen how you get into riding with Lou. You know you want to."

I did. I swallowed what little pride I had left and said, "Okay."

"Gotcha," he said. He flashed the gappy teeth. "You're not allowed on a bike with anybody but your dad. He told me that himself."

"I hate you," I said.

"I'm not that crazy about you either." He was still grinning.

"Is he making you do this?"

"Look, we're burnin' daylight. Are you coming or not?"

"Where are we going?" I said.

"To the Galleon for starters. I need a mocha."

Only because I saw caffeine in my future did I agree. Although as I marched down the sidewalk trying to stay just ahead of Rocky in spite of the fact that I didn't know where I was going, I wondered if Lou had told him not to let me drink anything but decaf. It wouldn't have surprised me. We got our drinks to go—I ordered a vanilla latte with two shots of espresso—and stood on the sidewalk across from the church, blinking in the sun. I fished my sunglasses out of my purse and put them on.

"Now you totally look like a tourist," Rocky said. "So where do you want to go? And just so you know, I don't shop and I don't do historical sites."

I took a long swallow of my latte. "Good. I want to see a historical site."

I actually did want to, and if it meant it would get rid of him, I won all the way around.

"Cool," he said. "The oldest house is only three blocks from here."

"You just said you don't do historical stuff!"

"I lied," he said. "Come on."

I practically had to run to keep up with him on the narrow brick streets lined with buildings that all looked like "the oldest house" to me, until we got to the one that was officially called that. Once we were inside, I could see why. The rooms were dark and tiny, and the kitchen was in a separate building out back and was even smaller than Lou's. It figured, since it was four hundred years old.

"Dude, I never knew some of that stuff," Rocky said when we were back outside.

"Did you just move here or something?" I said.

"Uh-uh. I've lived here my whole life."

"So you've been in there before."

He shrugged and headed around a corner with me in pursuit. "Once on a field trip in third grade. But who remembers anything from third grade?"

Definitely not me.

"Anyway, I got thrown out."

Of course you did.

"So, speaking of school, the oldest schoolhouse is back down on St. George Street." Rocky glanced down at me. "I suppose you want to see that too."

"Do you?" I said.

"No."

"Then let's go."

He took off again with me scurrying behind him like Rose. He was just doing it to tick me off, and I would have told him to get lost, except that then *I* would be lost.

There was a long line to get in at the old school so Rocky bought us ice cream and we hung out to wait. I was pretty sure by that time that Lou was paying him to babysit me. I checked my phone. It was already 4:15. Bummer. I really wanted to go to the fort.

"It's weird waiting in line to go *in* a school," Rocky said. "I can't wait to get *out* of mine."

"Me neither," I said.

"I hate it. One more year and I'm out of there."

"I wish. I have *three* more years. At least. More if I don't take ninth grade English over in summer school—" I stopped in mid-Blurt and wanted to cram my entire chocolate ice-cream cone into my mouth. Wonderful. Not only had I just agreed with Rocky about something—I'd also revealed that I was the ditz-queen airhead moron he already thought I was.

111

But he just said, "I bite at English. Who cares if you know what a semicolon is if all you want to do is tune carburetors, y'know?"

"I don't want to tune carburetors either," I said.

Rocky tossed his napkin in a nearby trash can and stuck his hands in the pockets of the denim jacket with the sleeves cut out that he wore over an also desleeved white T-shirt. "So what *do* you want to do?" he said, green eyes glittering. "Be a test-car dummy?"

I stared at him for all of a millisecond before I shoved all that was left of my ice cream right into the middle of his chest, cone and all. There were titters and muffled gasps all around us that I ignored as I turned on my flip-flops and started off down St. George Street.

"Hey!" I heard him call behind me. "Hey—wait!"

Why—so you won't get in trouble with Lou? Or so you can smack me in the face with another insult when I'm starting to think you're an actual human being?

"Come on, stop!" he said—right behind me—even though I was knocking people aside like bowling pins to get away from him.

He grabbed my arm. I tried to wrench loose but he had a steel grip. He even pulled me around the corner and pressed me against the wall of an art gallery and wouldn't let me go.

"Get off me," I said between my teeth. "Get off or I'll scream."

"Just listen, Jess, okay?"

I did, because his eyes looked scared and he wasn't flashing the gap between his teeth—and because it was the first time he'd ever said my name.

"Just listen to me, please," he said. "I want to say something."

"So say it," I said.

He sucked in air through his nose. "I was way out of line back there. I shouldn't have said that."

"Then why did you? No, I know why. Because you actually think that about me—only now you don't want to get in trouble with your precious Lou—"

"Would you shut up?" he said. "Look—I don't think that

about you. I just said it because I was trying to be funny. Lou says I sound like a jerk when I do that."

"Lou's right! You do!" I wriggled my shoulders. "Could you let go of me now?"

"Only if you accept my apology. And if you promise not to go anywhere."

I glared at him. He took his hands off my shoulders, but he planted one of them on the wall above my head and rubbed the back of his neck with the other one.

"What's with the Lou thing anyway?" I said.

"What Lou thing?"

"Is he like the substitute father for every kid in St. Augustine?"

"I don't know about every kid. He is for me."

"Oh," I said. Now I was the one who felt like a jerk.

"He's just been there for me since—well, he's just been there. Which is probably why I subconsciously wanted to make you look like a loser."

"Excuse me?"

"You cut in on my time with him. I know, it's immature—"

"You're as bad as the little Weezer," I said.

A grin spread slowly across his face. "The little Weezer," he said. "I like it. Hey, how did you get rid of her so fast last weekend? She's usually on Lou like Velcro."

"Simple," I said. "She hates me."

"She'll get over it. She's just jealous of you."

I let out a snort-laugh.

"What?" he said.

"Lou thinks that too," I said. "Nobody is jealous of me."

His smile stayed. "I doubt that. I bet a lot of girls hate you."

"Oh—thank you. Can you not go, like, two sentences without dissing me?"

He looked a little clueless. "I just meant I bet you have a lot of guys chasing you and the girls are jealous because the guys aren't chasing *them*."

I couldn't say anything. Not a thing—except "What-time-is-it-I-should-get-back" in one big breath.

"Not until you say you accept my apology," he said.

"Was it for real?" I said.

"I don't say I'm sorry unless I mean it."

"Lou said that too."

"Where do you think I learned it?"

Where else? I rolled my eyes. "Do you promise to stop calling me Crash?"

"Done."

"And will you never even mention the whole scooter accident thing, like, ever again?"

He gave me a blank look. "What scooter accident?"

"Okay," I said. "I forgive you. And I hope the chocolate comes out of your shirt."

"Is that *your* apology?" he said.

"Shut up," I said. But I smiled at him and followed him across the street and through the city gates.

"We return to the scene of the crime," he said.

"So help me, I'm warning you," I said.

"I figure I'm safe. You don't have a weapon—no killer ice-cream cone, no Formula One scooter—"

He dodged the arm I swung at him.

*

When I was down on the beach that night watching the water turn pink like I now did *every* night, Lou came down and joined me.

"Why are those fishermen giving me the hairy eyeball?" he said to me under his breath when he'd waded out to me.

I squinted at the two guys who were standing offshore with their long lines pulled tight over the water. "Does 'hairy eyeball' mean it looks like they wish we'd go away?"

"Pretty much."

I made a note to self to remember that next time Bonsai looked at me that way. "It's probably because they do wish we'd go away," I said. "Or at least me."

"What did you do, Jess?"

"The first night I came out here I was messing around in the water and that one guy said I was scaring the fish away."

"Define 'messing around,'" Lou said. His mouth was jittering at the corners.

"I was just bodysurfing and I went crooked and got tangled up in their thing—their line."

His lips stopped twitching. "Back up. You were bodysurfing?"

"Yeah. *You* taught me."

"You can't be out here swimming by yourself. It's too dangerous."

"That wasn't in the box."

"It is now. If you want to swim, let me know and I'll come be lifeguard."

First a babysitter. Now a lifeguard. What was next?

"We clear on that?" Lou said.

"Uh-huh."

"Jess."

I stopped scooping up sea foam and looked at him. He was swallowing the Ping-Pong ball again.

"This is serious," he said. "Look at me and tell me you get it."

"I get it," I said to the foam on my arm.

"Hey." Lou tilted my chin up with his finger.

"I get it," I said.

I tried not to pull my eyes away until he did. It didn't work. He let my chin go and glanced at the fishermen. "Just so you know, they don't own the beach. It's not like they're making a living at it."

"So, can I bodysurf right now?" I said. It was the only way I could think of to end this conversation.

"Absolutely. But let me get this out of the way first. Tomorrow is Friday. You know that means—"

"That I've been here a week, and my mom will be out of the hospital next week."

For probably the first time ever he looked like he didn't have a comeback. Then he shook his head.

"What do you mean, no?" I said, my voice heading upward.

"I mean, no, that isn't what I was going to say. Tomorrow is Friday, and Weezie is coming. You ready to try this again?"

I didn't ask if it mattered what I was ready for.

"I've talked to her, Jess," he said. "She won't be throwing anything in your face. I expect the same from you."

"I don't have anything to throw," I said.

"You have the fact that you're here with me all the time and she isn't. I know that isn't a big deal to you, but it is to her."

I couldn't help looking at him closer. His voice sounded sad.

"What's wrong?" he said.

"Do you want her to live with you all the time?" I said.

He tilted his head at me. "Of course I do. She's my daughter. It kills me that I don't get to wake her up every morning and make sure she's eating right and tuck her in at night."

"So you hate it that you can't torment her the way you do me." I immediately had my hands in the air, erasing the words. "Just kidding. Seriously, it was a joke."

He was already chuckling down in his throat. "She wouldn't think it was a joke. She thinks that's all torment too. So, are we good to go for tomorrow night?"

"She's not staying the whole weekend?"

"One day at a time, Jess," Lou said. "One day at a time."

*

I was actually in a good mood when we were on our way to Weezie's after work Friday. Bonsai hadn't given me the "hairy eyeball" once the whole day, and Rose had let me clean the bamboo mats he used to roll the sushi so I could finally see how they worked. Very cool.

And Rocky had shown up for my free time, which annoyed me at first because I hated that Lou still thought I needed a babysitter. But we went to the fort, and it was the single coolest place I'd ever seen. We went up and down the same stairs the conquistadores had used when they were watching for the British who were out to take their treasures. We walked on every outside walkway of the whole star-shaped fortress and sat astride the cannons until I could almost feel them shooting out over Matanzas Bay. Every time I looked at Rocky, he seemed to be as into it as I was.

Besides that, he kept his promise and didn't call me Crash. He had a new nickname for me.

"Have a good weekend with the little Weezer," he said when I was waiting for Lou.

I gave *him* the hairy eyeball.

"Aw, come on, Red," he said. "You know you love her."

"Shut up," I said.

Still, as Lou and I pulled up to Weezie's mini-mansion, I wasn't planning how to toss her in a dumpster. I wasn't even gritting my teeth.

That lasted all of about seven seconds.

She seemed to have a new tactic. Instead of making me feel like an intruder, she tried to make me feel invisible. Not only did she not speak to me on the ride to Lou's or while we were at the supper table having her coconut shrimp again, she didn't even look at me.

I was actually fine with that. Even when Lou went out to clean the grill and she turned to me in the kitchen where we were doing the dishes and said, "I guess you're wondering why I'm not speaking to you."

I blinked at her. "You aren't speaking to me?" I said.

She didn't get it. "No, I'm not. You want to know why?"

"No," I said.

She didn't get that either. "It's because my dad says if you can't say something nice to somebody, don't say anything at all."

I laughed right out loud.

"It's not funny!"

"Yes, it is."

She opened her mouth, and then she smacked her hand over it and darted out of the kitchen like one of those plover birds and slammed the bedroom door. For a very weird moment she kind of reminded me of somebody. Me.

I was putting the last of the dishes away when Lou came in. He was grinning.

"I was liking that," he said.

"Liking what?"

"You two laughing in here."

I shook my head. "That was just me. Weezie wasn't laughing."

An eyebrow went up. "What happened?"

I didn't have a chance to tell him. There was a shriek from the bedroom, followed by Weezie tearing into the kitchen, face flaming, screaming, "She took it! She took my shirt!"

"Whoa, Weezie," Lou said.

But she wasn't going to be put in her place this time. "That shirt is *mine! She* can't have it!"

"What shirt?" Lou said.

"The one you gave me to wear over my swimsuit. The Kennesaw's shirt that says 'Ride American. Eat Japanese.'" She thrust a finger at me. "She took it!"

"That was *your* shirt?" I said.

"Like you didn't know! Daddy, she stole it!"

I rolled my eyes. "I didn't *steal* it. I thought it was for me."

"No, you did not, or you wouldn't have hid it under your mattress."

I froze in the middle of another eye roll. "What were you doing looking under my mattress?"

"I can look anywhere I want in there. It's *my* room!"

"All right, enough," Lou said.

"Daddy—"

"I said enough—"

"You have to give her a consequence!"

"Louisa."

Weezie clamped her mouth shut, which was good because I was ready to shut it for her.

Lou looked at her like he was waiting to make sure she wasn't going to try again. "Last time I checked, I was the dad here," he said finally.

"My dad," I heard her mutter.

"Excuse me?" Lou said.

"Nothing."

Lou turned to me. I was in the corner formed by the counters, opening and closing a cabinet with my heel.

"You want to clear this up for me?" he said.

No, I didn't. Because I saw the doubt pinching the skin between his eyebrows. Maybe I *could* clear this up, but I hated that I even had to.

"She can have the shirt," I said. "I don't even want it."

"You just don't want *me* to have it!" Weezie said.

"You'll have your chance in a minute," Lou said to her. He scratched the back of his head and looked at me.

"What do you want me to say? The shirt was hanging on the back of the chair when I got here"—I squinted at Weezie—"before I even knew you existed. I thought it was for me, especially after Lou told me the helmet was for me. Then when I found out you thought I was, like, threatening to take your place as princess or something, I thought I should hide it when you were coming over so you wouldn't do what you're doing right now—which is pitching a major fit—"

"Okay," Lou said. "Weezie, do you see what Jess is saying?"

Weezie stuck out her lower lip so far I could have sat on it. "I don't believe her."

"Why not?"

She shrugged.

"I don't understand." Lou lifted his shoulders to his earlobes. "I need to hear a reason."

"You won't let me say it," she said. "So I'm not going to."

"Good choice." He didn't take his eyes from her. "You have anything else you want to say, Jess?"

"No. Yes." I stopped kicking the cabinet. "I want to know why you were snooping in my stuff, Weezie."

"I wasn't snooping. The shirt was sticking right out because you don't know how to be neat because you're—"

"Watch it now," Lou said.

It occurred to me that he hadn't cranked his voice up once during this whole thing.

"Is that acceptable to you, Jess?" he said.

"Yeah, and like I said, she can keep the shirt." I looked straight at her. "You can have everything."

I started toward the bedroom, but I stopped and turned around. "You don't mind if I go in *your* room, do you?"

"It's over, Jess," Lou said.

Yeah, it is, I wanted to say. It is definitely over.

CHAPTER THIRTEEN

Only two things kept me from busting right through the alarm system and walking back to Birmingham that night. One was the fact that Weezie went into her little coma on the couch instead of going to bed in our room—*her* room. The second was that Chelsea called me back.

"You actually have a cell phone?" she said when I answered.

"Chels?"

"Your mom finally gave in, huh?"

"No. I got it from my—this guy."

I only felt a little bit guilty that I hadn't told her about my father. After all, she wasn't exactly telling me her deepest secrets either. Donovan was probably getting all of those. He probably *was* all of those.

"A guy?" Chelsea said. "*That* sounds interesting. Where are you anyway?"

"Florida."

"Oh. The guy's your grandfather. I thought your mom was mad at him—"

"Have you talked to Marcus?"

"Not since he left for Canada."

"Canada?"

"He didn't tell you? Oh, I guess he couldn't—you left town, like, all of a sudden, without explaining anything to *any* of your best friends. Do I sound bitter?"

"Why is Marcus in Canada?"

"You're still mad at me because of Donovan. Forget about it. We broke up last night. It totally kills me to say it, but you were right about him. His teeth were, like, the least of his problems."

I was ready to scream. Was this how people felt when I babbled on and on and forgot what the point was?

"Forget Donovan," I said. "I'm over it. What about Marcus?"

"He went on some kind of wilderness trip with his uncle. You picked a great time to decide you like him, Jessie — they don't even have cell phone reception up there."

"Oh," I said.

That explained it, but it didn't make me feel any better.

"I don't think there are any other girls on the hike if that's what you're worried about," Chelsea said.

It wasn't. It so wasn't. I suddenly couldn't wait to get off the phone with her.

"I have to ask you something," she said.

"What?"

"I'm thinking I have a crush on Adam, but I know you kind of liked him, so I wanted to know if — "

"Go for it."

"You're mad at me again."

"No, I'm not."

"You know, you had your chance with him but you didn't want to get serious with anybody. Now that I want him, you're all funky about it." I could just see her tossing her hair around. "That is so immature, Jessie."

It wasn't her hanging up on me that stabbed me through the heart. It was that word. *Immature*. It came out of my mother's mouth at least three times a day when she was in a No-Bed Phase, but my friends never said it.

"You're such a ditz, Jess, but we love you. You never shut up and you flirt like no other. If you were any other way we'd go, 'Who are you and what have you done with our Jessie?'" Those things they would say. But I never thought they considered me to have "the maturity of an eight-year-old."

Maybe it was true. Lou sure seemed to think so. He did everything but put a chore chart on the refrigerator for me to stick gold stars to when I was a good girl. Using Rocky as my nanny actually went way beyond that.

I put the phone back in the drawer and rolled miserably

over onto my stomach, which was when I saw the RL book sticking out between the mattresses. Weezie must have pulled it from its place when she yanked *her* shirt out of there. Another pang went through me. Maybe that was why Lou started to believe her when she said I stole it. I'd told him I'd lifted the book at the airport, so why wouldn't he think I'd take her shirt too?

I shook my head at myself. Why did I even care that he doubted me, no matter what the reason was? I wasn't a daughter to him like Weezie was. I was more like a responsibility. Something he had to take care of because nobody else could do it.

Aw, man. I was feeling like I was going to cry again. I couldn't be doing that every five minutes.

I started to push RL back between the mattress and the box spring, but it wouldn't go, so I decided I might as well open it. I was going to go out of my mind if I didn't do something—and wandering around the house was out of the question with Weezer out there snoozing on the sofa. With my luck, she would wake up and accuse me of eating *her* banana.

I propped up against the pillows and found the place that came up to meet me.

He was standing on the shore of Lake Gennesaret—it said.

I figured "he" was Yeshua. He seemed to be the main character in the whole story. Wouldn't Mrs. Honeycutt be impressed that I could pick that out?

It was a big fishing lake. There were a ton of people there waiting to hear him teach, and they were seriously crowding him.

I couldn't imagine myself getting that excited to hear somebody teach.

He looked over and noticed a couple of boats tied up. The fishermen had just left them and were washing their nets.

At least they didn't use poles. I'd ticked off enough pole users on the beach. These guys must be professionals.

One of them was a guy named Simon. Yeshua got in Simon's boat and asked him to take it out a little from the shore, which he did—no questions asked. Yeshua sat in it and taught from there.

I sat up a little straighter. Now that kind of school I could dig. Sit in the sand, work on your tan, and listen to an interesting guy. He must have been pretty interesting or there wouldn't have been a whole crowd of people there hanging on his every word when they didn't even have to.

When he was done, he looked at Simon—the guy who owned the boat—and he said, "Go out where it's deep and let your nets out. Catch some fish." Simon said, "Look, you're obviously an incredible teacher. You're a master, even. But you don't know about fishin'. We were out all night and we didn't catch squat." Yeshua said, "Just do it." Simon said fine, and he did it—and his nets barely hit the water before they were loaded with fish—so many the ropes were about to break.

Something about this was sounding familiar, like maybe I'd heard it back when I was a kid. But it dangled just out of my reach, so I went back to the page.

Simon and his brother motioned to their partners on the beach to come help them, which was good because they filled both boats so full they could hardly get back to the shore. We are talking some serious fish here.

Simon threw himself down at Yeshua's feet and said, "Master, don't even look at me—just leave!"

Leave? That would be the last thing I would want him to do.

"I can't even handle being in your presence. You're too holy. Just leave me here in my unholiness."

Okay. I could understand that. I would probably have said, "Listen, Yeshua, you don't want to be around me. I'm a ditz-queen-airhead-moron."

I held the book away from me and looked at it from arm's length. What was it about this thing that made me feel like I was in the story? Weird.

I rolled over onto my belly with it and read some more as I knocked my feet together in the air.

By then, Simon's partners, James and John, the Zebedee brothers, were also standing there with their mouths open. It was obvious to all of them that they'd just witnessed a miracle. It got to Simon so deep he couldn't get up off the sand.

I could see that, although in that situation I would probably blurt out words that made no sense until somebody told me to shut up. Though maybe not Yeshua. He didn't seem like the "shut up" type.

Yeshua said to Simon, "Look, there isn't anything for you to be afraid of. From now on, you're going to be casting your nets for men and women."

Back the truck up. What did *that* mean?

So Simon and his brother and James and John pulled their boats up on the beach and left it all behind—boats, nets, the whole works—and followed him.

What about the fish?

They didn't need the fish now. They had Yeshua—and they had a new job.

Huh. I hoped they were better at the new job than they were at catching fish. They pretty much stunk at that, until Yeshua got in there and made it happen.

Too bad I didn't have a Yeshua.

Where that came from, I didn't know. But it was enough to make me close the book and press my cheek against it until I fell asleep.

*

We got through the weekend somehow. Saturday I slept in, and Weezie and Lou built sand castles while I took walks and chatted it up with the plovers and drew spiderwebs in the sand with a stick. That was the day I realized the whole beach was talking to me.

It was weird. I knew that. But how could I miss what the gulls were saying when they all landed in front of me and whined, longer and louder than Weezie even?

"I want that!" they wailed to me.

"What?" I wailed back. "I don't have anything!"

They didn't seem to care. They just kept begging. "I want. I want. I want."

The ocean itself, of course, kept calling to me in its splashes and swishes, to come out, and then come back in, and then out again, like it couldn't make up its mind. I could relate.

Even its foam had a life. It was always moving, always

bubbling—and then at times it just seemed to disappear. I could relate to that too.

But the plovers spoke to me the loudest and clearest, without even making a sound. They were hyperactive, skittering around just at the edge of the shore and always barely managing to avoid being swept away by the water.

"Stop for a minute, why don't you?" I said to them.

But I knew why they didn't. They couldn't. And although I could relate to that most of all, I knew right that minute that I didn't want to anymore. Not just because being hyper and over-bubbly and too-needy made me different from everybody else—but because it made me different from me.

So while Weezie and Lou built an entire kingdom in the sand, I found a place at the base of the dunes where I knew Lou could still see me, because he would probably send out the Coast Guard if he couldn't, and I just sat. For the longest I'd ever sat still when I didn't have to my whole life.

It was at least five minutes.

*

"You couldn't get rid of her this time, huh, Red?" Rocky whispered to me in church Sunday.

I glared at the back of Weezie's head. I'd volunteered to sleep on the couch so she could have her bedroom to herself, and I went out on the deck after supper and drew so she could be alone with Daddy and play Scrabble, my most un-favorite game on the planet—and she still wouldn't speak to me. That wouldn't bother me at *all* except that Lou kept getting quieter and quieter, which creeped me out. My mother always did that to me when she was getting ready for an In-Bed Phase.

"You need a mocha fix," Rocky whispered. "The Galleon, right after this."

I figured Lou must be paying him a *lot*. But the music got louder and everybody stood up to sing, so I didn't get to say it. And then I had to concentrate on when to sit down and when to kneel down and when to stand back up—it was like doing aerobics.

125

As soon as we got to the acting-out part, I totally forgot everything else. I wanted to see if Reverend Big Shoulders did the same thing he'd done the week before, and he did. This time I caught on that he was playing the part of Jesus, who I did know about from Sunday school days and "Jesus Loves the Little Children" (red and yellow, black and white, which I never did totally figure out). What I had never heard before was that when Jesus was serving the bread and the wine, he said it was his body and blood, which I thought was probably a metaphor—and wouldn't Mrs. Honeycutt have a *stroke* if she found out I remembered that? What it meant to be drinking and eating something that was supposed to remind me of Jesus' flesh and his red blood cells, I still didn't understand. But just like last week, I almost couldn't wait to get up front. And just like last week, I felt like we all knew each other and for a minute I belonged there.

Actually, when I was following Lou back to the pew, somebody whispered, "Hi, Jessie." It was one of the girls that had gone gaga over Lou in the coffee shop. I said "hi" back.

As soon as church was over, Weezie hung on Lou's arm like she owned it. Rocky nudged me.

"She's got no shame," he said. "I'm having a mocha attack. Let's go."

"I have to ask Lou," I said.

"I already did."

But I shook my head. I wasn't taking any chances.

I tapped Lou on the shoulder and got the hairy eyeball from Weezie.

"Relax," I said. "I just need to ask him something."

"What's up, Jess?" Lou said.

"Is it okay if I go over to the coffee shop with Rocky?"

"Absolutely—"

"I wanna go!" Weezie said. She sounded exactly like a seagull.

"I don't think you're invited," Lou said.

"I never get to see Rocky anymore!" Weezie latched onto Rocky's hand and pressed her cheek against his arm.

I thought I might throw up.

"She so just wanted to come because she doesn't want me to get anything she doesn't get," I said to Rocky as we hurried across the street *without* the Weezer.

He grinned down at me. "Nah. She wanted to come because she has a crush on me."

"I knew that kid had no taste," I said.

Rocky stopped outside the door to the Galleon and then pulled me by the wrist a few steps down the sidewalk.

"What are you doing?" I said.

He let go of my wrist, but it was like his eyes were holding me there. "I just want to know something," he said.

"What? I thought you already knew everything."

"I do — except for why it is that I had to promise not to put you down by calling you Crash and reminding you about your kamikaze mission at the city gates, but you get to put *me* down whenever you want."

I stared at him. He actually looked serious.

"This is the part where you say you're sorry," he said.

"But only if I mean it, right?"

"Forget it —"

"I'm sorry," I said.

He looked at me without smiling. I suddenly wanted to see the gap between his teeth.

"I guess it's just, like, a habit," I said. "Especially with people who annoy the snot out of me."

"I do that?"

"Hello!"

He finally grinned. "So, if I try not to annoy the snot out of you, you'll try not to do smackdown on my ego?"

"Try," I said.

"Well, yeah. That's all we can really do, right? Try?"

"What happens if one of us messes up?" I said. I made quotation marks with my fingers. "Will there be 'consequences'?"

"You've been living with Lou too long already."

"I got that from the Weezer. So —"

A green gleam came into Rocky's eyes. "Okay—if either one of us messes up, we have to answer one question the other person asks about them. Any question."

"Are you on drugs? There is no way I'm doing that!"

"You scared?"

"No," I said—although I was already getting butterflies the size of vampire bats in my stomach at the thought of it.

"Then what's the problem? I personally got nothing to hide."

"Neither do I," I lied.

"Then we're on." He put out his hand. "Shake on it."

I looked at it for a minute before I put mine in it. He pumped it one time and then spun me around so the back of me was pinned to the front of him.

I let out a squeal. "You are a—"

"Do I hear a put-down coming on? Watch it now—watch it!"

I opened my mouth and threatened my teeth against his arm.

"Hey!" He pulled away and looked at me, the greens still gleaming.

"You didn't say anything about biting," I said. I could feel my own blues gleaming back.

And then as he sauntered like a gangsta into the Spanish Galleon ahead of me, I felt them *stop* gleaming. I had a reputation back in Mountain Brook for being a flirt. And for running like a rabbit the minute a guy got all "serious." I couldn't afford to let any boy get that close. Not like Rocky was getting.

Not like I wanted him to get.

That was what stopped the gleam in me. He was never going to do more than flirt back at me. He was the Lou-appointed nanny.

I couldn't forget that—or that this was all temporary. I was going home soon.

*

And yet I did forget at times during that next week.

I got to do more and more at Rosie and Bonsai's and had fewer and fewer minor disasters, which meant I got fewer and fewer hairy eyeballs from Bonsai.

I rode on Levi with Lou every day except Friday, and I went down to the beach every night after supper and sat longer and longer in my spot by the dunes.

When three o'clock came around, Rocky was always waiting to babysit me, and that made me remember. But I couldn't help it: it annoyed me less and less as the days went by. Maybe that was because I got ahead on the "consequences." He slipped that Thursday at Rosie and Bonsai's, where he now came with Lou for leftovers every day, and asked Bonsai if he was sure there weren't any tips of my fingers in the California roll, since they were letting me use knives back there. I was on Rocky the minute we were out the door.

"I know, I messed up," he said.

He leaned against the wall and folded his arms. His muscles kind of bulged out of the no-sleeves jacket. I'd never noticed how much before.

"You aren't going to show me any mercy, are you?" he said.

"None. Here's my question." I sucked in a breath. "How much is Lou paying you to babysit me?"

"What are you talking about?"

"He called it being my 'personal guide,' but it's the same thing."

"You think he's *making* me hang out with you?"

"I may be a ditz-queen, but, come on—"

"Nothing," he said. His voice was a little stiff. "He isn't *paying* me anything."

"What is it that you owe him, then?"

"You only get one question."

"That's okay," I said. "I'll ask that next time. And there *will* be a next time."

"Whatever." He refolded his arms. "My turn."

I pulled in my chin. "What? I didn't put you down!"

"Yeah, you did. Here's my question: why don't you like living with Lou? Anybody in our youth group would sell their little sister to spend that much time with him, and you act like you're on death row."

"Youth group?"

"Yeah. At church. He's our youth leader—only Hank is doing it right now because Lou's taking time off from us to be with you. And you, like, blow him off half the time. What's up with that?"

"Lou's the youth group leader?"

"Quit stalling, Red. What's your deal?"

I couldn't see a way out of giving him an answer. If I said he was a jerk and it was none of his business, then I'd have two questions to deal with.

"Okay," I said. "I don't want to be here because it isn't my home."

"So, you're, like, close to your mom, then?"

"Not that close, no."

"You have a boyfriend in Birmingham."

"No."

"You've got a job there where you make money—you live on the beach—you ride on a Harley every day—"

"Uh, no."

"You've got somebody back there that totally gets you."

"No! And that's way more than one question."

Rocky put his hands behind his head, still leaning against the wall. It made his muscles look even bigger. "You still haven't answered the first one—not with the truth anyway. If you don't have any of that stuff back there and you have it all here, why is that better than this?"

"Because back there I could just be whatever and nobody cared, okay? They just left me alone!"

I swallowed and blinked and started to turn away. Rocky grabbed my wrist.

"I'm sorry, Red," he said. "I didn't mean to make you cry."

"I'm not crying."

"I just don't get it, that's all. Alone with nobody caring about you—I don't see that being a better deal."

"That's because you've never been there," I said.

"Yeah, I have," he said. "And I'm never goin' back." He dropped my wrist and peeled himself away from the wall. "You want ice cream?"

"No," I said.

"I don't think you know what you want, so we're getting ice cream. And I'm buying." He put his gleamy green eyes close to mine. "Not Lou. Me."

I had mint chocolate chip that day.

CHAPTER FOURTEEN

So do you want to see how this is done or what?" Bonsai said to me Friday morning.

I stopped wiping off soy sauce bottles for the tables and stared at him.

"Is that a yes?" he said.

Behind me, Rose giggled.

"You're not afraid I'm going to give somebody indigestion?" I said.

Bonsai grunted. "I didn't say I was going to let you do it, I just asked if you want to see how *I* do it. You haven't broken anything in three days. I figure it's safe."

I could feel the corners of my mouth going up to my earlobes. Who knew I'd ever get excited about watching somebody roll raw fish up in sticky rice and seaweed?

"Are you serious?" I said.

Bonsai gave me a blank look. "I don't joke about the art of sushi," he said.

"You don't joke about anything," I said.

Oops.

But I saw Bonsai snuff out a smile. "Stand right there, next to Rose. Watch. Learn."

I had wondered more than once how Rose could stand just out of Bonsai's elbow range for, like, hours, perfectly still, without saying anything. Now I was going to have to do it.

Once Bonsai flattened the fish, though—and then pulled out a ball of rice and pressed it onto the fish and put the whole thing on the little bamboo mat, I kind of forgot about myself.

The avocado bits went on next, and then he rolled it all up in the mat—the whole time dipping his hands into a pot of water to clean off his fingers. He moved fast, but soft at the same time, like he respected the fish he was serving up to eat. No wonder he was always telling me not to bruise it. I wondered if it was a piece of something I'd cleaned or picked out at the fish market. Weird how I felt like I was part of the whole process. That feeling didn't happen to me often.

Bonsai took the roll out of the mat and cut it into slices and arranged it on one of the wooden boats with a couple of curls of ginger and a dab of wasabi.

"Lunch," he said to me, and put it into my hands. "And don't let me catch you eating this with a fork."

"What's this one called?" I said.

Bonsai looked at Rose, who bowed, naturally.

"Eel and avocado roll," she said.

"Eel!" I said. I wanted to add, "Gross! I'm not eating that slimy stuff!"

But they were both looking at me as if I were about to take some kind of test. It was one I really didn't want to fail.

"Sounds yummy," I said.

And it actually was. It was sweeter than any of the other rolls I'd had. I scarfed down the whole thing.

"That was fab," I said to Bonsai.

He crinkled his disappearing eyes at my plate. "You eat like your father. Get that boat cleaned and put away and get ready."

"For what?" I said. "I've got all the chopsticks and napkins rolled. All the fish and veggies are chopped. I even made sure there are paper towels in the bathrooms. We ran out yesterday."

His face was blank. "You through?" he said.

"Yes."

"Then put on a clean apron. You're serving today. Rose will take the orders—you'll do the rest."

"Are you serious?"

"Don't I look serious?"

"Yeah," I said. "But, then, you always do."

I smiled at him. He almost smiled back.

I was pretty nervous at first. I was sure I was going to dump a bowl of miso soup in some biker's lap or drop a boat full of Futomaki, which was Bonsai's specialty and took the longest to make because he did these very-cool designs in it with dyed rice.

But the vampire bats in my stomach disappeared as I found out what happened when I placed a wooden bridge of Umeboshi plum rolls and Futomaki on a table. The HOGs— Harley Owners Group members, Lou had told me—sat back and made grumbling noises in their throats and said things like:

"You are an angel from heaven, girl."

"Look at this—I'm a happy dude."

"Now all we need is a little more wasabi. You think you could come up with some, Miss Jessie?"

Not only did I come up with some, I took a spoon and shaped it into a rose in its little bowl, the way Bonsai did his garnishes. Okay, completely weird, but I felt like I'd just completed the Mona Lisa or whatever that painting was we studied in art class.

"Would you look at that?" one of the bikers said when I set it on the table.

"That's actually cool, Red."

My head jerked up and I found myself looking right into Rocky's gleamy-green eyes. I could feel the red seeping into my cheeks, and there wasn't a thing I could do about it.

"Did she do that just for you, Oswald?" said one of the larger bikers in a bright-blue bandana.

"Who's Oswald?" I said.

Another guy, ultra-skinny and wearing an earring, put his arm around Rocky's shoulders. "You didn't know your man's real name is Oswald?"

"Are you serious?" I said.

"Shut up, man," Rocky said. His face was now a whole lot redder than mine, I was sure.

"Well," I said. "Good to know."

I flashed Rocky a smile, and he gapped his teeth at me, eyes still all glittery and gleamy. My face then passed him on the redness scale. I could feel it from the inside out.

"Watch it now," Rocky said, still grinning. "Watch it."

A loud chorus of "Oooh!" went up from the table. Rose tapped my arm and I had to follow her back to the kitchen for another order.

"You make the customers happy," she said to me. And I could have sworn she winked at me.

We were packed that day and I loved it. Bonsai couldn't give me bridges and boats and plates full of rolls fast enough, and I sailed to the tables without dropping a single one or getting anybody's order mixed up. It was delicious for me. Until the door opened, and Lou walked in with Weezie.

I darted back to the kitchen and almost ran into Rose, who was holding a square platter of nigiri jumbo shrimp.

"Table two," she said.

"You do it," I said. "I'll drop it or something."

A tiny line appeared between her even tinier eyebrows. "You not drop anything all day."

"I'm about to," I said. "Please — I'll mess something up."

For once she didn't smile, and she didn't bow. "No," she said. "You start. You finish." She pushed the platter into my hand. "Table two. You can."

I knew *all* the color had drained from my face as I took the platter and headed for table two. Rocky's table.

"Here she is!" Earring Guy said. "Put it right in front of me, darlin'."

"She's a keeper, Oswald." Blue Bandana twinkled his eyes at me. "How much is it worth to you to know his full name?"

"Whatever it is I'll pay double," Rocky said.

"You could make some serious money off of this, Wally," another guy said.

They laughed and dug into the shrimp, and I turned to go without looking in the direction of table four, where Lou and Weezie were snuggled up over the menu together. Rocky curled his fingers around my wrist and pulled me down so he could whisper in my ear.

"You're doing awesome," he said. "Don't let some ten-year-old mess you up."

I got a lump in my throat, but I still managed to whisper back, "Okay."

I collected the empty platters and took them back to the kitchen and picked up an order of Tekkamaki for the grandparenty couple by the window who looked a little freaked out by the two tables of HOGs.

"The food is great," the man said to me as I put it down between them.

His wife glanced at table two. "I'm so surprised that these men eat sushi," she said, in a too-loud voice. That must have been because of the hearing aid in her ear.

"They're the whole reason this is here," I said. "My dad got tired of eating hamburgers and french fries, and he loves sushi. He built the restaurant so he could have California rolls whenever he wanted."

I felt the smile returning to my face. Lou had told me the story one night over supper, but it was the first time I got to tell it to somebody else.

"Your dad is the owner?" the man said.

"That's him right over there," I said.

I turned and pointed, just as Lou and Weezie both looked up at me from the form they were filling out to order their sushi. Lou smiled and gave a little wave. Weezie narrowed her eyes until they looked like little dashes in her face.

"Then that must be your sister," the grandmother-lady said—loud enough for not only Weezie but the whole restaurant to hear. "She looks just like you."

"She's just my half sister," Weezie said—in that voice that made her sound like a dead ringer for a seagull.

Lou put his hand on her arm and she sat back in her chair, and I thought she was done. I looked at Rocky. He shook his head at me.

"Can I get you anything else?" I said to the grandparents.

"How about some jasmine tea?" the woman half shouted.

"I can do that," I said.

I made it to the kitchen before I doubled my fists and did a silent scream. What was Weezie doing here? This was my place to share with Lou—

I caught myself and listened to that thought shout in my head. Until Rose touched my arm and said, "They want tea?"

I was about to beg her to please serve it herself—and then I remembered Rocky whispering, "You're doing awesome." Saw him shaking his head at me. Heard Rose saying, "You start. You finish. You can."

"Jasmine," I said to her.

She nodded and bowed and smiled and set me up a tray. I took a deep breath and carried it halfway across the dining room, and then I stopped.

Weezie was standing at the grandparents' table.

I looked for Lou. He was bent over table two, laughing with Earring Guy and Wally and Rocky—obviously unaware that his princess was chatting it up with the customers. My customers.

I took the tea tray to the table and stopped behind Weezie.

"Excuse me," I said between my teeth.

She took about two steps to the side, but she didn't move away completely, which meant I had to hold the tray at a weird angle to get it on the table. I managed to do it without spilling it, but I couldn't pull off a smile at the same time.

"Wow, you did that good, Jessica," Weezie said—too sweetly.

"Jessica," Grandmother-Lady shouted. "Now, that's a pretty name."

"Thank you," I said. "I see you've met Louisa."

"Now those are good names," Grandfather-Man said.

He went on about how people needed to give their children the good old-fashioned names instead of all this yuppie nonsense parents were saddling their kids with—while I poured the tea and Weezie gave me eyeballs hairy enough to make a wig.

"And you're right, Louisa," Grandmother-Lady said. "Your sister does do a good job with the tea."

"Which is amazing," Weezie said. "Since she has ADHD."

Hot water sloshed onto my fingers and I dumped a half-full cup over on the tray. Grandfather-Man went after it with a napkin, but his wife didn't seem to notice.

"ADHD," she shouted. "Now what is that?"

137

"It means Jessica is hyperactive," Weezie shouted back—not so the deaf woman could hear her, but so that the entire restaurant would get the news.

I set the teapot down too hard and more hot liquid spurted from the spout onto Grandfather-Man's hand. Rose rushed over with several dozen napkins and bowed and didn't smile, and the grandparent-people both said it was fine, all fine, no harm done. Lou appeared and marched Weezie out the front door, and everybody else went back to their sushi and soup.

Except Rocky. I could feel him watching me. But I didn't look back. I brushed past him on my way to the kitchen where I untied my apron.

"What do you think you're doing?" Bonsai said. He was standing in the doorway with his hands drippy from the water pot.

"I don't think I can serve anymore today," I said.

"Why not?"

"You didn't see me just spill hot tea on that guy?"

"Who hasn't? Get back to work."

"I can't."

"You can. You start. You finish."

By the time I got myself back to the dining room, table two was gone, including Rocky. The grandparents were paying their bill, and Lou and Weezie were nowhere to be seen. But the fun had gone out of serving sushi. Maybe it had gone out of everything—because the ADHD demon was never going to leave me alone.

I would have given up my cell phone for a visit from Yeshua right then. I'd drop all this fish and take off with him and do the new job, whatever it was, and follow him. At least he didn't expect people to be perfect.

I choked back tears and cleared tables, and somehow got through the afternoon by promising myself I'd go back to the RL story as soon as I got home. It was the only place that was safe.

*

There was no way I was meeting Rocky in our usual place by the motorcycle trees that afternoon. I stayed inside and rolled enough chopsticks and napkins to feed most of Japan and scrubbed the bamboo mats until the string came off one of them. Bonsai was probably going to fire me now—who wanted a crazy chick working in their restaurant?—so I might as well leave the place clean. I was picking up grains of uncooked rice off the floor, one by one with my fingers, when a shadow fell across me from somebody in the doorway.

"That's what they make brooms for, Red," Rocky said.

"You're not allowed in the kitchen," I said.

"Then how come Rosie let me in?"

I looked up. His eyes weren't gleamy. They were soft. Like he felt sorry for me.

"Come on," he said. "Let's go for a walk."

"No," I said to the floor. "I've got stuff to do."

"Liar. Come on. I know a place we can talk."

Talk was the last thing I wanted to do. But what good did it do me, really, to refuse to go with him? Lou was making him pay back some kind of debt he owed him, only now there was probably nothing that was going to make this worth it for Rocky.

"Come on," he said again and put his hand out.

I pushed it away and stood up on my own, but I didn't look at him. Nobody said I had to watch him change from flirty to "poor baby."

Neither one of us said that much until we crossed Avenida Menendez and headed toward Matanzas Bay—the one that Lou and I went over every day on the bridge. A high wall ran along it, wide enough to sit on. Rocky sat and patted the stone for me to join him. I only did it because it was a great place to swing your legs, and I needed some serious leg swinging. But I sat as far away as I could without him calling Lou to say I was trying to escape.

"The little Weezer has a mouth bigger than the state of Florida," Rocky said.

"I don't want to talk about it," I said.

"Look, Red, if you stuff it you just end up having more to explode with—"

"I said no."

"It's not like you have AIDS or something."

I whipped my head around to look at him and saw the gleam in his eye. But it wasn't the same. It was a big brother thing. An "I better get her to talk or Lou'll make me hang out with her for *another* week"—that kind of look. I went back to bouncing my heels against the wall and watched a row of old-looking wooden boats bob in the water. Green algae climbed up the outsides of their cabins, and gulls perched on their vacant masts. Their sails waited, wrapped and roped, to be let out. I felt like that—like I just wanted to unwrap and go with the wind.

"Okay," Rocky said. "I'll talk."

"You do that," I said.

I folded my arms halfway around myself to cross him out, but he didn't go anywhere. He stretched out on the wall so that he was squinting up at the sun and me.

"Look, the little Weezer's messed up," he said.

How could she be messed up? She'd had the Father of the Year her whole life.

"She was only three years old or something when Lou and her mom got divorced. And he says he wasn't that much of a dad before that."

I grunted.

He opened his eyes and closed them again. "I better let him tell you about that if he wants."

"I don't care," I said, only because not talking never worked that well for me.

"Yeah, you do. Why don't you admit it? You want to be part of the family, and every time you get close she messes it up somehow."

He opened his eyes again and held onto me with them, so I couldn't look away. "If you want her to stop messing things up for you, you have to get to her."

I was interested in spite of myself. "You mean like get back at her?"

"Nah. You're better than that."

"I don't think so."

He sat up and pointed at me. "I get a question for that."

"Why?"

"It's our deal, and what I want to know is—"

He wiggled his eyebrows, and I tried to smack him but he got me by both wrists and grinned into my face even as I pulled myself back.

"I want to know if you ever rode your Big Wheel down a set of stairs when you were a kid."

I stopped struggling. *"What?"*

"Just answer the question."

"How do you know I even had a Big Wheel?"

"Didn't you?"

"Yeah."

"And did you ride it down any steps?"

I got one hand loose and covered my mouth.

"You did, didn't you?" he said. "I knew it."

I let out a big old sputtery laugh into my palm before he pulled it away from my face.

"Tell me," he said.

"Okay—me and my mom lived in an apartment over my grandparents' garage, and this one day, I pulled my Big Wheel out the door when my mom was drawing a pair of shoes, and I thought, 'I'm gonna do this,' and then I did."

"How many stitches did you have to have?"

"Eight. Right here."

He let go of me so I could pull back my bangs and bend my head for him to see the scar by my hairline. He rolled up the leg of his jeans and revealed one twice that long below his knee.

"You had a Big Wheel too?" I said.

"Yeah, but this is from riding a scooter down the—well, you know those wooden walkways through the dunes?"

"Yeah."

He shrugged.

"No way!" I said.

"I got drunk one night when I was fifteen and stole a scooter from your dad's shop and rode it all the way out to the beach and down the steps on one of the walkways."

I felt my eyes popping like a frog's. "Did you get arrested?"

"No, the cops didn't find me. Lou did."

They popped even farther.

"It happened down by his house, and he heard it and came out, and that's how we met."

"So—what did he do?" I said.

Rocky looked down at his hands. "He said I had two choices. I could either go to jail after he called the cops and my life would be pretty much over, or I could do everything he said and start a whole new life." He looked at me. "Like that was a choice, right?"

"Yeah," I said. "He does that."

"So he made sure I wasn't dying from my injuries, and he patched me up and called my mom—who couldn't have cared less—and he talked to me all night about stuff and—here I am."

"Why did he do that?" I said. "He didn't even know you."

"That's just who he is. It's like he gets how it is to be a complete screwup, and he doesn't want it happening to any other kid."

Oh. So basically, I was just any other kid.

And then something else clicked in my head. So this was what Rocky owed Lou for. No wonder he was still hanging with me. He'd have to babysit me until I was in college to pay that off.

"So," Rocky said cheerfully, "do you hate me now?"

"Huh?"

"Do you want to ditch me because you know I've got something 'wrong' with me?"

"I want to ditch you," I lied, "but that's not why."

Rocky blinked at me. "But isn't what I did worse than anything you've ever done?"

I went stubbornly back to the silent treatment. I could feel him watching me.

"It is worse," he said, "but I figure I'm too good of a person to try to get back at a ten-year-old, so why aren't you?"

I shrugged.

"If you want my advice—" he said.

"I don't."

He scooted himself next to me and swung his legs in time with mine, as if I hadn't just basically told him to buzz off.

"I say be so nice to her, she doesn't know what's going on."

I gave him a look. "Have we met?"

"I'm serious. You can totally do this. I've seen you in action with people, like in the sushi place—you're like ... a soda."

"A soda."

"You know, like, all bubbling over. Giggle, giggle, giggle—"

"Okay, okay—" I did Lou's eraser thing with my hands. I had to get him off this subject. "I *so* get a question for that. Is your name really Oswald?"

"Aw, man—"

"Come on. Dish."

"Yeah," he said, out of the side of his mouth. "Oswald Kenneth Luke."

"What's your last name?"

"Luke."

"Oh."

"Why?"

"I was hoping it was something like Snodgrass."

"You are so dead."

I squealed and scrambled to my feet and took off down the wall with him hollering behind me—hoping he would catch me. But when he did and got me into one of his half nelsons or whatever they were, I was sadder than I was before I admitted to myself that I liked this boy who could never like me that way. I liked him a lot. He made me feel like I could be nice to anybody.

CHAPTER FIFTEEN

My "nice" lasted until we got back to the shop. Lou and Weezie were waiting for me in Lou's office, and even from outside the window, Weezie looked like she was about to have a molar extracted.

I stiffened up to run, but Rocky gave me a poke and, after giving *him* my own hairiest eyeball, I went in. "Nice" must have left with him because I couldn't even make myself smile.

"Could you have a seat for a minute, Jess?" Lou said. "Weezie has something she wants to say to you."

I bit back all the smart remarks that crowded onto my hamster wheel and perched on the edge of a chair facing them.

Then we all sat there in silence until I was about ready to claw the paneling. Weezie finally mumbled, "I'm sorry I told everybody you had ADHD."

No, you are not! I wanted to say. Instead, I got out, "I thought we weren't supposed to say we were sorry if we didn't mean it."

Weezie looked at Lou. He didn't say anything. She squirmed. I enjoyed it.

So much for nice.

When it was obvious Weezie wasn't going to come up with an answer, Lou said, "That's true. I do say that. Are you willing to give Weezie a little more time, Jess?"

"She can have all the time she wants," I said.

Lou looked like he was going to say something, but he pressed his lips together and stood up. There wasn't a twitch within a hundred miles.

Why, I wondered, was I suddenly feeling guilty when I wasn't the one who had done something wrong? For once.

Nobody brought it up again that evening. I did see Lou talking to Weezie out on the deck when I was doing the dishes, and then she came in and said, "You can have the bedroom tonight."

I was glad. I needed to get to RL. It was the only way I could figure out how to get off the hamster wheel. And I wanted to—because being back on it after being free of it for a while made it feel crazier than ever, and I was tired of crazy.

I waited until I heard them start their Scrabble game in the living room before I pulled the book from between the mattresses. It opened easily in my hands, like it had been waiting for me.

Before we get to this next part, let me tell you about tax collectors in Yeshua's time.

Were we talking IRS? If so, all I knew about it was that every time we got something from them in the mail, my mom either screamed at somebody on the phone or pulled the covers over her head, depending on which Phase she was in. Marcus said his father wasn't that crazy about them either.

People had to pay taxes just like they do now, but the collectors back then were allowed to charge people more than they really owed so they could keep the extra money for themselves.

"Not fair!"

Exactly. Naturally, there was a lot of fraud and corruption and these guys were pretty much hated. People talked about sinners and tax collectors like they were the same thing. Which most of the time they were.

I wondered what all this had to do with the story, but I'd figured out by now that RL always had a reason for everything it said. I was liking that.

So, moving on. Yeshua went out of a house where he'd just healed a bunch of people, and immediately he had a run-in with some Pharisees on the street about where he got off thinking he could do what he was doing.

I kind of knew what a Pharisee was from somewhere, but I didn't ask to make sure. I wanted to get on with the story. Maybe later.

Yeshua saw a guy named Levi—

Levi? Seriously?

Levi was collecting taxes. What does that tell you?

Bad guy.

Right. But Yeshua said, "Come with me." And Levi did. He just left his entire tax collecting career and went with him.

This was the second story like that. Yeshua must have been kind of like Lou: When he told me to do something in that low-quiet voice he used, I did it, much as I hated to. Even Weezie did it. So maybe I could see how they all just dropped everything and followed this Yeshua person. I knew I would do it in a heartbeat.

Levi gave a huge dinner party at his house for Yeshua. All the people Levi normally hung out with were there—other tax collectors, shady types.

Maybe drug dealers? Gangbangers? Kids who got drunk and rode their motorcycles down steps?

The Pharisees and professors went to Yeshua's followers.

That would be Simon and that crowd, right?

Yeah. The Pharisees said, "What's up with this? Why's he eating with criminals and losers?" When Yeshua heard about that, he said, "Let me ask you something: who needs a doctor—healthy people or people who are sick and in pain? See, here's the thing—I'm here to invite the people you think are 'outsiders.' I'm not here to hang out with those of you who think you already have it all. What I'm about is bringing these messed-up people into a whole different life. A life that's for real."

I couldn't read any more because the page was blurry. It took me a minute to realize that it was because of the tears in my eyes. So—if Yeshua was into "outsiders," could I get invited to that party?

I closed the book and dropped it in front of me. What was I thinking? This wasn't about me. And it was fiction—it wasn't even real.

I ran my fingers across the carved-out RL letters on the front and the other initials someone—maybe even a lot of someones—had also etched into it. It sure seemed real to me. Maybe it had to these other people too. And if it wasn't, what else did I have?

With the book hugged to my chest, I curled into a ball and closed my eyes. "If you're real, Yeshua," I whispered, "help me."

*

I didn't wake up the next almost-afternoon without ADHD. I knew *that* the minute I moved in the bed and my phone, my flip-flops, and the RL book all tumbled off onto the floor. But I did feel different somehow—like maybe I ought to give "nice" a try. Yeshua was decent to people it was hard to be even half-way decent to, and Weezie was definitely in that group. It was the only way I could think of to "follow."

She and Lou were in their usual spot on the couch when I went out to the Everything Room. The second Weezie saw me she stopped whatever long story she was telling Lou and took a sudden interest in her glitter-pink manicure.

He grinned at me. "It's Rip Van Winkle."

"I know, right?" I said. "I'm starving. Do you guys want me to fix you some breakfast?"

"We already ate, like, two hours ago," Weezie said to her fingernails. "Can you even cook anyway?"

"Weezie," Lou said. He used his "sit down" voice.

Which I appreciated, because it took me a minute to figure out how to be nice to that question.

Weezie stuck her lip out, and Lou turned to me. "You really like working with food, don't you, Jess?"

"I guess so, yeah," I said.

"You did a great job in the restaurant yesterday. I was impressed."

I blinked. Did somebody just pay me a compliment?

"So now that she's up, can we go down to the beach?" Weezie said.

Lou shook his head. "We're about to have the mother of all thunderstorms. How 'bout we do a little shopping, maybe watch a movie?"

He looked at me. I glanced at Weezie, and for a second I thought she might have a hamster wheel in her head too.

"I'm fine with shopping if you are," I said.

"I'd rather watch a movie," she said.

Lou put his hand on her forehead. "You feeling okay, Weezie?"

"Yes. Why?"

"If you don't want to go shopping, you must be sick. You sure you don't want to go to the outlet mall?"

It looked like it was killing her, but she said, "I want to watch a movie."

"Great," I said. "Anything's fine with me. Except a Shrek movie. I've seen all of them twenty times."

"I was thinking *Shrek the Third*," she said.

"That's cool. I've only seen that one ten times."

Lou looked from one of us to the other and then said, "*Shrek the Third* it is. I'll make some popcorn."

"With butter," Weezie said.

"No butter and you know it. Except for pancakes."

"Aw, man," I said.

Weezie's eyes went into their little dashes. "That's okay. Butter's not good for you."

"Then I can definitely live without it," I said through my teeth.

It couldn't have been as hard for Yeshua to have dinner with the tax collectors as it was for me to be nice to this kid.

But I kept at it. When Weezie got bored with *Shrek the Third* just as I was getting into it and she announced that she wanted to go shopping, I was dressed and ready to go. When she whined because she would rather go to the mall on Levi — even though it was pouring down rain — I volunteered to stay behind. When Lou said no, and she pouted, I whispered to her that I was really sorry. Because I was.

I never had a worse time shopping than I did that day. We went in every tween store in the mall and looked at girly jewelry and cutesy clothes and shoes that would have given my mother a heart attack no matter what kind of Phase she was in. I actually missed my mom that day. When she was in a No-Bed Phase, she loved to shop, and she always knew where to go for the best stuff. Weezie's taste was, as Mom would have said, all in her mouth.

Yet even though we ate lunch where Weezie wanted to eat and yawned through what Weezie wanted to talk about and bought what Weezie wanted to have for supper, which was coconut shrimp again—being nice about all that became easier somehow. Once I got over gritting my teeth so I wouldn't blurt out, "Are you just the most selfish chick on the face of the earth?" it sort of became like a game to see how frustrated I could make her by not arguing with her. I discovered that she did not like Lou using his too-quiet voice on her. She clearly didn't want him even a little bit mad at her, so there was no way she was going to blow. But she wanted to, I could see that, and it made me feel kind of smug about my sweet self. Rocky, I decided, was right.

But then there was that moment after supper when she said she wanted to play Scrabble, and I said I'd just watch, and she said, "You just don't want to play because you—" and then she stopped and bit her lip and looked like she was going to cry—at that moment I had this weird feeling. Like I knew how she felt.

So I said, "I do want to play, but I'm not that good at it and I don't want to mess it up. This is a you-and-your-dad thing. I'll just go read."

"Stay, Jess," Lou said. "It's stopped raining. Let's go down on the beach and watch the moon rise."

"That's not fair!" Weezie wailed.

"Who ever promised you fair?" Lou said. "Get your shoes on."

She gave me a black look, and I didn't even enjoy it.

*

In church the next day, Weezie sat on the other side of Lou with her arms across her chest and her lip extended like a fold-out sofa. She actually kind of reminded me of myself.

Rocky gave me a nudge. "You didn't do the nice thing?" he whispered.

"Oh, yeah, I did," I whispered back.

He grinned at me. "You're good, Red. You're really good."

I wasn't sure I was. All I had succeeded in doing was making Weezie more miserable than she was before. I had to admit *I* felt better, but I found myself wishing for a different reaction from her. And I wasn't sure why I cared.

I stopped thinking about her when we got to communion, because it struck me as I was watching the people across the circle get their bread that maybe they weren't all good church people. That maybe some of them had as many problems as I did, had done as much stupid stuff, were dealing with demons of their own. But there we all were, like the tax collectors at the table with Yeshua. I liked that.

When the service was over, Rocky said, louder than he had to, "You want to go for a coffee over at the Galleon, Red?"

Before I even had my mouth open, Weezie said, "I want to go!"

"Okay," I said.

Rocky squeezed my arm, but I gave him a look and he got it.

"Can she come, Lou?" I said.

It was the first time I ever caught him by surprise. *I* was surprised he didn't drop his teeth.

"You sure?" he said.

I shrugged. "Why not?"

Weezie, meanwhile, was running her tongue back and forth over her braces and shifting her eyes like she couldn't decide where they should land. At last, she couldn't bring herself to throw my nice back in my face. She really must have a crush on Rocky.

I couldn't blame her.

I got busy trying to stuff that thought away while Weezie grabbed Rocky's hand and hugged his arm and tugged him toward the door. We were halfway across the street before he had a chance to whisper, "You owe me, Red."

"It was your idea," I whispered back.

*

It didn't seem to occur to Weezie that I was the reason she got to sit on a stool at the Spanish Galleon like a princess and drink hot chocolate with whipped cream and yak at Rocky until his eyelids were at half-mast.

Even in the truck on the way to her house, she went on and on to Lou about how Rocky rocked, and that must be why his name was Rocky, and how it double-rocked that he held her hand when they were crossing the street.

Like he had a choice. I tried to stop wishing he'd been holding mine. This was not the time to get weepy.

When we pulled up to the mini-mansion, Lou looked down at her without a twitch in his lips.

"Did you thank Jess for including you?" he said.

She cut a look at me like I was the one asking her to use some manners for once.

"You're the one who said I could go," she said to Lou.

"I was about to say you couldn't until Jess invited you. Jess, not Rocky."

I had to admit, the girl was a pro. She didn't even hesitate before she had her eyes rolling and a sigh blowing out of her nose.

"She only invited me to impress you, Daddy," she said.

Lou shoved the truck into park and snapped off the ignition. I curled my fingers around the door handle. So he *could* get mad. He did it in the same quiet way he spoke when he meant it. But it sent the message clearer than a full-blown fit.

"Would you mind waiting here for a minute, Jess?" he said.

I shook my head.

"You and me, Weezie," he said. "Let's go."

While he was getting her bag out of the back, she shot me another look. If she'd been Chelsea's Chihuahua, she would have bitten me.

I told myself I shouldn't watch as Lou pointed to the front step and she sat down and he stood there, one foot on the step, one hand on his hip, and talked in a voice so low there was no way I could hear it even with the truck window open. But I did watch, because Weezie did everything but put a bag over her head to keep from showing any expression in her face. How did she do that? He wasn't even talking to me, and I had a lump the size of a California roll in my throat.

When she'd gone into the house and he turned to come back to the truck, I saw by the way he was swallowing that he had one too.

He didn't say anything until we were out on A1A again,

and I sure wasn't going to start a conversation. When he did, his voice was sad.

"You were nothing but generous to Weezie all weekend," he said. "I'm sorry she didn't respond very well. It surprised me."

"It did?" I said, and then clapped my hand over my mouth. "Sorry," I mumbled between my fingers.

"Are you?"

"I kind of am. Mostly I'm trying to be nice." I probably should have added that it was Rocky's idea, but I didn't.

"Just because you're nice doesn't mean you can't be honest," Lou said. "It didn't surprise you that Weezie acted like a little brat to you when you were going out of your way not to cross her?" He gave me a glance. "And we'll get back to that part in a minute."

Oops.

We pulled up to a shaggy-looking building with a sign that said *A1A Crab Shack*. Lou turned off the motor but he made no move to get out of the truck.

"Let's face it," I said. "She hates me. You can say she's just jealous, but I think she proved that's not it. I basically told her she could have you—I mean, all to herself—and that wasn't good enough."

He nodded at the windshield. "She wants you gone."

"Yeah." I didn't add, "Duh."

"You like crab?" he said.

"I don't know," I said.

"Then let's find out."

He didn't start back in on the Weezie thing until we were sitting in a chipped, red wooden booth back in the corner of the place, each of us with a crab cake the size of a Frisbee in front of us. Lou let me go nutso over the amazing taste of it for a minute before he got serious again.

"Did your mother ever explain to you why she didn't tell me she was pregnant?"

I stopped chewing.

"I really am going somewhere with this," he said.

I shook my head.

"It was because she knew I would be a terrible father."

"How would she know that?" I said.

"Because I was a drunk."

I choked on a mouthful of coleslaw and had to drain half a glass of sweet tea. He waited until I could breathe again.

"We were the ultimate party animals, your mother and I," he said. "The only difference between us was that she knew when to stop drinking and I didn't. No—" He erased the air. "She *could* stop and I couldn't, only I didn't know that then. I didn't know I was an alcoholic until after I married Weezie's mother. I promised I would stop drinking when Weezie was born, but I found out I didn't have the power to do it myself, so I just kept on."

I put my fork down and started tearing up my napkin in my lap, just to make sure I was in a real place, hearing a real person talk.

"I don't know if Weezie remembers what kind of father I was before I moved out. She was only three, and I hope she doesn't." Lou sat back and stretched his hands out flat on the table and looked down at them. "But she does remember that I disappeared from her life for four years. And when I came back, sober and humbled and ready to be her dad, she wasn't all that excited about the idea." He looked up and tilted his head at me. "Sort of like you."

I just nodded. I was afraid to blurt out anything.

"For about a year she didn't want to come stay with me on weekends. Then when she did, she'd scream and cry and carry on every time I took her home, until I finally got it out of her that she was afraid I would disappear again and not come back. We've only had anything close to a decent relationship for the last year and a half."

"And then I came along," I said.

He leaned toward me. "I'm not excusing her behavior, Jess. I probably should have seen it coming. But I am asking you to be patient for just—"

"I am being patient. I was so nice to her this weekend."

"Yes, you were." The twitch came back to his lips. "And I suspect that wasn't all out of the goodness of your heart—

not that I didn't appreciate it, but didn't you have an ulterior motive?"

"What's that?" I said, although I actually knew. I was stalling.

"An agenda. Something you hoped to get out of it." He gave me the full grin. "Like seeing her go nuts."

There wasn't any point in denying it. I was convinced now that the man read my mind.

"Okay, at first, yeah. Rocky thought I should try it."

Lou's eyebrows went up, but he just motioned for me to go on.

"But once I got into it, I don't know—it felt kind of good. I really wanted her to stop, y'know, fighting me. I guess I should just give it up and leave her alone. Or maybe you should just send me home."

I really hadn't planned to say that. And even when I did, I wished I could take it back—because Lou looked as if I'd slapped him in the face.

"You still want to go back?" he said. "I thought you were liking being here."

"I am—I do—I mean, I think I do." The hamster wheel threatened to rev up again. I didn't know what to say about how I felt because I'd just now discovered I was feeling it.

Lou closed his eyes and nodded. When he opened them, they were strong again. "That isn't for us to decide right now anyway, Jess. I heard from your mother last night—well, from her doctor. I didn't want to tell you until we were alone."

"Tell me what? Is she okay?"

I was halfway out of the seat. Lou's eyes told me to sit down and I did.

"She's not making as much progress as the doctor would like, and he wants to keep her in in-patient care for a while longer, until they get her stabilized."

"She's in the hospital. She *has* to take her meds." Unlike me, who could flush them down the toilet. "What's to stabilize?"

"Bipolar disorder is hard to medicate. They have to get just the right balance so she won't keep going back and forth between—what do you call them—In-Bed Phase and No-Bed Phase?"

I wanted to cry. It was the first time anyone else but me had said those words that way. Weirdly, it was like Lou putting his arms around me. I was glad he didn't. I would have started bawling, and I wouldn't be able to stop.

"You okay?" Lou said.

I shook my head.

"Do you want to hear the rest?"

I nodded.

He still just looked at me for a few seconds before he went on. "Her therapy isn't going well. She isn't being as cooperative as they need her to be, and they still feel like she's a danger to herself. It doesn't matter how good the medicine is, she isn't really going to heal until she faces some of her issues."

"Her demons," I said.

Lou's eyes went soft. "Yeah," he said.

"Like being an alcoholic is your demon, and ADHD is mine."

He waited, like he knew there was more. And there was. I wanted to ask him if he ever heard of a guy named Yeshua who drove out demons. But for some reason I couldn't. Not yet.

"Will it be that hard for you to stay here for a while longer, Jess?" he said.

I looked down at my napkin, which was in shreds on my lap, the seat, and the floor.

"You don't have to answer that right now—"

"No," I said. "It won't be that hard. Where else am I going to go anyway?"

He pulled his eyes away and nodded. "Right," he said. "You ready for dessert? They have killer key lime pie."

"Bring it on," I said.

But I knew there was something else I should say. And once again, I couldn't.

CHAPTER SIXTEEN

When ten o'clock came around that night, Lou handed me my Sleepytime tea and put on the geezer rock CD and told me good-night from my bedroom doorway.

Before he turned to go, he said, "Are you sleeping better now?"

"Yeah," I said, "I guess I am."

"Must be the bedtime routine," he said. "I'm a firm believer in it."

He looked like he, too, wanted to say something else, something sad maybe, but then he just tapped the doorframe and said, "'Night, Jess," again and closed my door.

As soon as I heard his footsteps fade to his room on the other side of the kitchen, I slipped my hand under the mattress and went for the part of the bedtime routine he didn't know about. It was hard to even imagine going to sleep now without RL.

When it fell open in my lap, the words practically grabbed me around the wrist, kind of like Rocky always did.

Yeshua has something he wants to say to you, I read.

Me?

Okay, this was really getting weird. And yet—I dug it. I dug it like nothing else.

He originally said it to a crowd of people who came to hear him teach—and he's said it to everyone who's come to him ever since then. Since you keep coming back, he wants to say it to you.

So it was me, exactly me, Yeshua wanted to talk to, just like he did Simon and James and John and Levi—

Speaking of Levi, I'd meant to ask Lou why he named his Harley Levi. Just out of curiosity—just in case—

I shook my head. Lou had never read RL or he would have told me that day on the plane. This was obviously only for certain people—and I was one of them. Go figure.

I sank back, one foot propped over the other knee, book leaning against my thigh, and read on.

But I'm telling you up front: some of it you aren't going to like. Nobody does. But it's the truth, and if you don't believe it and live it, you might as well forget about reading it.

Like I was going to stop now. I scowled at the page. Get on with it already.

"If you're ready for the truth," Yeshua said, *"here it is: Love your enemies."*

"No way," I said out loud.

I told you you weren't going to like it. You ready to chuck this?

"No," I said. "Go ahead."

"Let your enemies bring out your best," Yeshua says. *"Instead of letting them make you lose it, take it as an opportunity to be your best self, your true self."*

"I'm going to do this how?"

"When someone pushes you to the limit, pray for her. If she smacks you in the face, don't hit back. If she tries to run off with your best jeans, give her the jacket that goes with them."

He was right. I didn't like it. But it was like a train wreck: I had to keep looking at it.

"If somebody does something to you that is totally unfair, see it as a chance to do the right thing. No more I'll-get-you-for-that, because if you're going to follow me, you're going to have to be more generous than that."

"If you're talking about Weezie, all bets are off. I'll be nice to her, but I can't love her." I wriggled to a sitting position. "Besides, who said I was going to follow you? I don't even know who you are!"

But you keep coming back to try to find out, don't you?

Okay, it had me there.

Yeshua makes it even clearer: "Just ask yourself how you want people to treat you, and then you treat them that way. Because, seriously, if you're only loving to people it's easy to be nice to, do you expect some kind of medal for that? Anybody can do that. If you only help the people who do stuff for you when you're in trouble, big deal. Gang members do that for each other. If you only give for what you expect to get out of it ..."

I got the idea, but I wasn't buying it. Did this guy expect me to be a doormat?

"I'm going to say this again: Love your enemies. Help and give without thinking they're ever going to do the same for you."

"You were right," I said, straight into the book. "I don't like it."

"But I promise you—I promise—that if you live this way, you won't be sorry."

I wanted to close the book and toss it in Weezie's little pink trash can. But I didn't, because I couldn't. It was like it knew me inside and out and I couldn't let go of that. But—dude—love my enemies? Love Mrs. Honeycutt? Love the doctor who put my mom in the hospital? Love Bonsai when he gave me the hairy eyeball and Lou when he planned out my life?

Love the little Weezer when she didn't even respond to "nice"?

I glared at RL again. "When's Yeshua going to drive out some more demons?" I said.

What do you think he's doing right now? I read.

That was enough weirdness for one night. I started to tuck the book back between the mattresses, but I changed my mind and put it under my pillow.

*

By Wednesday, I was pretty sure it hadn't been my imagination that Lou seemed like he wanted to say something sad Sunday night. Every time I caught him looking at me when he obviously didn't think I knew he was looking at me, his eyes were drooped at the corners and he was swallowing a Ping-Pong-ball-size lump in his throat. I missed that twitchy thing he did with his lips.

I almost asked him a couple of times why he was acting

like somebody had died and he was working up the nerve to tell me, but whenever I started to he'd smile and suggest that we go body surfing after work or hit the A1A Crab Shack for supper instead of cooking. If that wasn't a signal that he didn't want to talk about it, I didn't know what was. Besides, I was a little afraid of what it might be.

And everything else was going *so* better than its usual crazy, I didn't want to mess it up. For openers, Bonsai didn't fire me, which meant he either didn't hear Weezie that day or he didn't know what ADHD was. Maybe they didn't have it in Japan. Anyway, he said I could watch him cut the bamboo leaves into shapes, which was so completely cool it was all I could do not to grab the little knife out of his hands and beg him to let me try it.

Instead, I said, "I never saw anybody decorate food before."

Bonsai grunted. "You think this is all for decoration?"

"It isn't?"

He tapped the tiny net he'd just made with the tip of his pointed knife. "Shikibaran is put underneath to keep the sushi from drying out. Sekisho"—he directed the point at the cut-outs that looked like rows of grass—"go between the pieces of sushi like walls to separate them. The acid in the leaves kills the bacteria. It's all there for a reason."

It still looked like art to me, and I totally wanted to do it.

When I told Lou about it while we were doing the dishes that night, he raised both of his eyebrows about up to his red hairline.

"That's huge, Jess," he said.

"He only let me watch."

"He never let *me* watch. Not that many sushi chefs in America make their own leaf decorations. You go to any other sushi bar here and you get plastic leaves. Him letting you see how he does it is a big deal."

"Do you think I should ask him to let me try it?" I said.

Lou paused over the clam sauce pot he was scrubbing and looked at me. "What do you think?"

"I don't know."

"How do you think he'd respond if you asked him?"

159

"He'd probably give me the hairy eyeball," I said.

Lou let out one of his deep-down chuckles. "Then there's your answer."

"But I really want to do it."

"How have you gotten to do the other things you've wanted to do there?" Lou said.

I hoisted myself onto the counter and picked up a ladle to dry it. "He just out of the blue said, 'You're serving,' or 'You can watch me make an eel roll.'"

"So why fix something if it isn't broken?" Lou said.

"Excuse me?" I said.

Lou just went back to scrubbing the pot.

"So I should just wait until he asks me?" I said.

"Sounds like it."

"I wonder when *that's* going to be."

"Probably when you're ready," Lou said.

Evidently I wasn't ready yet, but watching Bonsai continued to be cool, and so did serving sushi and all the other stuff I did in the restaurant. And then, of course, there was my afternoon babysitting by Rocky.

I hated that I couldn't tease him about Weezie having a major crush on him, because if I did I would have been answering his questions for the rest of my life. Besides, most of the time we were too busy to spend much time pushing each other's buttons, as Lou would say.

We did everything in St. Augustine that we could do without wheels, and after I got my first paycheck—ever, in my whole life—I paid my own way when we went to the wax museum, the Oldest Wooden Schoolhouse, every coffee shop in the whole town, and even Ripley's Believe It or Not! "Odditorium"—which was full of some very strange things people claimed were real. That's where Rocky slipped up and got me another question—he pointed to the mummified cat and said he wondered if doing that to me would keep me from talking so much.

I made him suffer for a while before I asked my question. I waited until we were having raw oysters—which he bet I wouldn't be able to eat but I did—sitting outside at the Santa

Maria Restaurant on a pier sticking out over the bay. I actually liked the way they slithered down my throat.

"Okay, you're killing me," Rocky said. "Ask the question already."

"I want to know why your parents gave you a name like Oswald," I said. "Did they name you after some relative that had a lot of money or something?"

Rocky popped the last oyster into his mouth. I watched in fascination as he swallowed.

"Isn't it the weirdest feeling?" I said.

"What? Being named Oswald?"

"No, eating oysters."

"If I answer that, do I get out of the other question?"

"Hello! No."

He fiddled with the squeezed-out lemon on the plate. I suddenly felt squirmy.

"You really don't have to answer if you don't want to," I said. "It was kind of a rude question."

Rocky dropped the lemon and stared at me. "All right, who are you and what have you done with Red?"

My face, I knew, was turning the color of my nickname.

"Seriously," he said, "why do you all of a sudden care about my feelings?"

"I don't," I said. And then I wrinkled my nose at him to make him think I meant it. I didn't. Why was it the minute we were just ... being, I had to be reminded that this could only go so far?

"I read—someplace—" I said, "that you should think about how you want people to treat you, and then treat *them* that way. That's all I'm trying to do. You're just my guinea pig, okay?"

Rocky sat back and put his hands behind his head and I watched the muscles ripple. "I was named after my father. I'm Oswald Kenneth Luke Junior."

"Oh," I said. "Well, that's pretty cool, I guess. Weezie's all proud because she's named after *her* father."

"Yeah, well, my old man ain't Lou, trust me."

His voice had a sudden edge to it. It was my turn to fiddle with the lemon.

"If he was even close to being the man Lou is, I'd go by Oswald and deck the first kid that gave me grief about it."

The way his hands were now strangling the arms of the chair, I didn't doubt that for a minute.

"So that's why you'd rather be called Rocky," I said.

"Yeah. I figure if I try not to be like him in any way, I might not end up in prison."

"Your father's in prison?" It was my first Blurt in days and I immediately wanted to cut my tongue out.

But Rocky just nodded and said, "Armed robbery—assault—"

"You don't have to tell me," I said.

"It's not like it's a big secret. And Lou says it isn't about me so I don't have anything to be ashamed of."

"You don't," I said. "And I don't think you're ever going to be like your—like Oswald."

"Like you know me so well."

"If you keep messing up and having to answer my questions, pretty soon I'll know everything."

"Don't hold your breath, Red," he said. But he gave me the gap-toothed grin and I was glad.

So glad I wanted him to tell me his entire life history—everything that ever happened to him. And I wanted to tell him mine—while he put his arms around me and we stopped flirting and got the kind of serious I never wanted to be before.

I was that glad. Too glad. And I couldn't let it go any further.

"Insult me," I said.

Rocky blinked. "Excuse me?"

"Call me Crash or something. I want to ask you another question."

"I'm not doing that," he said. "Just ask me."

His eyes were some kind of soft, and I wanted to just forget it. But I couldn't. Not if I was going to do for him what I would want him to do for me.

I took in a breath. "Is it harder to do this for Lou now that you know about me?"

"What are you talking about, Red?" he said, but he put up his hand before I could answer. "You know what, there is nothing wrong with your attention span. You've got focus—and ALL you focus on is what's wrong with you."

I pushed my plate away from me, and I felt suddenly sick. This wasn't going the way I wanted it to.

"All I'm trying to do," I said, "is let you off the hook."

"What 'hook'?"

I motioned my hand back and forth between us. "This one," I said.

Rocky dragged his hand through his hair. And then he stood with a jerk and picked up the check from the edge of the table. "I'll get this," he said. "We've gotta get back."

I nodded—miserably—and watched him cross to the door and go into the restaurant, his arms rippling their muscles, his tall self telling the world he had it goin' on. I could've been walking with him, but I'd just blown it.

But I had to. Before I got any gladder every time he gave me that gap-toothed smile.

*

Lou and I picked up Weezie that afternoon. I was so crushed about Rocky and the way he'd had nothing to say all the way back to the shop and how I had no one to blame but myself—I wasn't even dreading trying to "love" my little sister. Rocky or no Rocky, I still had to do it.

At first Weezie continued to do her imitation of a Popsicle with me, but I still let her have the bedroom for the entire week-end and gave her my neon orange flip-flops that I saw her eyeing more than once. Saturday night when she and I were cleaning up after, yes, coconut shrimp, and Lou went to the store to get more popcorn so we could watch *Shrek* and *Shrek 2*, I even told her something I would have wanted to hear if I had been her.

"Your dad really wishes you lived with him all the time," I said.

She was careful not to look at me. "How do *you* know?" she said.

"He told me."

"No, he didn't."

I had to take a deep breath so I wouldn't stuff a dish towel up her nose.

"Yes, he did," I said. "He said it kills him that he doesn't get to wake you up every morning and make sure you're eating right and tuck you in at night." I smiled at her. "You know, all the stuff you hate."

"I don't hate it!"

"Look me in the face and tell me you don't hate broccoli and popcorn without butter," I said.

She twisted her mouth. "Okay, I do hate that."

"And going to bed at nine o'clock on a school night."

"If I lived here, he'd make me go to bed at eight thirty."

"Ouch."

"What time does he make *you* go to bed?" she said.

"Ten."

"Not fair!"

"That's still pretty tight when you're fifteen."

"I guess. I can't wait to be fifteen."

I hopped up onto the counter. She hopped up with me.

"How come you want to be fifteen?" I said.

"Because I wanna wear makeup."

"Why can't you wear makeup now?"

She rolled her eyes at me. "Are you kidding? Daddy doesn't even like it when I put on colored ChapStick."

"That's because you're his little girl," I said.

She rolled the eyes again, but a smile played at the corners of her lips. She was actually sort of cute in a preteeny way.

"So he won't let you wear makeup in public," I said, without adding that, hello, she was ten. "But does he say you can't learn how to use it so you'll be ready when you're fifteen and won't look like Ronald McDonald the first time you try to put on lipstick by yourself?"

Her eyebrows knitted together like she was trying to sort that all out, and then she slowly shook her head.

164

"So are you thinking what I'm thinking?" I said.

"Are you thinking that you could show me how to put on lipstick?" she said—almost shyly, almost like she was afraid that wasn't what I was thinking at all.

"A little lipstick," I said. "A little blush. No eye makeup—you're not supposed to share that—but I have some way-cool face glitter that'll go great with your nails."

"You don't think Daddy'll get mad?"

I pulled in my chin. "Does he ever get mad?"

"He got mad at me the other Sunday when I was a brat to you."

"That was mad?" I said.

She nodded, eyes round.

"Then I think we can handle that," I said.

But Lou didn't get mad. Not when he came home from the grocery store and found us in the bathroom together, Weezie sitting on the counter, me dusting clear glitter on her face, and both of us giggling like we were at a sleepover. In fact, he got the Ping-Pong ball going in his throat and pretty much had to force himself to say, "Now, you realize you can't wear that out of the house, Weezie."

"I kno-ow," Weezie said.

"Yeah, *Dad*," I said. "I mean, seriously."

He left the bathroom then. I heard him blowing his nose in the kitchen.

Meanwhile, Weezie was gazing at herself in the mirror.

"You do look fab," I said.

She didn't answer. But she didn't tell me I didn't know anything because I had a disorder, either.

The house phone rang and she jumped off the counter.

"That's probably my mom," she said. "I can't wait to tell her."

I couldn't hold back a grin as I followed her out to the kitchen. And then I felt it fade as Lou said, "Oh. Hey, Brooke."

It wasn't Weezie's mom. It was mine.

CHAPTER SEVENTEEN

Lou steered Weezie toward the bedroom while he listened on the phone. When I started to follow her in, he shook his head and motioned for me to go to the Everything Room with him and then closed the bedroom door. He didn't tell me to sit down and I couldn't have anyway.

We both just stood in the middle of the room while my mother shrieked on the other end of the phone line. I couldn't hear what she was saying, but I didn't really have to. The tone of her screeching told me everything I needed to know. She was flipping out.

When it was obvious she wasn't going to stop anytime soon, Lou just broke in with, "Brooke, where are you?"

She shrieked some more, but I could tell what was happening from the tight-tighter-tightest looks on Lou's face and the things he was saying:

"Okay—I just thought maybe you'd left the hospital ... Are you still on your medication?" There was a slight pause there while he winced. Then, "Why isn't that my business?... Does anybody know you're making this call?... Because you're out of control, Brooke, that's why I'm asking."

I shook my head at Lou. Not a good thing to say to my mother, especially when she was No-Bed, like she obviously was now. My grandfather's wife had said that to her once, which was one of the reasons we didn't see them anymore.

Lou nodded at me and closed his eyes. "Okay, poor choice of words. You just sound really upset and ... Yeah, you do have a right to your feelings but ... Absolutely not—I haven't said a negative thing about you to Jessie."

It hit me then that he was repeating things she said so I could be part of the conversation. I wasn't sure I wanted to be.

"If she wants to talk to you, yes, I'll put her on." Lou looked at me, eyebrows raised, and pointed to the phone.

Vampire bats were multiplying in my stomach, but I nodded and put out my hand. When Lou backed toward the kitchen, I shook my head at him so hard it hurt. He sat on the arm of the couch, but he didn't watch me as I put the phone to my ear.

"Hi, Mom," I said in a voice I could barely hear.

"Jessie?" she said. The shriek was gone, but she still sounded like one wrong syllable from me would fire it up again.

"It's me," I said.

"Is Lou still in the room with you?"

"Yeah," I said.

"All right, I'm going to call you back later on that other number you called me on before. What was that?"

"A cell phone," I said.

"Where did you get a cell phone?"

"Lou gave it to me —"

"The man is shameless." The shriek threatened, but I heard her breathe in shallow little gasps and it went back to where it had been hiding before. "I'll call you at that number so we can talk without him hearing every word we're saying."

"He can't hear you now," I said.

Lou's head jerked up. I shrugged at him.

"Don't bet on it," she said. "He probably has the phone bugged."

"Bugged?"

"Shhhh. Jessie, you are so dense." She breathed fast again. "That's why I'm going to call you on your cell. Does he ever leave you alone?"

"Well —"

"What time do you go to your room at night — or are you still roaming around at all hours like a raccoon?"

"Ten o'clock," I said through my teeth.

"I'll call you tomorrow night at ten fifteen. Do you think you can remember that?"

I didn't answer her. I was afraid I'd do some shrieking of my own.

"All right, whatever—just keep your cell phone with you, if you can find it. And, Jessie, for heaven's sake, don't tell Lou I'm going to call you. Do you get that?"

"Yeah, I get it," I said, and I handed the phone back to Lou and hurled myself out onto the deck so I could breathe.

Lou was beside me in about three seconds.

"What else did she say?" I said.

"Nothing. She hung up. You okay?"

I looked up into Lou's eyes, which were their saddest yet. I saw him swallow hard. I was right there with him.

"She sounded like she was losing it," I said.

"She's pretty unstable. Kind of disturbing, isn't it?"

"I didn't even know what to say to her."

Lou leaned on the railing. "Do you want to tell me what she said to *you*? You don't have to, but if you want to process it—"

"She said she's going to call me on my cell tomorrow night so she can talk to me when you aren't around."

For once I didn't regret a Blurt. Lou straightened up and stuck his hands in the pockets of his shorts.

"Do you want to talk to her alone?"

"I don't know," I said. "It's sort of creepy, her wanting to tell me something she doesn't want you to hear. She said you might have your phone bugged. It's like she's paranoid."

"We *don't know* if that's what it is . . ." He tilted his head at me. "Does it scare you, Jess?"

"Yes," I said, around the lump in my throat. "Can I just give you my cell phone tomorrow so I won't be there when she calls?"

"You can," Lou said. He dragged out the *can*.

"Why is there always a but?" I said.

I started to hoist myself up onto the railing, but he gave me a sit-down look. I paced the deck instead.

"Just take tomorrow to think about it," he said.

"You mean pray about it."

His eyebrows went up.

I shrugged. "That's what you always do, right?"

"I do. But that doesn't mean it's going to make her not call. It means maybe you'll know what you're supposed to say, either beforehand or when you open your mouth."

"I wish Yeshua would just come in and drive out her demons," I said in full Blurt mode.

Lou didn't have a forehead high enough for his eyebrows at that point. "I wish he would too," he said, as if he knew exactly what I was babbling about. "We can still pray for that, of course. But let's also pray that you'll know what to say to your mom when she calls you. If she calls you. She may not."

I stopped pacing. "You're going to make me talk to her, aren't you?"

"No. You don't even have to answer the phone if that's what you decide."

I leaned on the railing beside him and stared at my bare toes and wished my mind would go back to its hamster wheel and think about painting toenails with Weezie tomorrow or where I left my sunglasses or anything else—even Rocky— that would keep me from thinking about this thing that was choking me with its tears.

"Do you want me to pray with you, Jess?"

I looked up from my toenails. "On that kneeler thing?"

"You mean the prayer table?"

"In the Everything Room."

He formed that on his lips and then nodded. "We don't have to pray there—we can pray anywhere."

"I want to pray there," I said.

"Okay," he said. "I think there's room on there for all of us."

"Weezie's going to pray with us?"

"No," Lou said. "God is."

*

When I tiptoed into the bedroom to get RL after Lou prayed and I held back tears, Weezie squinted up at me and said in a voice that reminded me of mushy oatmeal, "You can sleep in here."

"You sure?" I said, hugging the book against me.

"Uh-huh."

I thought she'd drifted off again, and then she said, "Can I go to coffee with you and Rocky tomorrow? I promise I won't flirt with him. I know he's your boyfriend."

It was as if she'd stabbed me, and for once she didn't even know it. My phone rang and saved me—except for the chill of dread that wrapped itself around my chest. I grabbed it out of the drawer and hurried out to the kitchen before I answered.

"It's not ten o'clock tomorrow," I whispered into it.

"Jess?" said the voice I didn't expect.

"Marcus?" I said.

"Fine," he said. "Don't say hi to me."

"Hi!" I glanced at the door to Lou's room, but his light was off. Still, I took the phone out onto the deck so I wouldn't wake him up. A breeze was blowing the stars around out there and I could smell the ocean in its salty sleepiness. I felt like I could breathe for the first time since my mother called. It also occurred to me that the alarm didn't go off. That was comforting too—the fact that Lou hadn't set it.

"Are you still there?" Marcus said.

"Yes. Sorry," I said. "Are you back from Canada?"

"Yeah. When are *you* coming back?"

"I don't know. My mom is still away—" I squeezed my eyes shut. "You know what, she's not away. Not exactly. She's in the hospital, in the mental ward, and she's getting worse instead of better so I don't know when—"

"Could you come back if you had a place to stay?"

"I don't," I said.

"Yes, you do, if you want it."

So much for breathing.

"What are you talking about?" I said.

"My aunt and uncle I was on the trip with are staying in a condo here for two weeks. I told them about you, and they said you could stay there in the extra room. That's all you need, two weeks, right?"

It was the most Marcus had ever said to me at one time, and he wasn't done.

170

"I told them you were my girlfriend so they'd say yes, so you'll have to pretend you are. Unless you really want to be. I mean, do you?"

I got up on the railing and gripped it with my free hand. Don't blurt. Do *not* blurt.

"I guess not, huh?" His voice was small and hurt.

"No, wait. It's just a lot to take in all at once—"

"I did what you wanted me to do."

"I know, but things have changed. I'm not really with a 'relative.' I'm with my bio—I'm with my father."

"You said you didn't have a father."

"I didn't think I did. It's really complicated and—"

"So are you coming home or not?"

I heard something in Marcus's voice I had never ever heard there before and never thought I would. I slid off the railing.

"Are you mad at me, Marcus?" I said.

"Yeah. I am."

"I'm so sorry," I said.

But there was no answer. CALL ENDED, the screen on my cell phone said.

I had the feeling that wasn't all that had ended.

*

I didn't get to RL until late the next afternoon when we'd dropped Weezie off after the church service that Rocky didn't come to and had eaten lunch at the Crab Shack. It was raining and Lou was kind of quiet, so I said I could use some alone time. He seemed like he understood. But, then, when didn't he?

I was lonely. No big surprise. Sure, Weezie had been on me all morning like she was my Siamese twin, and two more girls said hi to me at church. And asked me where Rocky was.

It wasn't just that. Marcus had left a huge hole—even though I figured out that he really didn't know me, since everything I'd ever said or been with him had basically been a lie. Chelsea too. Maybe even my mom.

It was that—the thought of my mom's coming phone

call—that made me close the door and pull out RL. I didn't go back to "Love your enemies." I hoped Yeshua would have something new to show me that would help me, because in spite of the praying last night and in church, I still had no idea how to be with her now.

"One night, one of the Pharisees asked Yeshua over for dinner," I read.

I'd meant to ask somebody if the Pharisees were the jerks I seemed to know they were from somewhere.

The Pharisees, by the way, were this group of people who had the job of making sure everybody followed the rules of their religion. This wasn't bad in itself except that they'd gotten so into the nitpicky don't-do-this-don't-do-that, they'd pretty much forgotten about love and compassion and helping people. That's why watching Yeshua bent them out of shape. He was a threat to the control they had over people.

Oh. So they were like some teachers I'd had who claimed to care about our education but acted like they couldn't stand us. I got that.

Yeshua sat down at the dinner table, and a woman came in. She was, shall we say, a woman of questionable reputation.

I knew the type.

She'd heard Yeshua was having dinner there, and she brought a bottle of very pricey perfume. She stood in front of Yeshua, crying, just sobbing, so hard her tears were running down onto Yeshua's toes. Then she let down her long hair out of its clasp and dried his feet with it and kissed them. Next she poured the perfume on them like she was placing a blessing on his heels and soles and toes.

Part of me thought that was weird, bordering on gross. A bigger part of me could picture it as the most beautiful thing you could do for a person like Yeshua.

His host didn't think so. He thought to himself, "If this guy was the prophet I was starting to think he was, he would have known what kind of woman it is who's making a fool of herself over him."

"She is not," I said. "She loves him."

Yeshua just said, "I'll tell you a story. There were two men and both of them owed money to a banker. One owed five hundred silver pieces. The other one owed fifty. Neither one of them could come up with what they owed to pay back the banker. The banker told them both to forget it—they didn't have to pay the debt. Which one do you think would be more grateful?"

This was a no-brainer.

The Pharisee said, "I guess it would be the one who had the most to pay back. He was forgiven more so he'd be more grateful." Yeshua said, "Exactly. Now, do you see this woman?"

I could see her still rubbing Yeshua's feet and crying because he was letting her, instead of telling her she was a low-life tramp and to get away from him.

"I came to your home and you didn't have any water ready for me to wash my feet," which, incidentally, would've been dirty from walking around in sandals on unpaved streets all day. A decent host always had water available for guest foot washings. Yeshua said, *"But she washed my feet with her own tears and dried them with her hair. You barely said hello to me when I came in, but ever since I sat down she's been kissing my feet. You didn't offer me anything to make my visit comfortable, but she's still massaging my ankles with this incredible perfume. I'm impressed with her. And do you know why she's doing this?"*

I thought I might.

"Because she was forgiven many sins and she is extremely grateful."

Yeah. That's what I thought.

Then Yeshua said to the woman, "I forgive your sins." Well, THAT got everybody all worked up. The host and the rest of the guests muttered to each other, *"Where does he get off forgiving sins? Does he think he's God or something?"*

Yeshua didn't even let them know he could hear them. He said to the woman, "Your faith has saved you. Go in peace."

The page blurred just like it had before, only this time I didn't drop the book and call myself nuts. It *was* talking to me. I *could* be that woman, because I'd messed up so many times I *would* kiss Yeshua's feet if he forgave me. I believed it, and if that made me crazy, okay. For the first time in my life, I didn't care.

That was why I was ready for my mom when she called. She could put me down for forgetting stuff and being dense and roaming around like a raccoon all night. It didn't matter.

And not only that, but I knew what I was going to say to her, no matter what it was she had to say to me.

Still, I hung out with Lou in the Everything Room until the phone rang. When it did, he tilted his head at me and said, "You okay?" and I said yes and took the cell into the bedroom, closed the door, and answered it.

"It took you long enough," Mom said.

I had the weird feeling that we were just picking up last night's conversation—and every other conversation we'd ever had—right where we left off.

"Sorry," I said. "I had to get off by myself, like you said." More "treating other people the way you want to be treated." It was easier with Weezie.

"Good," she said, and her voice settled down some. "I want you to listen to me."

"Okay."

"And try to focus, all right, because this is important."

"Okay," I said again. My teeth were already grinding together.

"I'm going to be getting out of here soon. They aren't helping me at all so I'm going to find another doctor. They can't keep me here against my will."

In spite of the evening-still heat, I shivered and pulled the comforter over my lap.

"Are you listening to me?" she said.

"Yes."

"As soon as I get out, I want you home. Lou doesn't seem to think that's going to happen, but he has evidently forgotten who he's dealing with. He says it's your decision, but I don't believe that for a minute. He's always been a control freak. Like most alcoholics. Has he told you he's an alcoholic? Oh, excuse me—a *reformed* alcoholic."

She was babbling on in a way that was so familiar it made my mouth go dry. She sounded just like me.

"Hello?" she said.

"I'm here," I said.

"In body maybe. Jessie, have you heard a thing I've said?"

"Yes," I said. "It *is* my decision. Lou says I always have a choice."

"Sure, as long as it's the one he's already made for you."

Her voice was hard and nasty. I had to grit my teeth even harder to keep from blurting at her.

"All right, so what is your 'decision'?" she said.

"I'm going to stay here with him."

She actually laughed. "And how long do you plan for that to go on?"

"I don't know. Until you're completely better, I guess."

"Until Saint Lou says I'm better is more like it. Why did I not know that he would completely snow you like he did me way back when? And that was even before he had the Twelve-Step Program." She coughed out another laugh that reminded me of sandpaper. "You have no idea what he's doing, do you?"

I didn't answer.

"It's the same thing they try to make you do in here," she said. "Go through the twelve steps to recovery and you will be healed. He's just doing this to complete Step—what is it—Nine? Just like he did with his other kid. What's her name? Wheezer?"

I was suddenly sorry I'd ever called Weezie that. And sorry I'd answered the phone.

"Yes, this is Step Nine," my mother said, still sputtering away.

"I don't care what step it is," I said. "I'm staying here."

She stopped laughing. "All right, enough with this. Lou might let you make 'decisions,' but I don't parent that way. You are coming home when I get out of here, and that's it. Start packing. Am I clear?"

I wasn't sure which one of us hung up first.

CHAPTER EIGHTEEN

I didn't tell Lou what my mother said, even though he stayed up until I was off the phone and gave me every head-tilting, eyes-soft, "you okay?" chance to. I just couldn't say it to him — all that hateful stuff she'd spewed out like she was coughing up phlegm. I wouldn't have wanted him to say it to me.

But it kept coming up inside for the next three days.

Anytime any phone rang anywhere I was, I panicked that she was calling to take me back home to the very place I'd been dying to be and now couldn't stand the thought of.

Every time I heard Lou talking in a low voice so that I couldn't hear everything he was saying, I started to come apart, because I was sure he was talking to some official somebody who said he had to return me like stolen goods.

By Thursday I finally couldn't stand it. I had to talk to somebody. But it had to be someone who wasn't going to go to Lou and tell him the things I didn't want him to hear. That left out Weezie — who wasn't even a candidate anyway — and Rocky — who was, after all, Lou's babysitter and who was avoiding me anyway. There basically was nobody who didn't seem to talk to Lou about everything.

Nobody, that is, except the one person who didn't talk much to anybody at all.

I didn't think of it until Rose and I were in the kitchen together and she was showing me how to put the vinegar dressing in the rice. I had the feeling she was only letting me do it because Bonsai wasn't there at the moment. As I watched her and copied her, it made me think about how the way she moved was so soft

176

and quiet and how she didn't say anything but I felt like she was talking to me anyway ...

"Rose," I said. "Can I talk to you about something?"

She smiled at me and bowed and went back to spreading the rice out with the paddle. I decided that was Rose for yes.

So I took a deep breath and I told her. Everything. How I felt about Lou when I first had to come here. How I couldn't stand Weezie for a long time. How I hated it when he planned my whole life out for me and when Weezie announced to the world that I had ADHD. How all of that had messed things up with Rocky so I couldn't even hang out with him anymore because it hurt too much. Then I had to back way up and tell her about my mother before I could go on and explain what I really wanted to talk about, which was all the things she said about Lou.

Up 'til then Rose just nodded and kept lifting and mixing. But when I told her about my mother saying Lou was just helping me because of some step thing he was doing, she stopped and put down the paddle. Her face went hard like one of those porcelain dolls.

"No," she said.

"No what?" I said.

"She wrong about Lou."

Rose went to the doorway and looked into the part of the kitchen where Bonsai usually worked, like she was making sure he wasn't there. When she came back to me, her eyes were stern as a math teacher's. I put down my paddle too.

"Lou help Bonsai," she said. "He come here poor—no green card."

"You mean like an illegal alien?" I said.

She nodded. "Bonsai steal food from Lou—" She seemed to be searching for a word and then pointed to the refrigerator.

"From his fridge?" I said. "At his house?"

"No. Here." This time she pointed out toward the shop. "Lou find him but he not call—" Again she searched.

"The police?" I said.

"Yes. He help Bonsai—give him this." She waved her

177

hand around the kitchen. "Pay for me come. Give him name Bonsai. Help him become American citizen. "

"Wow," I said.

"No 'steps,'" she said as if she had just tasted some bad sushi. "Lou do this because he—"

She stopped and blinked her tiny crinkly eyes, and I saw tears streaming from their corners. She crossed her hands over her heart.

"Lou did it because he loved Bonsai," I said.

"Yes," she said, in a voice so firm I had to look twice to make sure it was still her. She pressed her fingertips on my forehead and said, "Remember, Yes."

Then she went back to the rice. I sighed all the way from my knees.

*

I didn't know what to do with myself after I got off work, now that there was no Rocky to be with. I didn't realize it until I was just sitting on Levi in the parking lot and waiting that he'd become like a best friend. If he'd been a girl, we'd still be together. If he'd been like Marcus, I could have thought of him like he was a girl. But he wasn't. He was different from everybody, and it hurt even to think about him.

It would hurt worse to have him keep babysitting you, I told myself. So get over it.

"Are you in as bad a mood as I am?"

I looked up, accidentally jerking the handlebars. Rocky put a hand out to steady them and touched the side of mine with his fingers. I wanted to curl my own fingers around them. Instead I said, "Do I look like I'm in a bad mood?"

"You look a little cranky. 'Course, it's kind of hard to tell—"

He cut himself off and scrunched his face up, but he was too late.

I couldn't remind him how far ahead of him I was in questions, though. We would start bantering and I'd be right back where I was before.

"Go ahead," he said. "Ask."

I shook my head. He stuck his hands on his wonderful skinny hips.

"Then I'll ask. Are you, like, the most stubborn woman on the face of the earth?"

"I guess I'm probably in the top twenty percent," I said.

Instead of grinning, he seemed to sag. "Did you ever wonder how I got a Harley?"

Actually I had, and although I had no idea where this was going, I nodded.

"When Lou was pretty sure I was going to straighten out, he said I could have his old bike in exchange for working here. He taught me how to fix it up."

One more reason for him to do absolutely anything for Lou. This wasn't helping me.

I started to climb off Levi, but Rocky put his hands on my shoulders and pushed me back to the seat. He didn't let go as his green eyes bored into mine.

"Just listen to this one thing," he said, "and then if you still want to dump me, I'll go."

I was too stunned to say anything.

"I told you that because I know you think I hung out with you because I owe Lou something. I also know you think I hated doing it when I found out you were hyper. But here's the thing: Lou never asked me to hang out with you. I asked *him* if you ever had any free time, and after he made me promise not to try anything with you or break your heart or let anything happen to you, he said I could. I knew right away you were a crazy chick, and I knew I loved that about you."

Not only could I not speak, I couldn't move except to try to swallow.

"So I don't know why you think you were some kind of job for me. I never did anything to make you think that. And you know what—it's a total insult to me that you see me as that kind of person." I saw him try to swallow too. "So, look, if you don't want to be with me because I come from trash or I'm not your type or whatever, fine. Just tell me. But don't back off

179

from me because you think I feel sorry for you or something. It's me I feel sorry for."

"Why?" I said in a tiny voice.

"Because it's tearing me up that you don't want to be with me."

I shook my head because I didn't know what else to do. He closed his eyes and dropped his hands from my shoulders and turned away. He was halfway to the garage before I slid off of Levi and went after him. And careened on something and sprawled face-first onto the parking lot.

Rocky was on me before I could even catch the breath that knocked out of me.

"Red?" he said. "What the—"

"Don't say it," I said to the grease smear that was now wiped across my face.

"Say what?"

"Don't call me Crash."

And then I started to cry. Rocky rolled me onto my back and stared down at me, his eyes gleaming with—no, those had to be my tears I was seeing.

"I just can't let anybody get close or they'll find out who I really am," I said.

"I know who you are," Rocky said.

"A ditz-queen-airhead-moron?"

He pulled me up by my shoulders again so that I was sitting up close to his face. Mine, I knew, was blobbed with grease, proving my point—

"I don't know any ditz-queen airhead moron," he said. "I just know Red. Except for one thing."

I swiped at my face with the back of my hand. "What?"

"I don't know how you feel about me. And I need to."

What was I supposed to say? That I thought he was the most amazing guy I'd ever known and I wanted to—

"Okay, if I asked you to go out with me, what would you say?"

"I'd say yes. Oh my gosh, I would so say yes, only—"

The smile he'd begun stuck halfway. "What is so hard about that?"

"I don't know."

He twisted his neck and looked over his shoulder. His face was turning as red as I knew mine already was.

"That's like the worst possible answer you could say to me."

"No—Rocky—I want to! I just don't know if I'm allowed to. I mean, my mom doesn't let me date, but I never asked my—Lou—if I could."

Rocky shook his head at me. "As far as I was concerned, that's what we've been doing every day for the past two weeks."

He looked beyond me, over my head, and put his hand over my mouth, which I had just opened to answer him.

"You want to ask permission, go for it," he said. "Here comes Lou."

He kept his hand pressed to my lips, which I thought was pretty brave considering I'd threatened to bite him once.

Lou came over to us, helmet on his hip, and broke into a full grin. "That's one way to do it, Rock," he said. "I hadn't thought of that." Then he looked at me more closely. "What happened to you, Jess? What are you doing in the middle of the—"

"She just wants to ask you something," Rocky said, and pulled his hand away.

"Okay." Lou gave my greasy face another look and went back to having what was obviously a very good time. "Ask away, Jess."

"I want to know if I'm allowed to go out with Rocky."

"I see. Where were you planning to go?"

I looked blankly at Rocky.

"To the youth group beach party Saturday," Rocky said.

"Ah. Well, I don't see why not."

My face broke open into a smile in spite of me, and in spite of the I-won look on Rocky's face. Or maybe because of it.

"Good to know you trust me, Lou," Rocky said.

"Of course I trust you." Lou's lips twitched in a way I hadn't seen them do all week. "Especially since I'm going to be there too."

I looked at Rocky, but he squinted his eyes at me so hard I didn't dare say a word. But he still said, "Watch it now, Red. Watch it."

His eyes were gleaming at me again.

*

I wondered a couple of times between then and Saturday what Chelsea would say about my father chaperoning my first real date. Weezie was even going to be there. She was already whining about not being allowed to wear lip gloss like me.

Saturday night Rocky pulled up to the house on his motorcycle and came to the door, and I opened it—after Lou put Weezie in a headlock so I could answer it myself. I forgot about what Chelsea would say when Rocky said, "Hey, Red."

He gave me the smile. "You ready to be babysat?"

"Shut up," I said.

And then I smiled too, right into that fabulous gap. Weezie got away from Lou and squeezed between us in the doorway and hugged Rocky's leg while I laughed silently in his face. Lou peeled her off and looked out at Rocky's bike.

"You're planning to *walk* Jess down to the beach, right, Rock?"

"Yes," Rocky and I said at the same time.

"Just wanted to make sure you remembered."

"It's not like she's an airhead, Daddy," Weezie said.

Rocky opened his mouth. I told him to watch it. Weezie rolled her eyes at me.

It was one of the happiest moments of my life.

*

I had never been to a beach party before, but within about five minutes I decided it was my new favorite thing.

A bunch of kids were bodysurfing. I gave them all a run for their money.

Four guys had set up a volleyball net and had a game going. I told Rocky I didn't want to play because I stink at sports where other people expect me to be any good, but he made me get out there anyway and he hit every ball I missed so I didn't feel like a loser-klutz.

The three girls who had said hi to me at church—Simone and Emma and Katrina, who introduced herself as "Katrina, and, no, I'm not the hurricane"—dragged me over by the dunes and questioned me about whether Rocky and I were "going out." I didn't mind it. It made me not miss Chelsea so much. I really, *really* didn't mind it when they said Rocky never had a girlfriend before—and not to think they hadn't all tried.

The Reverend Big Shoulders, who everybody called Hank, was there, and before we ate he prayed in a big booming voice I was sure God could hear wherever He was. At the end of it he said, "And all God's people said—" and everybody yelled, "Amen!" I wanted him to do it again so I could join in. I would know next time.

Next time. I really wanted there to be a next time.

We all sat in a circle on the beach and ate cold fried chicken and potato salad and honkin' chocolate chip cookies. I looked across at Lou and held up my cookie and gave him a question face. He got the sad-happy look on his and gave me a thumbs-up. I ate the entire thing. A lot of things had changed, but my being a sugar-holic wasn't one of them.

The water was turning pink by then, and although the air was still warm, Lou built a fire in the center of the circle and everyone moved in closer. Rocky got closer to me than he needed to and picked up my arm and shook it up and down so my hand would flop around. Then he held onto it and didn't let go. I didn't pull away. Halfway around the circle, Simone and Emma and Katrina-not-the-hurricane gave me girlfriend smiles.

"Has everybody greeted our new member?" Hank said. "Jess?"

"Hi, Jess," they all said in unison just like the group at the coffee shop that first Sunday.

"What is that about, anyway?" I whispered to Rocky.

"Jess wants to know what that's about," Rocky said to the entire circle, and probably the people a mile down the beach as well.

"It's kind of a joke," Simone said. She turned to the kid next to her. "You tell it."

The kid—a dark-haired guy Chelsea would have been all over like a coat of paint—said, "It's not exactly a joke. You know about AA, right? Alcoholics Anonymous?"

I forced myself not to look at Lou.

"Yeah," I said.

"Whenever somebody new comes to a meeting the person'll say, 'I'm So-and-So and I'm an alcoholic.' And then everybody says, 'Hi, So-and-So.' Lou told us about it, and we just started doing it."

"But it doesn't mean we think you're an alcoholic," Simone said, eyes round.

"I'm not," I said. "Just so you know."

They all laughed.

"It probably sounds kind of weird to you, though," Emma said.

She looked at Lou.

"It's okay, Em," he said. "You can tell Jess."

Emma rearranged herself like she was about to give a report. "Okay, well, a lot of us ended up at youth group because we were messed up. I can only speak for myself—but, like, I was into cutting—"

Simone raised her hand. "Smoking pot."

A boy on the other side of the circle said, "I just generally hated everybody."

"I, on the other hand, was perfect," Katrina said, and then ducked as several people threw stuff at her.

"So anyway," Emma said, "Lou was just, like, okay, you're a mess but Jesus can help. So he sort of combined the Bible and the Twelve Step Program and now—I think we're all gonna make it."

I felt the beginnings of a chill. "Twelve-Step Program?"

Emma looked around the circle. "Somebody else talk."

"I will!" Weezie said.

"No, you won't," Lou said.

She was sitting between his knees, leaning back into his

chest. He put his hand playfully over her mouth and grinned at Rocky.

"Hey—it works," he said.

"Okay, I'll tell," said the guy who'd said he used to hate everybody. "I'm Travis, by the way. So here's the deal—when you have some thing that, like, has control over you—drugs, booze, anger—"

ADHD.

"—you can't handle it alone, or you would. So alcoholics who want to recover use the Twelve Step Program that they do with the support of a group, and then they don't have to be a slave to their addiction."

I knew I shouldn't ask it, but if I didn't, I knew I would Blurt it anyway, at some moment when it would make me look like a moron. "What are the steps?" I said.

"Number one is admit you're powerless over whatever it is—that you're out of control," Simone said.

"Number two," Travis said, "is believe that a power greater than ourselves can restore us to wholeness—in our case, that's Jesus Christ. Number three—"

"What's number nine?" I said.

There was a funky silence around the circle, probably because they'd never heard somebody Blurt like that before. A couple of people counted on their fingers. One of them said, "Make amends to the people you've hurt because of your alcoholism or whatever it is."

Maybe they backed up to the ones I'd skipped or went on to ten, eleven, and twelve. If they did, I missed it. All I could hear in my head, going round and round on my hamster wheel, was my mother's voice: *He's just doing this to complete Step Nine. Just like he did with his other kid.* But I also heard Rocky telling me, *That's just who he is. It's like he gets how it is to be a complete screwup, and he doesn't want it happening to any other kid.* And Rose telling me Lou helped Bonsai because he loved him.

And Lou saying, *Weezie does remember that I disappeared from her life for four years . . . I came back, sober and humbled and ready to be her dad.*

I looked around the circle at the kids who had broken into private conversations as if the group discussion had completely weirded them out. Most of them were projects of Lou's too. Only they didn't care because he wasn't their father, who they were just starting to trust—just beginning to believe that they really mattered to him the way Weezie did—more than they mattered to their mother—or anybody else in the world.

Hank suddenly had a guitar in his hand and people were calling out songs to him. Across from me, Lou had his arms crossed over Weezie as she snuggled back against him, and they both glowed in the light of the fire like they were one person. Like I would never be with Lou. What if I was just Step Nine like my mother said?

Nobody was looking at me anymore. I could leave without being noticed—

"You want to go for a walk?" Rocky whispered.

I nodded and got up and half ran down the beach. He caught me by the arm until I slowed down.

"What's going on, Red?"

"Nothing," I said.

"You're a liar."

"Yes, I am. See—you do know everything about me."

I was running out of breath. Rocky got in front of me and stood there. I folded my arms and looked down at the water lapping over my feet.

"Where's all this coming from?" he said. "Five minutes ago you were having a blast."

"That was before the whole group told me my mother was probably right. She might be crazy but she isn't stupid."

"What did she say?"

"I'm not going to tell you because you'll tell Lou and I don't want him to know—but I guess it doesn't matter now if he gets his feelings hurt or not. It's the truth."

"What's the truth?"

I dug my toes into the sand.

"Okay, look, I'm not gonna run to Lou and tell him something you confide in me—unless you're planning to kill yourself."

I jerked my head up. He took that opportunity to put his hands on the sides of my face. I didn't pull away, because he wasn't being rough. And all of a sudden, I needed a place to rest my head, because it felt too heavy for my body.

"No, I'm not going to kill myself," I said. "That's my mother's kind of crazy, not mine."

"You can trust me, Red."

I wanted to. And I wanted him to tell me I was wrong. So I told him about Mom and Step Nine. And he listened.

And then he pressed my forehead against his chest and said, "You really are a crazy chick if you believe that—and I don't think you are and I don't think you do."

"Are you sure?" I said, to the T-shirt that said *Kennesaw's Cycles* and smelled like salt air and mocha and all things Rocky.

He was quiet for a minute—a terrifying minute when I thought he was going to say no and all my hope would be gone.

"I don't know how much you know about Jesus," he said finally, "but Lou is more like him than anybody I ever met. Jesus didn't use people to make himself feel better and neither does Lou." Rocky pulled me face-out to look at me. "I bet you never thought I'd be preaching to you, did you?"

"Do you swear to me that's true?" I said. "You have to tell me if it's not, because if it is, then I'm going to tell Lou—"

I had to stop and swallow. Rocky pressed his hands into my hair.

"Tell Lou what?"

"Tell him I never want to go back to live with my mom. That I want to stay here with him forever."

Rocky closed his eyes and wrapped his arms around me, hard, and rocked me back and forth. "It's true, Red," he said. "It's true. I swear to you it's true."

I almost let myself cry—but a whistle from down the beach jolted Rocky away from me, hands up like the cops were after him. When I looked up, though, he was grinning. I turned to see Lou, hands at his lips in post-whistle.

"We're on our way!" Rocky called to him. To me he said, "Busted." He grabbed my hand and we ran.

"The party's over," Lou said when we got to him. "Or didn't you two notice?"

His lips were twitching. I couldn't wait to tell him everything.

*

Rocky took off on his motorcycle and I watched until I couldn't see him anymore, and then I told Lou I would stay with Weezie while he took some of the kids home. She was dead asleep before he even carried her into the house and rolled her into her bed.

I stretched out on mine and smiled at the ceiling. I didn't know how to be as happy as I was, but I wanted to practice. When my cell phone rang, I was sure it was Rocky and I answered with, "I believe you."

"It's a good thing," my mother said.

I came up off the bed like somebody had shot me in the back.

"Are you packed?" she said.

"No," I said.

Her voice was shrill and it brought back the vampire bats. I tried to think of Rocky, to hear Lou's voice, even to think of Yeshua.

"We don't have time for me to go into detail, Jessie," she said. "The bottom line is, Lou is trying to take you away from me permanently.".

"Mom—"

"Listen to me. You have to leave tonight, as soon as he goes to sleep. Don't bother to pack. Grandpa can buy you new clothes."

"Grandpa!"

Weezie stirred. I hurried out into the hall with the phone and started for the kitchen. My mother's voice screeched me to a halt.

"Just get as far away from there as you can on foot. Take your phone with you, of course, and then wait for my call. Are you getting this, Jessie?"

"No!" I said.

"What is so hard about it? Sneak out—you know how to do that—"

"Lou has an—"

"Do what I say! Get out of there or he is going to ruin your life just like he did mine. You have no idea."

"Yes, I do," I said.

My voice sounded like a piece of wood. She didn't seem to notice.

"All right—I'm going to repeat this because I know you didn't get half of it. You run—get to a safe place—and I will call you and you'll tell me where you are. I'll notify your grandfather and he'll bring you home."

"Are you out of the hospital?"

"Jessie—can you focus for five seconds? Just do it. Do you hear me?"

"Yeah," I said. "I hear you."

She hung up. I dropped the phone and shook. And then I ran to the kitchen window and looked out. Where was Lou? What was taking him so long? My mother had gone completely off the deep end and I needed him. I couldn't do this by myself—

The phone rang and for a wild second I couldn't think where it was. When I finally remembered I'd dropped it in the hallway, I was afraid to answer it. Except that when I looked, the screen said ROCKY.

I fumbled for it, talking almost before I turned it on. "Oh my gosh, I'm so glad it's you!"

"Now that's what I'm talkin' about," he said.

I could almost see his grin. I sank to the floor with the phone.

"Red?" he said. "What's wrong?"

"My mother just called," I said. "She wants me to run away. She says Lou's going to ruin my life. I'm scared she's going to—"

"Where's Lou?"

"He's taking some people home."

"Okay—I'm coming over."

189

"Your bike will wake Weezie up."

"Meet me on the beach."

"I can't leave her—"

"If she wakes up and sees you like this, she'll freak out."

"Okay—the beach," I said. "Hurry."

"I'm only five minutes away."

Still shaking, I put the phone down and peeked into the bedroom. Weezie was so far under the covers I could hardly tell she was there except for the breathing. Still, I was afraid to go in and look for shoes.

Just go. Just go to Rocky and it'll be all right.

I told myself that, over and over, as I tore barefoot down the road past the condos and onto the sand. I'd never gone down there in total darkness before, and it felt like a strange place. Everything, in fact, felt different than it ever had before.

My feet hit the wood and I ran faster, bumping into the railings on both sides as I tore blindly forward, gathering splinters in the soles of my feet. I couldn't see the beach yet, but I could hear it talking to me and I flung myself toward it.

Until I missed the turn in the walkway and smacked straight into the railing and over the top of it. Before I knew it I was headed straight down on the other side, and my face hit something sharp and pointy. One of its points went into my cheek.

I yanked it out and rolled over on my back in the sand and the underbrush. Above me the sky was almost starless. Its blackness came down on me like a suffocating blanket and I couldn't fight it back. Not until I heard the Harley growling its way down the beach.

I screamed Rocky's name and tore across the dunes. He was just pulling the Sportster to a stop at the base of the steps when I stumbled out of the brush, still screaming for him. He met me before I could fall down again and held onto me.

"Dude, is somebody chasing you?" he said.

"I think *I* am." I pulled back from him. "This is a bad idea—I'm too freaked out. I need to go back."

"Yeah, as soon as you chill. Come here—sit on the bike."

I could do that. He led me to the Harley, and I climbed on

and leaned back on the sissy bar. He got on too, backward, facing me. I saw his eyes flicker fear.

"What?" I said.

"You're bleeding," he said. "Here."

He pulled the bandana off his head and pressed it against my cheek. It hurt, but I didn't care. I was safe now.

"So what's with your mom?" he said.

"She wants me to run away so my grandfather can come get me. She says Lou's going to ruin my life."

"And we already get that she doesn't really know anything about your dad, right?"

"Right."

With every word my heart was slowing down a little more.

"I just gotta ask this," Rocky said. "You're not doing it, right?"

"Running away? Are you serious? No!"

He nodded at me. And then he closed his eyes and turned around on the bike. With his hands on the handlebars he let his head hang forward.

"What?" I said.

"Just give me a minute," he said.

"What are you doing?" I said.

"This is called being so relieved you aren't leaving I might cry like a little girl."

"Oh," I said.

I didn't know exactly what to do. And then I leaned forward and rested my good cheek against his back.

"We can go now," I said.

"No, Jess. You aren't going anywhere."

We both startled up like rabbits as a flashlight shone in our faces. Behind it I could see Lou's face.

Only it couldn't have been Lou's face—because it was very, very angry.

CHAPTER NINETEEN

Lou snapped off the light when he got to us at the bottom of the steps, but I could still see the blotches of red on his face and his neck, the bulging vein in his forehead, and the grind in his teeth that made his jaw hard and square.

But it was his eyes that scared me the most. They didn't spit sparks like my mother's did when she was mad, or frost the scene the way I'd seen my angry grandfather's do. They bored right into me, yes, but all around them were deep creases of disappointment. I didn't know what to say to that.

When I didn't speak, the eyes went to Rocky.

"Dang it, man," he said. "What were you thinking?" He put up his hand. "You know what—I can't even talk about this right now, Rocky. That's how—"

I pulled the bandana from my cheek. "He didn't do anything!" I said. "He just—"

Lou put his hands on the back of my head and pulled me toward him. Even in the dark I could see all the color drain from his face.

"What happened?"

He wasn't using the low, quiet voice. This one was hard and full of something I couldn't even name.

"Jess—answer me—what happened?"

"I fell," I said.

He pulled my face even closer—and then he examined my arms and my legs, where gashes and scratches that hadn't even started to hurt made me look like someone had beaten me with a palmetto bush.

"Get off the bike, Jess," he said.

"I didn't—"

"I said get off."

I would have killed right then for the sit-down voice. I swung my leg over and yelped when pain fired through it—which drove Lou's voice down, into some dangerous place.

"Go home, Rocky," he said. "We'll talk later."

"It's not her fault, Lou. I made her come down here—"

"Are you trying to make this worse?"

"You just need to listen to her—"

"What am I going to listen to?" Lou turned his sheet-white face to me. "Weezie tells me you talked to your mother, your mother told you to run away, then you called Rocky for help. I find you with no cell phone, you've been on a bike I told you never to ride on, no shoes, no proper clothing, banged up and bleeding—"

"Okay, fine!" I said. "I'm a ditz-queen-airhead-moron who's never gonna change no matter what step you're on so you might as well send me back to my mother where I belong because she's crazy too—just like me!"

I couldn't look at either one of them then. I went for the steps, and I ignored Lou calling my name. I took them two at a time, no matter how much the pain shot up my legs and the blood poured down my face, and got myself to the house. The whole time I knew Lou was right behind me, but he didn't say a word.

Even when we got inside, he just said, "Let's go in the bathroom and get you cleaned up."

"I don't want to talk to you," I said.

"I don't think you *should* talk to me right now," he said. "And I'm not so sure I should talk to you either."

I wouldn't let him touch me. I cleaned all my cuts myself and bandaged them up. Nothing hurt as much as the broken-heart pain in my chest.

Lou fixed my usual Sleepytime tea, which I didn't drink. He turned on the geezer rock I tried not to listen to and sat on the edge of the coffee table until I fell asleep on the couch. When I woke up the next morning, he wasn't there.

Neither was Weezie. There was just a note that said he was taking her home. The only thing that kept me off the hamster wheel was that he'd left me there by myself, that he knew I wasn't going to run. And then I remembered the alarm—the alarm he had stopped setting.

I was afraid to check it, but I had to.

It was turned off.

I went into the bedroom and dropped onto the bed and then yelled, "Ouch!" because everything on my body hurt. It was no big deal that Lou hadn't set the alarm when he left. He knew I didn't have anyplace to go anyway. I was cut off from Chelsea and Marcus. I couldn't trust my mother. Rocky probably hated me now because I'd gotten him in trouble with Lou, who he loved more than anybody on the planet. And I knew down in the pit of myself that Lou wasn't going to want me anymore—not after I went off on him like that.

Something came to me that Rocky said to me once. *If you blow, you got nothin'.*

I now had nothin'.

I pulled the pillow out from under my head and started to put it over my face, but I felt something under me.

It was RL. A stupid leather book that—

That understood me.

I sat up and opened it and searched the page with desperate eyes until some words rose up to meet me.

Yeshua and his followers went by boat to the county of the Gerasenes, just across from Galilee.

I wanted to go with him.

He was barely out of the boat when a seriously crazy man from the town was screaming at him. This guy was really, sadly sick in his mind. We're talking more than one demon. He wouldn't wear clothes. He was totally naked. He wouldn't stay in his house, hadn't for a long time. He lived in the cemetery where they had him chained like an animal.

My hands were suddenly clammy.

He threw himself down on the ground in front of Yeshua and screamed. Yeshua, of course, ordered the thing in him that was tearing his soul apart to come out. But the guy just shrieked, "Why are you messing with my head? You're Yeshua. I know you're the Holy One, but why do you have to pick on me?"

"He's trying to help you," I said. "Can't you see that?"

It didn't seem to be working. The man was having one seizure after another, so violent his chains and shackles were breaking. His sickness—his demon—just seemed to be driving him further and further into insanity.

I felt sick.

Yeshua said, "What is your name?"

"Jess," I whispered.

"Mob," the crazed man said, because there was a whole mob of demons terrorizing him. There was a lot going on with him. Yeshua looked deep into the man, and the demons pleaded with him not to order them to come out.

Well, of course they'd say that. They knew they were safe as long as they were tucked in there, and this guy didn't know how to get them out himself. The whole thing was so clear to me, I could almost feel the chains on his wrists, taste the nasty dry mouth of fear.

Close by there was a herd of pigs that some pig herders were allowing to feed. The psycho-demons begged Yeshua to order them into the pigs so they would have someplace to go. So Yeshua did. Those pigs went ballistic, worse than the guy himself. They were so insane they panicked and jumped off a cliff into the water and drowned.

My heart was pounding.

The pig herders' hearts were pounding too. They took off running into town where they told everybody what had happened. You know people—they had to come out and see for themselves. And what they found was Yeshua and the crazy guy. He was sitting there at Yeshua's feet, fully clothed and talking like the sane person he now was, making total sense. It was one of those scenes that makes you want to kneel down and pray, you know?

I did know.

They, naturally, all wanted to know how it had gone down, so the people who'd been there at the time told the story of Yeshua ordering the demons into the pigs, and the pigs going out of their minds and committing suicide.

Good. I sat up straight. Maybe now they'd all believe Yeshua and stop dissing him all the time.

It wasn't long before a bunch of people from the Gerasene area formed a delegation and went to Yeshua and asked him to get out of town.

"No!" I said. "Were *they* crazy?"

They'd seen too much that they didn't understand, and believing it was going to mean major changes in their mind-sets and their way of doing and being, and it scared them spitless. You can understand that, I'm sure.

I couldn't even answer.

So Yeshua got back in the boat to leave. The man who'd been saved from his insanity asked if he could go with, but Yeshua said, "What I want you to do is go home and tell everybody what God did in and for you."

What God did? Did I miss something? I skimmed back several paragraphs. No—it said *Yeshua* ordered the demons into the pigs. How did God get in there? It hadn't said anything about God before, had it?

Look again.

I looked at the page, but there were no words that read "Look again." The chill zipped up my spine.

"Look where?" I whispered.

The part where I talk about loving your enemies.

It didn't say that on the page either. I heard it like a whisper, my voice but not my voice.

Look again.

My fingers shook like little plover wings as I turned back the pages and found the spot.

"'Love your enemies,'" I read out loud. I ran my finger down the page. No God there. Oh—wait: "I promise that if you live this way you won't be sorry. This is the way God loves you, so you have to love this way too."

I stared, hard, but the words stayed.

"You weren't there before," I said. "I know you weren't."

No answer. I flipped back to the crazy-man story. It still said, "Go and tell everyone what God did for you and in you."

"This is about God?" I whispered. "Yeshua is God?"

*

I was still staring at RL when Lou appeared in the bedroom doorway. I hadn't even heard him drive up or come in the front door.

"You ready to talk?" he said. His voice was Lou again. His eyes were sad.

"Yes," I said. "Why did you give your Harley the name Levi?"

His eyebrows went up. He nodded his head toward the hallway. "Come on out here," he said.

I hugged RL against my chest and followed him to the deck. He pulled two chairs up to the railing so we could sit with our feet on it. I didn't let go of the book as I sank into mine. My heart pounded against it.

"So—" he said. "You want to know why I named him Levi."

"Yes."

He leaned his head back and looked up. "It's the name of a guy in the Bible."

"What guy?"

"He was kind of a sleazeball, actually—"

"A tax collector?" I said.

Lou turned to me, eyebrows sprung. "Yeah, he was. Jesus called him to be a follower and he—"

"Jesus?"

"Right. Jesus Christ."

"And Jesus is God."

"Right—God who came to be with us." He tilted his head at me. "Where's all this coming from, Jess?"

I hugged RL harder and closed my eyes. A thing wrapped itself around me—like a warm blanket—no, like a pair of arms—no, better than that—like a peace. I just didn't know it at first, because I had never felt it before. Never in my life.

"You okay?" Lou said.

I sat up and looked right into his eyes-like-mine. "You can

197

be as mad at me as you want and never feel the same about me again, but if Yeshua is God—I think I'm going to get rid of my demons."

"Whoa, whoa, whoa." Lou pulled his feet off the railing and peeled his back from the chair so he could twist to face me. "Why would you think I don't feel the same about you?"

"You got so mad at me," I said. "You never get that mad. And then I blew and—"

I stopped because he had his hand up.

"First of all, I was the one who blew. I think I told you once the only way you could drive me over the edge was to get hurt."

"I didn't get hurt on the bike."

"I know that now. I should have listened to you, and I'm sorry, Jess. I'm more sorry than I can even tell you."

He swallowed and pulled his hand across his eyes.

"And you don't say you're sorry unless you mean it," I said.

He lifted his hand like a visor. "That's right."

"I should have waited for you," I said. "I shouldn't have left Weezie here by herself. I didn't think she'd wake up, but I shouldn't have gone anyway. I know you love her more than anybody in the entire world."

"I do love her, yes."

"And it's okay that you guys have this daddy-daughter thing that I can't be part of. I can live with that."

Lou let a long breath come out of his mouth, so long I thought it would never end. When it did, he said, "I loved Weezie the minute I saw her, but not because of anything she did. I didn't even know her."

"What was she—like two minutes old?"

"Less than that. I loved her because she was my child. There have been times since then when I didn't *like* her very much, but I have always, always loved her."

This was not helping me. At all. The lump in my own throat wasn't going to block the tears for much longer if he kept on.

"Do you remember me telling you that it killed me not to have Weezie here with me all the time?"

I nodded.

"That I don't get to wake her up every morning and make sure she's eating right and tuck her in at night."

It couldn't have been more like torture if he'd pushed things under my fingernails.

"All of that, Jess—all of it—is how I feel about you."

I shook my head and tried to get up, but he put his hands on the arms of my chair and I had to stay.

"I loved you from the first moment your mother told me you were even in the world—because you're my child. And when I learned how to be a father to Weezie, it killed me every day that I couldn't wake you up in the morning and make sure you were eating right and tuck you in at night. I spent an entire year trying to find you, and when I took one look at you in your mother's kitchen, I fell in love with you—because you are my daughter." He swallowed—hard. "Since then I have loved waking you up every morning even though you hate it—and making sure you eat right even though you go for ice cream every time you're out of my sight—and seeing that you are tucked in at night even though you think I'm tormenting you. And when I started to think that I wasn't going to get to do that every day until you're grown, it killed me all over again, because—" He stopped and put his hand on his mouth, and his face looked like it was working hard. Then he moved his hand and said, "Because I love you, Jess. You are my firstborn child, and I love you."

He looked like he didn't know what to do then, but I did. I flung my sobbing, weeping, nose-running self into his arms, crying into his neck.

Crying until I stopped. Crying until I could say, "I love you too."

CHAPTER TWENTY

We didn't make it to church that day, so I asked Lou if we could take Weezie with us to lunch. When he called her, she said she didn't want to go, but he told me he thought he knew why and he went to get her anyway. I stayed home to wait for them, kind of wandering around the little house and wondering how it had ever seemed like a cage to me. It was the safest place I knew.

I stopped wandering at the prayer table and ran my hand across the top of it. Lou had done all the praying when we'd knelt there together that one day, but—could I actually pray by myself? Did I know how?

I looked around, and then felt stupid because who was I worried about seeing me? I got on my knees on the padded part and closed my eyes the way Lou did and couldn't figure out what to do next. What was I supposed to say to God...Jesus...Yeshua.

"I want to follow," I whispered. "So would you please call the demons out of me so I can?"

"Hi, Jessie," someone whispered.

I choked—until I realized it was Weezie behind me.

"Where's Lou?" I said.

"He's in the car. He said to come out when we're done."

"Done what?" I said.

So far she hadn't looked at me. Her blue eyes went to the door, the floor—they practically went into her armpit—but they couldn't seem to find their way to mine.

I patted the kneeler next to me. "Want to join me?"

She nodded and sat on it. Her eyes were now on her knees.

"Did you want to say something?" I said.

"Yes. But I'm scared."

"Of what?"

"That you won't."

"Won't what?" It was starting to feel like I was pulling out her nose hairs or something.

"That you won't forgive me—because I'm really sorry that I told on you—but I only did it because I was scared you were really gonna run away, and I wouldn't ever see you again, and that would be horrible because you're my sister." She looked up at me with her eyes all wet, ready to overflow. "Aren't you going to say something?"

"As soon as you give me a chance," I said.

She pressed her lips together over her braces.

"So—you say you're sorry."

She nodded.

"Do you mean it?"

"I never say I'm sorry if I don't mean it."

"Because your dad says so."

"I do mean it!"

I put my face down close to hers. "I believe you. And I forgive you, okay?"

You would have thought I told her she was going to meet Hannah Montana. She wrapped her arms around my waist and squeezed until I was sure she was going to cut off my circulation. I let her do it, though. It felt kind of good.

"You want to go to lunch with us?" I said. "They have coconut shrimp there."

"Okay," she said—all fuzzy-voiced.

"I have to go get my phone or your dad will give me the hairy eyeball," I said.

"Okay."

"That means you have to let go of me."

She did, but she trailed me like a bloodhound into the bedroom. I found my phone and my flip-flops, and she sat on my bed and picked up RL.

"You like this book, huh?"

"Yeah," I said.

She ran her fingers across the letters. "Real Life," she said. "I don't know if that's what it means."

"That's what it means when me and my friends text message each other."

"Seriously?" I said.

"Don't you text?" she said.

"Your dad didn't get me texting."

Weezie rolled her eyes. "You know, Jessica, he's your dad too."

I didn't tell her not to call me Jessica. I was afraid I'd cry again.

*

Even though we spent the whole day with Weezie, she still begged to be allowed to spend the night. Lou said no. We all had to get back to our routines. For the first time ever, I liked the way that sounded.

On the way back from dropping her off at the mini-mansion, my cell phone rang.

I looked at the screen and got an instant attack of vampire bats.

"It's my grandfather," I said. "Do I have to answer it?"

"Not if you don't want to. But I think you can handle him."

That was the only reason I said hello.

"Jessica," he said, "this is Grandpa."

"I know," I said, although I wouldn't have recognized his voice. He sounded old and tired.

"Have you heard from your mother?" he said.

"Last night," I said.

"Not today?"

Something unfamiliar was gathering in me. I sat up straight in the seat.

"No," I said. "And I don't want to do what she told me to do. I want to stay here."

"When exactly did you talk to her?" It was as if he hadn't

202

even heard me, which *was* exactly like the grandfather I remembered. And exactly like his daughter.

"I told you, last night," I said between my teeth.

"Then you're the last person that's heard from her."

"Didn't you call the hospital?" I said.

"I was *at* the hospital, Jessica." He gave an impatient sigh. "I'm at your house now. It looks like she left here in a hurry."

"I don't get it." I looked at Lou with what must have been wild eyes because he slowed down. "The doctors let her out?"

"Incompetent bunch of — all right, look, if you hear from her, you call me, do you hear?"

"I hear."

"This is a mess."

"Well," I said, my voice stiff, "I'm sure you'll clean it up."

He was only silent for about a breath. "You still have a smart mouth," he said. "You're just like —"

"Don't say I'm just like my mother."

"I was going to say you're just like your father. You call me immediately if you hear from her."

I didn't have to answer because he hung up. We were in the driveway by then.

"Did you get all that?" I said to Lou.

"I got enough."

His face was serious.

"You okay?" I said.

He hung his thumbs on the steering wheel. "Listen, Jess, I want to say something to you about your mother."

"Do we have to talk about her?"

"Yeah. We do. Your grandfather's right about one thing: she's in a mess and I don't think it's over. But I just think you ought to know that the way she's treated you isn't because of anything you've done —"

"I know," I said.

He looked at me.

"She's got 'demons.' Bad ones." I pulled my feet up onto the seat and hugged my knees. "I prayed today."

"Yeah?"

203

"I asked Jesus—Yeshua—they're the same person, right?"

"They are. Yeshua is the Aramaic word for Jesus. How is it that you know him by that name?"

"It's a long story."

His lips twitched. "Then we'll save that for another time. Back to your prayer."

"I prayed that Jesus would call out my demon. I think it's going to happen."

"You're talking about your ADHD."

"Yes."

He gazed through the windshield for a minute like he was seeing an answer out there. I started to squirm.

"What?" I said.

"I think Jesus is already working on that. You've improved a whole lot in the short time you've been here."

"But that's because of the medicine and you making me have a routine and all that. I'm talking about being cured."

He scratched the back of his head. "There isn't a cure for ADHD, Jess."

"Then what about Jesus pulling the demons out of Mob and putting them into the pigs? What about the guy that was foaming at the mouth in church and Jesus cured him? Is all that stuff just fiction?"

He was staring at me, mouth halfway open. "I think I want to hear that 'long story.'"

"That doesn't answer my question," I said.

"No, it isn't fiction. Jesus did call out the demons—which could have been the hold those people's mental illnesses had on their lives. They weren't slaves to their insanity anymore—just like I'm no longer a slave to alcohol and you're no longer a slave to that merry-go-round I bet you have in your head."

"It's a hamster wheel."

"Jesus is already taking away the power ADHD has over you, but you still have to work with him. I go to AA meetings. I don't go to places where they serve alcohol. I'm constantly praying—and reading the stories about Yeshua driving out the demons."

"Where?" I said.

"In the Bible," he said. "Isn't that where you read them?"

"I don't know," I said.

His eyebrows went up.

"It's part of the long story," I said.

He nodded and opened the truck door. "Let's go have some popcorn, and you can tell it to me. I've got all the time in the world."

*

The vampire bats in my stomach were having babies the next morning when we pulled up to the shop on Levi. Rocky was standing there waiting for us.

I must have squeezed my dad hard around the waist because he said to me through his visor, "I think you can be a little late for work. You better take care of this first."

"Does he know you're not mad at him?" I said.

"He and I are cool."

Of course they were. Lou could probably bloody Rocky's nose and he'd still forgive him. But me — that might be another story.

I swung my leg out to get off the bike and caught it on the sissy bar and dumped myself onto the ground. When I looked up, a boy-creature with an adorable space between his teeth was grinning down at me.

"That's one way to do it," he said.

"Shut up," I said.

He put a hand down to me, and this time I took it. And when I was on my feet, he took my helmet off me and tucked it under his arm.

"Did you tell your dad you thought you were Step Nine?" he said.

I looked around, but my father was gone.

"No," I said between my teeth, "and if you ever do — "

"You've already forgotten."

"Forgotten what?"

"That I said you could trust me."

205

Rocky wasn't smiling now. He was looking all serious, and he shifted the helmet to the other arm.

"I remember," I said. "I'm sorry."

"Mean it?"

"I don't say I'm sorry unless I mean it."

His green eyes began to gleam. "So that's it? That's all you have to say?"

"What else do you want me to say?"

"Nothing. You just usually go on for, like, ten hours—"

"You are just begging for a question, aren't you?"

"Aw, man."

"Lucky for you I only have one left."

"I doubt that—but go for it."

I took my helmet and hugged it to my chest, just in case I didn't get the answer I wanted and I needed something to keep me from bursting into tears.

"Do you still not think I'm a basket case after I went off the other night? You can tell me if that changed your mind and I'll understand—"

He didn't stop my lips with his hand this time. He stopped them with his.

*

I still went down to my place by the sand dunes before sunset that night. I just didn't go there for the same reason I did before. I actually wasn't sure exactly what I was doing because I didn't know that much about praying yet, but it seemed like a good place to try. I did know it involved closed eyes, and I was getting comfortable with that when someone said my name.

It was my mother.

Although, as I sat there, frozen in the sand, staring up at the bony form above me, I wasn't sure it really was her. I'd seen her at her worst, going without showering or changing clothes for days, eyes with carry-on bags underneath them. I'd also seen her at the top of her form, polished to a gleam and snapping her French manicure at the world. But this woman was neither one of those. She wore a hot pink jacket over a T-shirt, and both of them hung on her like they were on a hanger. So did the jeans. My mother never went out looking like that.

It was her eyes, though, that really seemed to belong to someone else. They were cloudy and bloodshot, and they couldn't seem to be still even as she tried to stare me down.

"He said you'd be down here," she said.

The voice was the same. Sort of brittle, maybe, but still so sharp it brought me to my feet and yet made me want to start compiling excuses to get through this. I suddenly felt like I was on an old escalator.

"Hi," I said.

She brushed that off the same way I was brushing the sand off the back of my shorts.

"Are you packed?" she said.

"No," I said.

"Did I not tell you on the phone to get packed? I knew you weren't listening to a thing I was saying." She gave me the first look that indicated she was even seeing me. "What are you waiting for, Jessie? Let's go."

"Go where?" I said. I was hating myself for even asking, but the familiar escalator was almost to the bottom, and I couldn't see how to climb back up.

My mother tossed back the hair the wind was blowing in her face—what little there was of it. It looked like half of it had fallen out. "Where else would we be going?" she said. "Home."

"I don't want to go back there," I said. I couldn't bring myself to even say the word *home*.

She didn't seem that surprised. "It isn't about what you want. It's about what's going to happen."

"What—"

"Honestly, Jessie, you still have the emotional maturity of an eight-year-old. Let me spell it out for you." She spit some sand from her mouth and looked up at the wind like her annoyance alone was going to stop it. "I'm out of the hospital.

I'm taking you away from Control Freak, who I should never have left you with in the first place. I don't know what I was thinking—"

I felt myself stiffen. "He's not a control freak," I said.

"—and we are going back to our life. That clear enough for you?"

She gave me the look I hated. The look that said I was a ditz-queen-airhead-moron. The look that wasn't true anymore.

"No," I said. "It isn't clear."

"Jessie, for Pete's sake—you are still a—"

"Don't tell me who I am."

She stopped, mouth open. That unfamiliar thing gathered up in me again, the way it had with my grandfather. Only now I knew what it was.

"You don't know who I am," I said. "And that's why I'm not going back with you. I'm staying here."

She crossed her arms over her chest like a pair of sticks. "Am I hearing this right? You're telling me what you are and are not going to do?"

"Yes."

"Oh, no, ma'am."

She reached out to grab me, but I pulled away.

"He might let you get away with that kind of attitude, but I—"

"He?" I said. "You mean my dad? No, I don't have to pull attitude with him. He doesn't put me down every single chance he gets. He doesn't treat me like a moron. He doesn't ignore me for weeks and then get up and try to run my life. That's why I don't pull attitude with him. And that's why this is my home now."

She shook her head for so long I thought she really was possessed by demons. When she stopped, she batted her hair out of her face again and lowered her voice to someplace dark and menacing. Someplace meant to scare me.

"You don't have the maturity to make this kind of decision," she said.

"Yes, I do."

"You have a mental disorder!"

"So do you."

"And you have a smart mouth that I'm about to smack."

I backed up, but only to get out of her reach. Inside, I wasn't backing up an inch. "I know I have a smart mouth," I said. "Just like I have a smart mind. Because I'm just like my father."

I had never seen anybody shudder before, but she did it. And then she suddenly seemed so weak and small, I thought maybe the wind might blow her away.

"This isn't over, Jessie," she said in a very different voice.

But as she staggered away, fighting the ocean breeze that was almost too big for her, I could tell it *was* over. I could tell by the now-familiar gathering feeling. The feeling that was Yeshua, driving out the demons.

*

The Atlanta airport seemed different when we were waiting for our flight to Birmingham. I didn't get the feeling that I was trapped in a squirrel cage, or that I was about to be picked up by the airport police. I was pretty sure you didn't get arrested for putting back something that you thought you stole.

"Where are you going to leave it, Jess?" my dad said.

I hugged RL like I'd been doing ever since we left Jacksonville. It was kind of comforting, because even though I knew we were only going back to Mountain Brook so I could tell the judge I wanted to be with my dad and he could sign the final papers that said he had full and permanent custody of me, I still had a few baby bats in my stomach. He'd promised me fifty-seven times that we were coming back to Florida. The last time I'd said we had to, because Bonsai had promised I could make my first California roll when we returned. I was pretty sure Rose had put him up to it.

I brought RL up to my nose and smelled its leather. "It's hard to let it go."

"I can understand that."

"What if I'm not ready to go on to the regular Bible?"

"The 'regular Bible' is still going to speak to you, Jess. That's the way it works." He reached over and squeezed my knee. "Besides, RL says you're ready, right?"

That was true. The night I'd told him about the book, I'd opened it to the last page I'd read and new words came up to meet me.

You've discovered why I was left for you, the words said. *It's time for you to leave me for someone else who is hungry for me. But you are not alone. You will always have Yeshua. You will always have his Word.*

"You okay?" my dad said now.

"Yeah."

He let go of my knee and stood up. "I'm going to see if I can get us in the exit row." His lips did their twitchy thing. "Any problem with that?"

I wrinkled my nose at him. He wrinkled his back. I was sure anybody watching would have known we were father and daughter.

He started toward the counter.

"Dad?" I said.

It was a second or two before he turned around, swallowing that Ping-Pong ball.

"Do you have a pen?" I said.

He nodded toward his bag, eyes all swimmy. "Look in the outside pocket."

I did and found one and put RL on my lap. Other people had carved their initials into the cover or drawn pictures on the empty pages, and I felt like I should do something too. I didn't know what until now.

Now I opened to the back and formed the words in my head first so I wouldn't spell them wrong and then decided it didn't matter.

"If you ever want to talk about what you learned from RL," I wrote, "call me. Meanwhile, I'll be praying for you."

I signed it Jess K. and wrote my cell phone number. Then I closed the book for the last time and held it close to me and whispered, "Thank you."

"You ready, Jess?" Dad said from a few steps away. "They're boarding."

"Okay," I said.

I looked around and saw a bench, outside a bookstore, where somebody searching for something to teach them might go. I wove through the people going past and put RL on the seat.

Then I turned to my dad and walked to the gate to start my new life. My real life.

ABOUT THE REAL LIFE BOOK

You might have figured out before Jessie did that when she opened the leather Real Life book, she was reading stories from the Bible. They aren't the actual Scriptures, of course, but they are inspired by what Eugene Peterson did in *The Message*, which was to use modern, everyday language that makes you realize the Bible is for and about you. Jesus spoke in the street language of his day, so it only makes sense that we should be able to read his words that way. In fact, Eugene Peterson was inspired by a man named J. B. Phillips, who in 1947 wrote *The New Testament in Modern English* so his youth group could understand the Bible and live it!

Of course, no matter what translation of the Bible you read, it doesn't actually "talk" to you the way Real Life carried on a conversation with Jessie. Or doesn't it? Scripture is the Word of God and a Word is meant to be spoken. When you really settle in with the Bible,

- *doesn't it make you ask questions?*

- *doesn't it answer the questions that pop into your head?*

- *doesn't it seem weirdly close to the exact things you're going through now, even though the stories were told thousands of years ago?*

- *doesn't it sometimes say something you didn't see the last time you looked at that very same part?*

Reading the Bible really is like having a conversation with God, and I hope the Real Life book helps you open up your own discussion with our Lord, who is waiting for you to say, "Can we talk?" Comparing what Jessie read to the actual passages in the Bible might help you get started. All of them are found in the gospel of Luke, who even more than Mark, Matthew, and John, showed the love and sympathy Jesus had for the people who didn't fit, the people who others said were weird, sinful, and not to be hung out with. Luke also shows how much Jesus respected women. It seemed like just the thing for our Real Life girls—and for you.

THE SCRIPTURES

WHO HELPED?

One of the most fun parts of writing a book is working with experts who know all kinds of things that I don't. These are the pros who helped me make *Motorcycles, Sushi & One Strange Book* feel like real life.

Max, chef and owner of Sushi Max in Lebanon, Tennessee, who showed me how sushi is made (and fed me the best eel and avocado roll this side of Japan).

My husband, Jim, who took me to St. Augustine and carried me on the back of Headley, our Harley, wherever Jessie would go.

Two books about ADHD in teenage girls, which helped me understand Jessie: *A Bird's-Eye View of Life with ADD and ADHD: Advice from Young Survivors* (by Chris A. Zeigler Dendy and Alex Zeigler); and *Understanding Girls With AD/HD* (by Kathleen G. Nadeau, Ellen B. Littman, and Patricia O. Quinn).

Katie, Regan, Liana, and Julia, my blog buddies, who named Rocky, right down to the Oswald Kenneth Luke.

Madison McGinn and her mom Kristen Richardson (both my nieces!), who shared Mountain Brook, a suburb of Birmingham, Alabama, with me. We even had ice cream at the Mountain Brook Creamery.

Eugene Peterson, the author of *Eat This Book*, who showed me how the Real Life book could speak to Jessie.

BOYFRIENDS, BURRITOS & AN OCEAN OF TROUBLE

[REAL LIFE]

a novel by

NANCY RUE

CHAPTER ONE

I didn't wish the car accident had killed me. But lying there on the table in the emergency room as that bald doctor with the tangled eyebrows shined his tiny flashlight in my eyes, I would have settled for unconscious. Just a nice coma so I wouldn't have to answer any questions. My few seconds of blackout didn't seem to count, because no one had stopped interrogating me since the paramedics had arrived on the scene.

The doctor—*Jon Wooten*, it said on his name tag—dropped the flashlight into his coat pocket and put his warm hands on the sides of my face. I tried not to shiver.

"So, you hit your head on impact?" he said, nodding at my throbbing forehead.

"No." I hoped what I'd learned in my drama classes would kick in as I faked a smile. "The air bag hit *me*. Those things are dangerous!"

"It got you right here."

He brushed his fingers along my cheek, and I winced.

"We'll clean that up and get you some ice for the swelling," he said. "It's an abrasion—it won't leave a scar."

I was *so* not worried about a mark on my face. What I was worried about was getting out of here before—

"All right, we're going to have you change into a gown so I can examine you."

Before that.

"I'll have a nurse help you." He nodded at my father, who was standing in the corner of the curtained cubicle where he'd been asked to stay. "She's definitely had a concussion. I may want a CT scan to rule out internal injuries, but let's see if there's anything else going on first."

He motioned for Dad to follow him and then swept out.

Dad nodded, but he came to me and leaned over the table. His face was gray, his pale blue eyes wet around the edges. In the harsh hospital light, I saw lines etched in his face that weren't there when I left the house that night, as if he'd just gotten old that very minute. He had to be even skinnier now too, and the thinning place on top of his head made him seem somehow fragile. My father never showed much emotion except when he had to put a young dog to sleep. The way he was looking at me, I could have been a terminal puppy.

He was a veterinarian, but a doctor's a doctor. He couldn't be missing the fact that my heart was slamming at my chest and taking my breath away. "Bryn, this is serious," he said. "Don't downplay it—tell them everything, you hear?"

His Virginia-soft accent didn't usually affect me that much. Probably because he didn't actually talk to me that much. But right now it was doing me in. I swallowed back the sob that threatened to burst from my chest. At least he wasn't asking me what I'd been doing in a car alone with Preston.

"Brynnie?" he said.

"Okay," I said. "But I'm really not hurt."

Except for the pain in my stomach and the ache in my arm and the throbbing in my head, that was the truth.

As soon as he disappeared through the curtain, panic grabbed at my insides and climbed all the way up my throat and gagged me. I plastered my hand over my mouth and prayed I wouldn't throw up. Then I prayed that Dr. Wooten would learn about a sudden outbreak of the plague in Virginia Beach and forget about me, and Dad and I could go home and pretend to forget this whole thing happened.

But there was as much a chance of that as there was that once I was clad in a flimsy gown, that doctor wasn't going to see what was under it. I wasn't so worried about tonight's injuries. Those bruises wouldn't rise to the surface until at least tomorrow.

It was Wednesday's evidence I was worried about. I couldn't let him see that. Not with Dad standing there. At least my mother wasn't here. At least there was that.

A nurse in turquoise scrubs and a messy ponytail slipped in through the curtain, a gown and a sheet over her arm. She looked at me like I was one of Dad's patients, recently brought in from a storm drain.

"Hey, girlfriend," she said. "I'm Cindi. How you doin'?"

"I'd be better if I could just go home," I said. "I bet you have people way sicker than me to take care of."

"Nope. You lucked out tonight."

She put her hand on my shoulder, and I tried not to cringe.

"I'm going to need you to take everything off and put on this precious gown." She gave me a winky smile. "It's not a good look for anybody, but it's all we've got."

If she was trying to get me to relax, it wasn't working. My mouth dried up, and I could feel my hands oozing sweat.

"Once you get that on you can lie back, and I'll cover you with the sheet." She tilted her head at me. "Are you cold?"

I was, even in my pink sweater, even though it was June and everybody else at the party had been in tank tops. It was pointless to pretend I wasn't shivering now. I could almost feel my lips turning blue.

"I'm going to go get you a blanket," she said. "If you even start to feel dizzy, lie down and I'll help you get undressed when I come back."

When she left I fought back more panic. Jesus, what do I do?

I wasn't swearing. I was really asking Jesus, just like I'd been doing for the last three months. I hadn't gotten any answers. I would have given up a leading role for one right now — because if there was any way out of this beyond a miracle, I wasn't seeing it.

I pulled the thread-thin blue gown to my face and breathed in the hospital smell and begged Jesus to make me disappear. Outside the cubicle, sneakers squealed past on the linoleum. I could either do it now or do it ten minutes from now or two hours from now. But they were going to make me do it, and the longer I put it off, the more suspicious they were all going to be.

I pushed the gown from my face. Okay—do it fast—like it's no big deal. Make up a story about the bruises. Promise to be more careful with my bird-boned, five-foot-one self in the future.

I couldn't come up with anything else.

I pulled off the sweater, the one Preston said back in the beginning made me look delicious, and yanked the deeper-shade-of-pink long-sleeved tee over my head. The pain seared through me like I was being sliced with a bread knife, but I was now beyond crying. Fear steals your tears—I'd learned that. Still, I didn't dare look at myself as I fed my arms gingerly through the holes in the gown.

Tying the thing in the back was almost not worth the agony involved, but it might keep the doctor from seeing that part. Not that he would need to. The black-and-purple handprint around my bicep told enough of a story by itself. I was going to have to think of a better one, and tell it with a sheepish smile. Assure them it would never happen again.

Please, Jesus—don't let it ever happen again.

Things were tangling in my head and I couldn't allow it. I put all my focus on wriggling out of the rest of my clothes and tucking the gown tightly around my legs and draping my hair over my shoulders. Maybe they'd believe some lame story because I was blonde. I was about to pull the sheet up to my neck when Nurse Cindi slid the curtains apart, already talking.

"Are we set?" she said.

Her lips stopped moving in mid-word. Even while I was retreating behind the sheet, I caught the flicker that went through her eyes. It was gone almost before it was there, a trick they must teach in nursing school. But it had lingered long enough for me to know she knew.

Any story I came up with was going to be perfectly useless. I buried my face in my knees.

"I'll be right back," she practically whispered. "No worries, girlfriend. We'll take care of this."

No. Jesus, please don't let them "take care of it." *You* take care of it. Make it go away.

He didn't. Instead, the curtain parted again, and I groped for my smile and the strands of my story. Everything on Dr. Wooten's face came to a suspicious point. Nurse Cindi wasn't even trying to hide the pity on hers.

"Where's my dad?" I said.

"Filling out some paperwork," he said.

I let go of a ragged breath that dragged through my ribs. Good. I didn't want him here for this.

Without a word, Dr. Wooten pulled back the sheet and examined my arms with only his eyes. I could feel him taking in the bruises — some of them pale blue and red, some dark purple, a few a sickening yellowish green. Cindi watched him, watched me, looked at him again. A whole conversation went on while nobody said a word. I had to stop it.

"Those are old bruises," I said.

"I know," he said.

"I got them playing football."

"I'm going to have you lie back for me."

"Seriously. I'm a double linebacker."

"There's no such thing as a double linebacker, Bryn."

"Single?"

Doctor Wooten pressed his hands on my abdomen and that's when I lost it all — my smile, my loser attempt at a story, my hope. The sucker-punch pain in my stomach throbbed worse now than it had when it first happened. I squeezed the sides of the table and cried without making a sound.

"This one is new," he said. "Were you wearing a seat belt?"

I shook my head and waited for the lecture. The doctor only frowned and pulled the sheet back up to my chest. Nurse Cindi smoothed and tucked and bit at her lip.

He rolled a stool close and sat looking at me long and hard. I should have seen it before: he had eyes you didn't lie to, even if you thought your life depended on it.

"Let's talk about how this happened," he said, "without the football scenario."

He put his hands on my neck and felt around, his eyes

never leaving mine alone. He wouldn't find anything there. It never happened in a place I couldn't keep covered up. I didn't own any turtlenecks.

It was a random thought to have at that moment, but my mind was trying to leave my body. This doctor with the bald head and the intense brows and the eyes that saw everything must have seen that too, because he said, "Who did this to you, Bryn?"

"It was an accident," I said. My voice was so thin I could hardly hear it.

"Was it an accident every time?"

"He didn't plan it. He just got mad and it happened."

"And he hit you in the stomach."

I started to shake my head, but he went on. "You have a large hematoma that's rising even as we're looking at it. Probably a broken blood vessel in your abdominal wall, which could be serious. If you weren't wearing a seat belt—"

"Maybe I was—"

"Bryn. Who did this?"

His voice had gone soft around the edges. I closed my eyes and felt the tears slither into my ears.

"I'm sorry this has happened to you," he said. "We don't want it to happen again, so you need to tell us who's been hurting you."

"I can't." I opened my eyes and let them plead for me. "I'll make it stop, I promise."

"If you could have stopped it, you would have." His voice got firmer. "This is not your fault, Bryn."

"Yes, it is. Please—I'll take care of it."

He folded his arms and looked at me so sadly I thought for a minute he was going to let me.

"Your dad's *Doctor* Christopher," he said.

"He's a vet," I said.

"Does he have his own practice?"

"It's next door to our house." I didn't know where we were going with this, but at least it was away from my beat-up body.

"Is he under a lot of stress?"

"My dad?" I would have laughed if I hadn't been crying. My

father was more laid back than Winnie the Pooh.

"Does your mom live with you?"

"Yes, sir, but she's away on a trip." Thank goodness.

"How long has she been gone?"

"Two weeks. She won't be back 'til the end of July."

I closed my eyes again. Suddenly I was so tired I could have faded away—if he hadn't said what he said next.

"I don't have a choice, Bryn. You're only fifteen. I have to report this."

My eyes sprang open.

"You're the victim of assault."

I tried to sit up, but I flopped back like a helpless fish. "He didn't assault me." I said. "He just—"

He just what? Was I going to tell them his eyes had gone wild and the veins in his neck bulged like purple cords and I knew he couldn't stop himself? That I knew it was going to be worse than last time because it always was?

Dr. Wooten stood up. "I'm going to send you down for a CT scan so we can be sure of what's happening with your belly. That will give you some time to think it over." He brushed my hand with his fingertips, like he knew that was the only place on me that didn't hurt. "I want you to know there's nothing to be afraid of, for you or your dad. He can get help—"

In spite of the breath-stealing pain, I sat right up on the table this time.

"My dad?" I said. "You think my dad did this?"

"No matter what you feel you did to deserve it, it's child abuse."

"You don't understand!" I grabbed for his wrist and caught a handful of his coat in my fingers. "My dad would never do this."

"Then who was it, Bryn? Because if you don't tell us, the police are going to assume it was him."

"The *police?*" I let go of his sleeve and shoved my hands into my hair. And then I let go of the words that were going to change my life forever and ever.

"It wasn't my father," I said. "It was my boyfriend."

Real Life Series
by Nancy Rue

A mysterious book unites four teen girls and unlocks the secret that will get each of them through the real-life struggles they face in their lives.

Boyfriends, Burritos & an Ocean of Trouble
Book Two

Bryn O'Connor is good at keeping secrets. But when a car accident reveals the marks of her boyfriend's physically abusive behavior, the truth is unleashed.

Tournaments, Cocoa & One Wrong Move
Book Three

Sixteen-year-old Cassidy's promising basketball future is threatened when she finds herself a victim of Female Athlete Syndrome.

Share Your Thoughts

With the Author: Your comments will be forwarded to the author when you send them to *zauthor@zondervan.com*.

With Zondervan: Submit your review of this book by writing to *zreview@zondervan.com*.

Free Online Resources at
www.zondervan.com

Zondervan AuthorTracker: Be notified whenever your favorite authors publish new books, go on tour, or post an update about what's happening in their lives at www.zondervan.com/authortracker.

Daily Bible Verses and Devotions: Enrich your life with daily Bible verses or devotions that help you start every morning focused on God. Visit www.zondervan.com/newsletters.

Free Email Publications: Sign up for newsletters on Christian living, academic resources, church ministry, fiction, children's resources, and more. Visit www.zondervan.com/newsletters.

Zondervan Bible Search: Find and compare Bible passages in a variety of translations at www.zondervanbiblesearch.com.

Other Benefits: Register yourself to receive online benefits like coupons and special offers, or to participate in research.

ZONDERVAN®

ZONDERVAN.com/
AUTHORTRACKER
follow your favorite authors